A DANGEROUS MASQUERADE

"I should have guessed you would be involved with smugglers," Brienne whispered.

"Me?" Evan laughed. "You were the one negotiating with Marksen for passage across the Channel." Leaning forward so his face was close to hers, he added, "How in hell did you get involved with Marksen?"

"On my way from London, I asked for the name of a captain who was interested in making some money," Brienne replied stiffly, looking past him to where Marksen and his surly crew waited.

Evan settled his hand on her shoulder to keep her from edging away. "Running off like this was crazy. You need protection now, and I am going to give it to you whether you like it or not. Cooperate, Brienne, if you value our lives."

Waiting for him to reveal some great plan, Brienne stiffened when his arm slipped around her and brought her tight to him. As his lips captured hers, he pressed her to the wall, warning her that his desire for her was very real. Brienne's fingers crushed the wool of his coat as she tried not to be swept into the eddy of passion.

Finally Evan raised his head and whispered, "Very good, honey. Every man in the room is watching. I knew you would put on a good act for them."

Brienne shrugged off his arm, furious with herself for believing once again that he found her enticing. He had never wanted her as much as he wanted what he thought she could bring him. . . .

Dear Reader,

Last month, we launched the Ballad line with four new series, and each month we'll present both new and continuing stories set everywhere from medieval England to the American West—the kind of passionate, romantic stories you love best, written by the most gifted authors. At the back of each book, we'll tell you when you can find subsequent books in the series that have captured your heart.

Veteran author Jo Ann Ferguson explores the shattering results of the French Revolution in the first *Shadow of the Bastille* book, **A Daughter's Destiny.** In this sweeping series, a mysterious thunderbolt crest will reunite siblings separated by the Terror—and whose destinies have been forever changed by love. Next, newcomer Shelley Bradley takes us back to medieval England with **His Lady Bride,** the first in a series called *Brothers in Arms* which introduces three daring knights fostered together as boys who have become men of strength, honor—and breathtaking passion.

Experience the extravagance and splendor of Georgian England with Maria Greene's *Midnight Mask* series, beginning with **A Bandit's Kiss,** which introduces us to the secrets of a notorious highwayman and the hearts he has stolen. Finally, Sylvia McDaniel presents **The Rancher Takes A Wife,** the first in *The Burnett Brides* series set in rough-and-tumble 1870s Texas, where one matchmaking woman is determined that her three stubborn, handsome sons will marry the right women—even if she has to find them herself! Enjoy!

Kate Duffy
Editorial Director

Shadow of the Bastille:

A DAUGHTER'S DESTINY

Jo Ann Ferguson

ZEBRA BOOKS
KENSINGTON PUBLISHING CORP.

http://www.zebrabooks.com

8203

For Dot,
Sister-in-law and friend

Other books by Jo Ann Ferguson

Sweet Temptations
The Captain's Pearl
Anything for You
An Unexpected Hero
Mistletoe Kittens
An Offer of Marriage
Lord Radcliffe's Season
No Price Too High
The Jewel Palace
O'Neal's Daughter
The Convenient Arrangement
Just Her Type
Destiny's Kiss
Raven Quest
A Model Marriage
Rhyme and Reason
Spellbound Hearts
The Counterfeit Count
A Winter Kiss
A Phantom Affair
Miss Charity's Kiss
Valentine Love
The Wolfe Wager
An Undomesticated Wife
A Mother's Joy
The Smithfield Bargain
The Smithfield Bargain
The Fortune Hunter

And writing as Rebecca North

A June Betrothal

Chapter One

London, 1811

There it was! Again!

Brienne LeClerc dropped the knife onto the kitchen table and rushed to the back door. Throwing it open, she looked both ways along the alley.

Fog twisted as if in pain through the trash pressed up against the walls of the buildings. A cat yowled in victory at catching its dinner. Rain splattered the ground that was the same gray as the fog.

But no one was in the narrow space. From the street, she could hear the calls of teamsters and the clatter of wagon wheels. Not the whisper of a footfall intruded in the empty alley.

Brienne shut the door and frowned. The first time she had caught the motion out of the corner of her eye, she had guessed it belonged to the delivery boy from Covent Garden. He was late. The next time she had thought she had seen someone, she had waited for his knock. Now, this third time ... mayhap it had been just Madame Dumont's cat.

Although the kitchen was hot while this evening's selections cooked on the iron stove, she shivered. Odd things had been happening lately. Grand-mère had laughed at Brienne's disquiet. So many people traveled in London's crowded streets; therefore it was not strange that a man should follow the same route through Soho as Brienne did while on her errands yesterday and the day before. She must not be fanciful when so much work waited here at L'Enfant de la Patrie.

She laughed softly, not wanting to disturb Maman,who was resting upstairs. Grand-mère would be pleased to hear that any man was paying attention to Brienne. A young woman should have many callers, Grand-mère believed.

Brienne had no time for callers. Her hours were filled with the chores necessary to keep the salon open and her patrons well-fed and eager to return.

Taking a deep breath and savoring the aromas of red wine and garlic, she went to the table where she had been chopping carrots. Her patrons among the *ton* would not arrive at the salon off Tottenham Court Road until long past dark, but she still needed to iron the napkins and arrange the flowers for the tables in the salon.

The bell over the front door chimed. At last! The delivery boy must be here, because no one else should be entering at this hour. *Should be*. Another tremor cut across her shoulders. She tried to shrug it away. Grand-mère was correct. She was too fanciful.

She drew the pass-through aside. "Tip, how many times have I told you to make deliveries to the kitchen door?"

"If I were Tip, I might know the answer." The deep voice resounded in the salon as if heralding the Prince Regent.

Stop being fanciful!

Putting down her knife, Brienne peered through the small window. Her view was blocked by a stack of extra plates on the sideboard. She gasped as a shadow cut across the window, just as it had at the back door. Tempted to ask if he had been in the alley, she could not as her gaze met eyes the same blue as the plates. Those eyes pierced her as fiercely as a shard of china. Mesmerizing, they refused to let her look away.

Then, so abruptly her breath caught, the eyes crinkled in amusement. She clutched the sill of the pass-through. Who was this man who could unsettle her with a mere look?

"I am looking for a Miss Laclerk," said the voice that belonged to those extraordinary eyes, which were ringed with a deeper blue.

His appalling pronunciation freed her from his spell-binding gaze. Maman always was distressed by how the English slaughtered their name. Of course, Maman hated everything English. Brienne could not share that prejudice, for she had been only an infant when the Terror had forced her family to flee Paris. England with all its quirks was home.

"One moment, sir," she said, closing the small window.

Leaning against the wall, she forced her heart to slow its frantic beat. The man's voice was quality. Her flighty thoughts must not betray her into insulting a potential patron.

She straightened her unbleached muslin dress and grimaced when she noted the spots splattered across the high bodice. No apron ever caught everything she splashed. She pulled off her apron and tossed it onto the table.

Gathering up the carrots she had chopped, she dropped them into the soup. She dipped the spoon and took a sip. Grand-mère was appalled at the very idea of such samples, but Brienne could not cook without them. After pinching a bit of sage into the bubbling pot, she hurried to the salon door.

The room was as elegant as the kitchen was utilitarian. White latticework climbed one wall where she struggled to keep flowers alive amid the smoke and dust of London. With the salon boasting walls the color of a summer sky and a stone floor and bricks edging the room's single window, she hoped her patrons would believe they had entered a hushed garden.

As she walked past the half dozen tables, Brienne wondered what the tall man, now standing by the front door, wanted. He glanced around the salon with disinterest, but his clean-shaven jaw was taut.

He was dressed well enough to be part of the *ton*, but not as grand as a peer. A younger son, mayhap, or a gentleman aspiring to match his money with the hand of a penniless lord's daughter to gain a title for his son. His brocade waistcoat was shadowed to a dusky maroon by the lowered shades over the window. He wore tan breeches beneath a perfectly tailored coat of cocoa-colored wool that was lightly spotted with rain. Above his white cravat, which was tied as fashion dictated, his hair was a warm, light brown. He carried a silk hat in his hand.

"I am Brienne LeClerc," she said as his gaze came back to her. Again her heart started to thud against her chest, for those eyes were even more powerful at close range.

"A pleasure, Miss LeClerc." When she smiled at his proper pronunciation, he took her hand in his, which was gloved in walnut-colored leather. He bowed over it, but did not raise it to his lips. "My name is Evan Somerset. I had the honor of dining here last evening. The meal was one of the finest examples of French cuisine I have ever sampled. I wanted to tell you that, so please forgive my intrusion at this hour."

She smiled. Grand-mère would be pleased to hear of this

call. "Mr. Somerset, I hope you will join us at L'Enfant de la Patrie again some evening."

"I had hoped to speak with you now, Miss LeClerc," he said as she turned toward the kitchen door.

"About what?" She did not have time to waste on idle chitchat, but she must not antagonize any patron. "I should warn you, Mr. Somerset, that I do not share my recipes with anyone's kitchen."

"Wise of you." His eyes narrowed, although his face did not lose its polished smile. "If I may . . ." He pointed to the sideboard beneath the pass-through.

"If you may what?"

"Indulge me, Miss LeClerc. I need to satisfy my curiosity."

"About what?"

His eyes crinkled again, but she was not fooled. They were cool and appraising every motion she made. What could he possibly be interested in on the sideboard? The wrinkled napkins? She bit her lip. The silver was spread across it. Could he be a thief disguised as a gentleman? Had he been checking out every entrance and exit to the salon in hopes of robbing her?

"I intend you no harm, Miss LeClerc."

"I am pleased to hear that." She wondered if he could read her thoughts. *Don't be fanciful!* She was standing as stiff as a Beefeater at his post. Anyone with a hint of insight could see she was disquieted.

"I know this is a most unusual request." His deep voice took on a soothing warmth. "Do humor me, mademoiselle."

Brienne gestured toward the sideboard, not wanting to own that she was more than a bit curious to discover what had intrigued him enough to bring him out on this foggy, rain-swept day. She watched him walk to the old oak cabinet. Every step was measured yet graceful. The image of Madame Dumont's cat stalking some hapless creature burst into her head. What was Evan Somerset on the prowl for?

She frowned as he reached behind the pile of unironed napkins and picked up a vase. Held in his broad hands, the vase seemed even smaller than its scanty six inches. Why was he interested in that? For years, it had been collecting dust upstairs. When Brienne had noticed it last week, she had brought it down because its blue color complemented the dishes. She had since decided not to use it because the gilt bolt of lightning slicing across its side ruined the serenity of the salon.

When he turned it upside down, she cried, "Mr. Somerset, no!"

Water splashed over his breeches and shoes, and he cursed. She shoved several napkins into his hand. He dabbed at his shoes without putting the vase back onto the sideboard.

"You could have warned me a bit sooner," he said with a grin. She was amazed, because she had guessed he would be furious. His golden brown eyebrows arched to a rakish angle. "I trust that was not the excellent white wine sauce that I enjoyed last night."

"No, only water." She was astonished at her reluctance to own that. Mr. Somerset, with his practiced smile, alarmed her more than he should, and she wished he would take his leave.

"Is that so?" He balanced the vase on his palm. "Miss LeClerc, I am prepared to offer you Ł50 for this lovely vase."

"I beg your pardon?"

"Is that too little?"

She plucked the vase from his hand, then drew herself up to her full height so her eyes were level with the cleft in his chin. "Are you mad?"

"I would prefer to think not."

His composure threatened to undo hers even more.

"Then, why are you offering me Ł50 for a useless piece of bric-a-brac?"

His gaze glided along her. She wanted to flee back to the safety of her kitchen, but she could not move, save for her heart that sped like a racehorse. The strong emotions in his cobalt eyes confirmed what she had guessed. Evan Somerset was a man who guarded the truth as closely as a miser watched every ha'penny.

"Mayhap the vase has been useless to you," he said with that smoothness that was no longer soothing, "but I suspect you might be willing to part with it for Ł100."

"Ł100?"

"I am willing to pay twice that, but no higher. Surely Ł200 would be of some use to you."

Brienne faltered. So much money would have many uses. A new coat for Grand-mère. Flowers to brighten Maman's room. A new stove for the parlor upstairs. There might even be enough for a visit to the theater, a treat she had not enjoyed in more than a year.

He smiled and ran a finger along the lightning bolt on the vase. She pulled back, holding it against her splattered bodice. A mistake, she realized instantly, for his gaze followed. The heat from his eyes seared her breast, and she did not dare to breathe.

His voice became hushed. "Very beautiful. I would say exceptional."

"Would you?"

"The gentle curve, the smoothness, the warmth." His eyes sparked like iron wheels on the cobbles. "All in all, exceptional."

"I would not have described this vase as exceptional."

"Neither would I."

"But you just said . . ." Her face became hot.

"By Jove, I believe I have insulted you when I meant only to pay you a compliment." He reached under his coat. "And Ł200 if that is acceptable to you."

"It is not!"

He frowned, and she took a step back, for his eyes were as cold as a frost fair day. "Please be careful, Miss LeClerc. That vase is very valuable."

"Its only value is sentimental, for my father gave it to my mother before he died."

"My client has seen it and is willing to pay highly."

"Client?"

He withdrew a leather folder from beneath his coat. Pulling out an engraved card, he offered it. She looked at his fake smile. What was he hiding?

"Miss LeClerc?" he prompted, pressing the card into her hand.

When she was about to put the vase on a table, he tensed. Would he try to snatch it? She tightened her grip around its slender neck as she looked at the calling card.

EVAN SOMERSET

DEALER IN FINE ART AND ANTIQUITIES

GROSVENOR SQUARE

She held the card out to him. "I suspect you have been the butt of a very expensive prank, Mr. Somerset."

"It is no prank. I must have the vase. I have offered you Ł200. Be reasonable, Miss LeClerc."

"The vase is not for sale."

"Not for sale?" His smile became as frigid as his eyes. "My dear Miss LeClerc, everything is for sale. All one needs to do is find the price."

"You are mistaken. Everything is not for sale at L'Enfant de la Patrie."

"A shame."

"I bid you good day, sir. If—"

His arm around her waist tugged her to him. His gaze held hers again as his fingers splayed across her back, pressing her to the hard planes of his chest. " 'Tis a shame, Miss LeClerc," he said softly, "that you are so sorely mistaken. Everything and everyone has a price. Find it, and what you want is yours." His hand slid up her back to curl around her nape as he whispered, "And I have found what I want right here in your salon."

She stared up at him, unable to look away. Something glittered in his eyes as they lowered toward hers. His fingers tilted her mouth beneath his. The warmth of his breath caressed her face as his arm tightened around her waist.

The door from the kitchen opened, and Brienne jerked herself out of Mr. Somerset's arms. *Mon Dieu*, was she mad?

A lad peered past the door, his eyes growing wide. A sly grin inched across his freckled face. "Didn't know I was interruptin', Miz Laclerk. Do ye want me comin' back in a while? Don't want to get in yer way with yer fancy gent." He snickered behind his dirt-encrusted hand.

Brienne fought the heat climbing her cheeks. Why had Tip arrived *now?* She fought to keep her voice steady. "Tip, wait in the kitchen." When the door swung closed, she whirled and spat in a furious whisper, "Mr. Somerset, I want you out of my salon. You have ruined my reputation with your antics."

He pointed to the vase she held. "Let me give you the Ł200 for the vase, and I will be glad never to return."

"No."

"No?" He reached toward her again.

She backed away. "I will not listen to this nonsense any longer. Will you please leave before I have no choice but to send for the watch?"

"Miss LeClerc, I—"

"Good day, sir." She glanced at the kitchen door. It was ajar. Blast Tip! The lad would soon be spreading the tale of the outrageous Mr. Somerset holding her in his arms.

Catching her by the wrist, Mr. Somerset spun her back to him. "You must listen to me."

She choked back a gasp. His easy smile was gone, replaced by a fury that burned blue-hot in his eyes. Her first impression had been right. He was hiding something—a temper too fierce to be voiced. If she did not convince him to leave. . . . She was not sure what he would do.

As she drew back, she was surprised he released her. Quietly, she said, "I have listened to you and have given you my answer. The vase is not for sale." Again his gaze locked on the vase that she held close. The heat in his eyes seared her skin. When he took her hand in his, she gasped, "Sir, if you do not leave posthaste, I shall scream."

"And embarrass L'Enfant de la Patrie? I doubt that, Miss LeClerc. The tale of such a public spectacle would be repeated in your patrons' ears."

"Are you threatening me?"

"Me?" She did not know if his astonishment was real or feigned. "I wish only to close this business deal. Why don't you sit down while we discuss this like two reasonable people?"

Brienne pulled her hand away. She wondered how many other business deals he had closed with this charm. It would not work on her . . . again. "That is quite impossible."

"Why?"

"Because we do not have two reasonable people in this room." She smiled coldly. "Good day, sir."

As she put her hand on the kitchen door, she heard Tip scurry away. Behind her, Mr. Somerset's angry steps stamped toward the front door. The bell sounded over the door as it opened and closed.

She glanced over her shoulder to be sure he had left. When his shadow passed the front door, she shuddered.

Had it been Mr. Somerset's shadow that had caught her eye in the kitchen?

She wrapped her arms around herself, but fear enveloped her in its serrated claws. Evan Somerset would not accept defeat this easily. His eyes had glowed with obsession when he spoke of how each person had a price, warning how sincerely he believed that.

And one thing she believed. He would come back to the salon to get the vase and to find out exactly what her price was . . . and then do whatever he must to be sure she paid it.

Chapter Two

Brienne shoved the kitchen door open. Setting the vase on the table, she asked, "Tip, do you have fresh green beans for me today?"

"Well 'e was quite a dandy. Who was that bloke?" The delivery boy gave her a bawdy grin.

"Someone who has learned to mind his own business!"

"Looked like 'e was mindin' yers, Miz Laclerk." He crowed at his jest.

"I could use you tending to your business and letting me tend to mine. He will not be returning." She drew on her apron.

" 'E'll be back. No gent looks at a lady like 'e looked at ye and don't come back."

"You are wrong. He—" When he laughed again, she shook her head. "Dash it, Tip! Where are those beans?"

After haggling with the lad, who always tried to add on a few pennies profit of his own, she bought what she needed and sent him on his way. She checked the simmering broth, then began to cut the beans.

"You look busy."

Brienne smiled as her grandmother came down the stairs. She carried an armload of clean tablecloths, and the warm smell of freshly ironed linen swarmed over Brienne. With the soup's aroma, it combined into the fragrance Brienne loved most.

"Good afternoon, Grand-mère." As always, she spoke in French while *en famille*.

Setting the linens on the table, Grand-mère picked up the small vase. She ran a gnarled finger along the design. A sad smile deepened her careworn face beneath her thinning, white hair.

"Why did you bring this vase down here, *ma petite?*" asked her grandmother. "I thought Lucile had it in her room."

"Take it if you wish." Brienne was tempted to add that she would be delighted never to see the vase again.

"It may ease Lucile's discomfort."

Brienne nodded. Maman had always been sickly, and the sooty air of London made it impossible for her to leave her bed. Every year, she grew weaker.

Grand-mère walked to the door opening onto the stairs. "I am going to get the desserts Lord Grantton ordered. Do you need anything while I'm out?"

"I have everything ready for tonight. Finally." She gestured toward the table. "Tip just arrived with today's order."

"So it was his voice I heard?"

"Yes." She looked away, not wanting to let her beloved grandmother know she was not being completely honest.

"I shall be back within the hour, *ma petite.*"

"That will—Oh, no!" Brienne whirled as a telltale smell warned that the broth needed stirring.

Grand-mère chuckled. "I believe the broth needs more basil."

Kissing her grandmother's cheek, Brienne smiled. Cooking here was always a cooperative task, as long as Grand-mère did not catch her tasting the sauces.

Brienne went into the salon. Seeing a man's hat on a table, she sighed. Mr. Somerset must have left it. Dash it! That meant he would be coming back. Mayhap he would send a servant to retrieve it. She put the hat on a peg near the entrance. If she met Mr. Somerset at the door, she could have him on his way without delay.

As the door opened, Brienne glanced over her shoulder. Her lips tightened, and she prepared to tell Mr. Somerset to take his hat and himself from L'Enfant de la Patrie.

Her eyes widened as two men entered the salon. They were dressed in the shabby clothes of seamen.

"May I help you?" she asked, hoping they would realize their mistake and leave.

The taller man ran his fingers through his greasy, black hair and leered a broken-toothed smile. "Ye ain't Brienne Laclerk, are ye?"

"I am Miss LeClerc."

"Listen to that Frenchie talk. Right out of Boney's court, eh, Lefty?"

She followed his gaze to the man by the door. He reached for the drapes and closed them.

"What are you doing?" Brienne asked.

The black-haired man grabbed her arm. She gasped when he spun her to face him. Her breath snagged as she stared at the long blade of a knife he held close to her face.

"Be quiet, darlin'. I wouldn't want to be cuttin' yer pretty face."

"Wh-wh-what do you want?" About a dozen guineas were cached in the box on the top shelf in the kitchen. Would that be enough to satisfy them? It must, because she could not let them upstairs where they could hurt her invalid mother.

He shoved her into a chair. "Miss Laclerk, make it

easy on yerself. Tell us what we want t'know. Where is it?''

"Where is what?" She stared at the blade.

"C'mon, darlin'. Tell us. If you don't . . ."

Scowling, she ordered, "Begone!"

He laughed. "As soon as ye tell us where it is."

"Where what is? I don't—" She gasped as he raised his hand. He would not strike her . . . would he?

"Tell me, darlin'. Otherwise, I'll 'ave to be searchin' this place. Ye won't be liking it." He cracked the knuckles of one hand.

"There, Ep! Look over there!" called the other man.

When the black-haired man went to the sideboard, she started to rise. A heavy hand pressed her onto the chair.

"Don't be moving, lass," the second man warned. "Give us what we came for, and we'll be on our way."

"What do you want?" she whispered.

"Shut up!" snapped the black-haired man. "Shut up, or I'll be shuttin' ye up." He examined the vases Brienne had yet to fill with flowers.

Horror filled her. Vases? Had Mr. Somerset sent them? Was this what he had meant when he told her she would regret not selling him the vase?

"Where is it?" the black-haired man demanded.

"If you would tell me what you want, I could—"

With a growl, he swept everything off the sideboard. Dishes crashed to the floor, splintering. When he scowled at her, she feared her punishment was just beginning.

If only they would explain. . . .

"Where is it, darlin'?"

"Please tell me what you want."

"All right, darlin'. We'll pretend yer as stupid as ye act. The vase. The one with the lightning bolt. Where is it?"

In disbelief, she stared at him. For almost twenty years, the vase had been here. Why was someone interested in it now? "I don't know." She could not take them upstairs. Maman was too fragile. The shock of seeing these wretched men could kill her. "Honestly, I . . . d-d-d-don't know."

He seized her hair, tilting her head back. "When yer brains are loosened a bit," he growled, "ye might be more likely to be rememberin' where ye put it."

"Stop," she whispered, but he did not heed her as he raised his hand again. It swung at her.

The pain lasted only a heartbeat before it, along with her fear, disappeared into blackness.

The warm, sweet scent of starched linen teased Brienne. Slowly she became aware that she was moving. Odd, for her feet were not on the ground. It was as if she were floating.

Sound intruded. A low, repetitious rumble close to her ear, like a distant church bell tolling matins. The cadence grew more rapid as she heard a soft squeak. A door opening?

"Miss LeClerc?"

A man's voice! Whose?

Something hard and flat pressed against her back. Cool dampness caressed her forehead. She tried to reach up to touch what lay across her brow. Her arm was too heavy.

"Miss LeClerc, can you hear me?"

Yes, she could hear him. She tried to find words to answer.

The dampness moved from her forehead to her cheek. Agony erupted through her. Her eyes opened as her hand clasped a wool sleeve. She stared up at Evan Somerset.

"What . . ." She groaned when the single word ached through her head.

"It might be better if you don't say anything right now."

Brienne looked past him. She was in the kitchen. She was lying on the kitchen table if her blurry eyes were not playing her false. That smell—the broth was burning! With a moan, she pushed herself up to sit.

"Be careful," he warned.

She cradled her throbbing head in her hands. She doubted if she could move any way but carefully right now. Any sudden motion threatened to send her head flying off.

"The stove," she whispered, closing her eyes. "The broth . . . it needs stirring."

He muttered something; then she heard his footsteps cross the wood floor. He yelped. Metal clattered. She moaned as the noise struck her.

"Those handles were hot," he grumbled as he came back to the table.

"You should have used a cloth."

"Thank you for the sympathy."

"I'm sorry." Weak tears billowed into her eyes. "I don't have much sympathy for anyone else at the moment. My head hurts so horribly."

His arm slipped around her shoulders as he put the damp cloth in her hands. She raised it to her forehead. When she swayed, he placed her cheek against his chest. The scent of starch and the low sound of his heartbeat were shockingly familiar.

"I brought you in here," he said as if he could hear her confused thoughts, "because I did not want you to wake up and see the other room."

"What is wrong with the other room?"

"How much do you remember?"

Brienne frowned, then wished she had not. Another slash of pain cut across her face. She touched the puffiness by her left eye. What had happened? Her eye was as sore as when she had fallen as a child and suffered a black eye. What if she had another one now? How was she going to explain that to her patrons or to Grand-mère?

"Brienne, how much do you remember?"

She stared at Mr. Somerset, shocked he would use her given name. As the fuzz clouding her vision cleared, she saw his straight lips.

"Brienne?"

"I remember you," she retorted, irritated at his impatience. "What are you doing back here?"

"I came back for my hat, but I found something quite unexpected." He pushed aside the door to the salon.

Brienne slid from the table. Smoothing her dress around her, she took a single step, then wobbled. She forced her feet to take another step.

"*Mon Dieu*," she whispered.

Every table and chair in the salon was upset. Shards of broken glass and mounds of dented silver covered the floor. All the cabinets gaped open. Even the plants edging the window had been tipped over.

She shivered as memory burst upon her as viciously as the black-haired man's blow. "Two men came in here and did this. Did you send them?"

"Me? Why do you think I sent them?"

Evan Somerset tried to be patient when Brienne did not answer him, but he could think of only one reason why she would accuse him of having a hand in this. He hoped he was wrong.

She lurched to the window. Kneeling, she set a plant on the sill. Her shoulders quivered, but when he put his hands on them, she shook them off. She stood and crossed the room, clearly trying to keep as much distance between them as possible.

Pretty Brienne LeClerc was anxious to be rid of him. Pretty . . . she was that. Her trim figure was outlined so perfectly by her plain gown. She did not need the bows and flounces that decorated the frocks worn by the *élite*.

Her loosened hair cloaked her in an ebony sheen, tempting his fingers to entangle in it. How soft it had been when it had draped over his arm as he carried her into the kitchen!

He went to the sideboard. It had been knocked onto its side and one leg broken off. Ramming his fist against his other palm, he wished he could find the blackguards who had attacked this salon . . . and Brienne. He *would* find them. Then they would rue this.

He knew who was responsible for this. Evan Somerset. How could he have been so stupid? That he had come to L'Enfant de la Patrie twice must have tipped his hand. He had been a complete idiot not to expect competition. Lagrille trusted him as much as England trusted Napoleon.

The vase! If those men had the vase now, he should be giving chase.

Instead, he went to where Brienne was struggling to lift a table back onto its legs. Without a word, he set it upright. He smiled as she held out his ruined hat. Taking it, he poked his fingers through the holes. "What did they want, Brienne?"

"Ain't it obvious?" At the deep, frigid voice, Evan turned to meet the iron gray eyes of the man entering the salon.

Evan recognized the stench of authority. Although he usually found it prudent to stay far from any forces of the law, he did not move. He recalled a headmaster who once had tried to daunt him with a superior scowl such as this. That teacher had suffered many cruel tricks before Evan had ended their mutual duress by leaving school on a moonless night.

"I am Evan Somerset," he said with a cool smile. "Who are you?"

"Haviland. I oversee the watch here."

"Do you? Then, what pub were you hiding in instead

of protecting this woman and her business as you are paid to do?''

Brienne surprised him by saying, ''If you gentlemen wish to talk, please do it outside. I must restore my salon for my patrons.''

''Let us help,'' said Haviland so kindly Evan chuckled under his breath. The watchman must be smitten with Brienne, although not enough to risk his skin.

As Haviland seated Brienne at the table, she hunched her shoulders to avoid touching him. Good. She was sensible. Haviland would be no help, but Evan had to make certain that calling in the Bow Street Runners was not suggested. Those lads might find the men who had done this before he could. That would lead to all kinds of complications.

He had to get that vase! Even a piece of it would be enough. Why, he had no idea. Nor did he care, for all he wanted was to find the vase, collect his pay, and go on to his next assignment, which he would make sure was less complicated than this one was becoming.

Leaning against the wall, he crossed his arms over his chest in a negligent pose guaranteed to bring out the worst in Haviland.

Haviland glowered at him. ''What in the hell—Excuse me, Miss Laclerk. What are ye doin' here, Somerset?''

''This is a place of public business. I came here on business.''

''What business?''

''My business.''

Haviland kicked a table. It collapsed with a crash. He ignored the flare of dismay in Brienne's eyes as he stepped toward Evan. ''Somerset, if ye don't cooperate, ye'll find yerself rottin' in prison.''

''No!'' cried Brienne, leaping to her feet. ''You cannot put a man in jail for no reason.''

Haviland whirled to face her. "I can give ye lots of reasons, Miss Laclerk. One is gettin' in my way."

"Now, now," Evan said, "there is no cause for such words to Miss *LeClerc*."

When Haviland growled something incoherent, Evan looked at Brienne. Her dark eyes still flashed. Her impassioned defense was a surprise. He would have guessed she would gladly pay the turnkey to put shackles on him.

She rocked almost off her feet as Haviland pushed past her, and Evan swore under his breath. This was not the time to enjoy poking fun at Haviland. She was ready to collapse. That was no surprise either.

Evan grasped her hand and drew her to him. She almost tumbled into his arms. When she stiffened and was about to pull away, he murmured, "I need *you* to cooperate if you want to get rid of him."

She glanced at Haviland, then nodded.

Slipping his arm around her shoulders, he turned her to him. The lush softness of her breasts against his chest threatened to take his breath away. His fingers sifted through her thick hair that swept over his arm, and he gazed down into her eyes which were lustrous with unshed tears. He had never seen such courage . . . or such temptation.

He brushed his lips against hers, savoring the sweet flavor of her mouth. She stared up at him, astonishment lighting her eyes until they glowed like dark jewels. Smiling, he kissed her forehead. She closed her eyes and rested her cheek against his chest.

Looking over her head, Evan said, "As you can see, Haviland, I am here because Brienne is my dear friend."

"Dear friend?" He snorted. "She don't have gentleman callers."

"If you watch this salon closely enough to know that, you should have seen the two men who attacked her."

"Two?"

Evan cursed his own glib tongue. If Brienne's warmth were not so distracting, he might keep his mind on getting rid of Haviland and getting his hands on the vase. Although, he had to own, getting his hands on Brienne was not a bad consolation at the moment.

"Miss Laclerk, is this true?"

Brienne hesitated, not wanting to lie. Mayhap with this bit of information, Mr. Haviland would leave. Her salon was destroyed. It would take more money than she could imagine to repair the damage. Money! Mr. Somerset would give her Ł200 for that silly vase. As soon as the watchman left, she would sell it to him.

"Yes, Mr. Haviland," she said quietly. "Two men. They smelled of the docks."

Mr. Somerset tilted her face toward his. "*Ma chère* Brienne, how will you ever forgive me for letting you face this alone? How can I ever forgive myself for allowing such evil to hurt the one I love most in the whole world?"

She bit back her retort that Evan Somerset loved no one but himself. His blue gaze surrounded her as his fingers stroked her arm. The light touch urged her to forget everything else as she brought his mouth to hers again.

"Brienne!"

Pulling away from Mr. Somerset, Brienne ran to her grandmother, who was staring at the broken chairs and tables. "Grand-mère, be careful! Will you go to Maman? She must have heard the noise here."

"No doubt about that." Grand-mère picked up a table-cloth and frowned at the dirt on it.

"Please reassure her that everything will be all right. I can handle this."

In haughty, very correct English, she demanded, "Will you handle this, *ma petite*? Or will you be the one handled?"

"Grand-mère!" She forced a smile. "Please do not tease me about Evan. Have you forgotten what he asked me this afternoon?" She hated lying, but she did not want to see anyone, even Evan Somerset, sent to prison. She had heard too many stories of the horror of the Bastille.

"This afternoon?" Her eyes narrowed.

Evan stepped forward, took the old woman's hand, and bowed over it. "*Bon après-midi, madame. Je voudrais—*"

"Do not try to charm me by speaking French, young man." A smile tipped her lips. "However, you do speak it well for an Englishman."

"A friend taught me well."

"A friend? A friend like Brienne?"

Amusement glittered in his eyes. "A very different type of friend, madame. I should have said a business acquaintance."

"I shall not ask what business that was."

"A wise decision."

With a chuckle, Grand-mère turned to Brienne. "We still have much to discuss before I allow you to mix up your life with such a scoundrel, *ma petite*." She did not give Brienne a chance to answer as she added to Haviland, "I trust you have suspects to capture and be tried for this crime against us, sir."

The watchman opened his mouth, then clamped it closed as he strode out of the salon. The door crashed behind him, rattling the gilded glass.

"Good riddance," Evan said with a return of his smile. Bowing his head, he said, "Evan Somerset, madame—"

"I am Yvonne LeClerc, Monsieur Somerset. I owe you a debt of gratitude for coming to my granddaughter's rescue."

"Too late, I fear."

Brienne stepped back to keep her grandmother from examining her face. "I am fine, Grand-mère. 'Tis nothing. Thank you for your help, Mr. Somerset. I regret that your hat was ruined. However, I assume you came back because you are still interested in the vase.''

"The vase?'' He caught her hands in his. "What about the vase?''

Before she could answer, Grand-mère said, "I hear your mother's bell, Brienne. Go and let her see that you are safe.''

"Maman has not rung. She—'' The distant sound of a handbell contradicted her. "I will return quickly. We have much to do if we plan to reopen tomorrow night.''

"Tomorrow night?'' Mr. Somerset asked. "How can you expect to clean this up in such a short time?''

"Because we have to. Mr. Somerset, if you would be so kind as to wait.''

"Of course, Miss LeClerc.'' Evan laughed as Brienne glanced at him, surprise again in her expressive eyes, as he addressed her as formally as she had him. When she rushed out of the room, he smiled at her grandmother. "I trust I may wait here?''

"You may, although you may have to wait a while. If my daughter is distraught, Brienne will have to calm her.''

"Daughter?'' He swallowed the rest of his question as the old woman arched a single snowy brow. If Brienne's surname was LeClerc as was her maternal grandmother's, that suggested Brienne was the product of an illicit union. Mayhap Brienne had inherited some of that ungovernable passion. No, he had no time for such enticing thoughts. He had to get that vase, not imagine delighting in the innocent fire on her lips.

"Lucile is not well, Monsieur Somerset.''

"I am sorry to hear that.'' He looked around the room. "And this will not help.''

"Do you always exhibit such a gift for understatement?'' She lowered herself to a chair. "I was right. You are a scoundrel.''

"You are insightful, madame.''

"My eyes are clearest with matters concerning my granddaughter. From what Brienne said, I assume you called earlier."

"Yes."

She shook her head and sighed. "I fear this cool, subdued English climate has washed away Brienne's *joie de vie*. She thinks solely of the salon."

"Madame, I assure you that my interest in Brienne is purely business."

She smiled. "There are many kinds of business."

"True." He drew off his coat and hung it by the door. "Where do you keep your broom, madame?"

"A broom? I do not understand."

Making sweeping motions with his hands, he repeated, "A broom. To clean the floor. If your granddaughter wishes to reopen tomorrow evening, you will need every hand to clear away this mess. I offer you my services."

"No, thank you, Monsieur Somerset. Brienne and I shall tend to that after we deal with our other problem."

"Other problem?"

"You. What is it that you want, young man?"

"Me?"

Madame LeClerc chuckled heartily. "You, sir, are a rogue. Do not misunderstand. I do not dislike rogues. Men with few scruples make fine ministers for a king and fine lovers for a woman. However, I am old, and I have seen a king beheaded and watched as a peasant has dared to call himself emperor of France. There is a place for rogues in this world."

"Thank you," he said, his smile broadening.

"Do not think you can deceive me as you have tried to deceive Brienne."

Evan bent to pick up scattered napkins. Regret creased his forehead as he looked at the ruined furniture. The men had come from the docks, Brienne had said. He should not be delaying here. He should be on his way to the

Pool. A few questions there might gain him the answers he sought. He hoped his pockets were plump enough to pay for those answers.

Setting the napkins on the table, he said, "I have not fooled Brienne. She does not trust me."

"You are correct about that!" Brienne came from the kitchen. She forced a smile as Grand-mère gasped. With her hair back in a simple braid, the marks left by the man's hand must be visible. She had avoided the glass upstairs and had clung to the shadows while speaking with Maman. "Thank you for waiting, Mr. Somerset. I wanted to thank you again."

"Thanks? That is why you wanted me to stay?" He edged around the broken tables and put his hand on the doorframe beside her. When she started to back away, he clasped her arm. "Brienne, I thought you might want to speak to me about the vase."

"No." She dared say no more. The silly vase was so precious to Maman that Brienne would not ask her for it, not even to help resurrect L'Enfant de la Patrie.

"It is no longer here?"

"Yes." That much was the truth. It was not in the salon.

A soft sound intruded.

"That is Maman," Brienne said. "I should go, and—"

"She will want me." Grand-mère stepped between her and Mr. Somerset. "It has been most interesting to make your acquaintance, Monsieur Somerset. I bid you a good day."

Before Evan could do more than give a half bow in her direction, she trotted through the kitchen door. The light sound of her footsteps on the stairs leading up from the kitchen confirmed what he had guessed. The LeClerc family lived upstairs.

"Your grandmother is quite a lady," he remarked with a smile.

"I do not wish to speak of Grand-mère."

"And of what do you wish to speak, then?"

Her lowered brows could not cool her fiery beauty. "I do not want you to come here again. Play your games elsewhere, Mr. Somerset."

"Game, Brienne? Hardly a game, as you have learned today."

"I thought you did not know the men who did this."

"No, I do not." He laughed without humor. "I disdain violence myself." He grasped her shoulders. "Just remember this, Brienne. If you are lying to me, you are hurting yourself. This was just a warning. Those men will come back if they did not get the vase. They will come back again and again and again until they get what they want or they destroy you and this salon."

Brienne backed away. "No," she whispered.

"Then, be honest with me."

For a single heartbeat, she was ready to agree. Then, as she gazed up at him, she knew she would be a fool to trust him. If Evan Somerset refrained from violence, it was a conscious decision, because his intense eyes warned he could be a fierce foe.

"Where is the vase, Brienne?" he asked quietly.

"I told you—"

"You have told me nothing but lies." He cursed, then smiled as his hands slipped along her shoulders. As she tried to pull away, his fingers encircled her throat.

Her heart faltered. This was no jest, for his eyes narrowed with fury. Would he strangle her? She held her breath.

In a blistering whisper, he said, "Mayhap they will be interested in selling it to me for Ł200."

She put her hands over his. His grip tightened on her, but she gasped, " 'Tis my vase!"

"Is it? Not if you no longer have it."

"You would deal with the men who attacked me?"

With a shrug, he slid his hands up to curve along her cheeks. His mouth grazed her unbruised cheek. She fought the thrill rushing through her. She should despise him, not be taunted with the yearning for his lying lips.

"Business is business, my dear Brienne," he murmured against her ear. "You cannot sell me the vase if you do not have it. What do you expect? That I will find your trinket and then pay you for it? Why would I do that?"

"It would be the decent thing to do."

"I have never been described as decent."

Pulling out of his grip, Brienne stepped behind the kitchen door. She needed some barrier between her and his tempting touch. "Put the Closed sign in the window on your way out."

All humor left his face. "Brienne, for the love of heaven, I am just trying to help you."

"And yourself."

"Where is the vase?"

She did not answer. Running up the kitchen stairs, she paused at the top. She flinched as the street door slammed. Slowly she inched back down the steps. After turning down the lamp by the kitchen door, she drew back the torn curtains on the window.

Evan Somerset was stepping into an elegant carriage. She frowned. Only a fine lord or a wealthy businessman could own something so grand. Had he been honest with her?

No! He had been lying.

He must be lying. Otherwise, those men might be coming back.

"Brienne, what are you doing?"

She turned. "Grand-mère!"

Her grandmother leaned a broom against the wall. "May I assume that loud sound was Monsieur Somerset taking his leave?"

"Yes." She wrapped her arms around herself and walked into the kitchen. "I am glad he is gone."

"Are you, *ma petite?*" Grand-mère blew out the lamp. "Is that why you watch from the window?" She smiled. "He makes no secret of his pleasure with you."

"Do not play the matchmaker. He only wants to cause trouble for us."

"Are you certain of that?"

"More certain than I have been of anything in my life."

"Then, you must decide how you will deal with him, *ma petite.*"

She faced her grandmother. "What do you mean?"

"Monsieur Somerset will be back." Grand-mère's smile was as strained as her voice. "Of that, I am more certain than I have been of anything in my life."

Chapter Three

Brienne rushed to the apartment door. The loud rapping sounded like a drummer going mad in the midst of a symphony. She threw open the door. "Evan!"

"Brienne, I see we are friends once more," he said with a smile. Again he was dressed as a stylish gentleman should during the Season. Taking off his hat, which was as fashionable as the ruined one had been, he asked, "May I come in?"

"No." She pushed the door, but his arm kept her from closing it. "Mr. Somerset—"

"Miss LeClerc, I do think you need to decide what you are going to call me."

"How did you get in here?"

His smile broadened as he slowly forced the door open wide enough for him to enter. Putting his hat on a nearby table as if he were a regular caller, he said, "You should be more cautious, Brienne. Your kitchen door is unlocked."

"It cannot be unlocked. I locked it last night after you left."

"Mayhap a breeze blew it open."

"That is impossible. It—" She saw amusement twinkling in his eyes. He knew any breath of wind that might find its way along the alley would not have been strong enough to ruffle a hair on a lady's coiffure. Someone would have to help that breeze open a locked door. And that someone must have been Evan Somerset, fine gentleman. On the outside, that was, but what was behind the façade?

"What do you want?" she asked, too tired to argue. She had spent the night tending Maman and cleaning up downstairs.

"Just now? I would like to talk with you."

"If you want the vase—"

"I said I wanted to talk, Brienne. I said nothing about buying anything."

Stepping aside, she agreed, "All right, but you can stay only a few minutes. I have more work to do downstairs."

"You have done wonders in the salon." He brushed invisible dust from the navy coat he wore over a sedate, light blue waistcoat. "It looks almost as pleasant as it did before."

"May I remind you," she retorted in her haughtiest voice, "that you alone doubted we would reopen tonight? I knew I could count on my neighbors to lend me what I needed."

"Probably because they have been able to count on you many times in the past."

"How did you know that?"

"You are well known about here."

"Have you been asking about me?"

He shook his head. "No need. The hubbub here yesterday is all that is being talked about along the street. Everyone is agog about it."

Walking across the parlor, he paused by the settee which once might have been gold but had faded to a sad tan.

He looked around the room with indifference, but Brienne recognized this pose. It was the same one he had used in the salon yesterday before he offered her all that money for Maman's vase.

When a frown ruffled his brow, she resisted defending her home from his upper-class snobbery. She knew the parlor looked threadbare compared to the fine townhouse where he claimed to live. But this room, along with the two bedrooms and the tiny storeroom, held the memories of generations past. The furniture was shabby, but the wood glowed with care, and the tops of the two small tables were covered with books and lamps.

When Mr. Somerset picked up a framed miniature, Brienne took it from him. "Be careful with that!"

He tipped her hand so he could see the face in it. "Is this your father?"

"Yes."

"Where is he?"

"Dead."

At her terse answer, he said, "You don't sound very sad."

"He died when I was not much more than a baby. I find it impossible to mourn for a man I never knew." She put the portrait in its special spot on the table.

"Yet he gave you a legacy."

"A legacy?"

"You cannot have failed to note how much your eyes and stubborn chin are shaped like your late father's."

"So Maman has said often."

"May we sit while we talk?" He lavished that charming smile on her again.

She pointed to the settee. "Please make yourself comfortable, Mr. Somerset."

"You should call me Evan, as we are about to become business partners."

His words froze her. When she realized she was poised

halfway between sitting and standing, she dropped onto the chair. "Partners?"

From beneath his coat, he pulled a handful of pound notes. He tossed them on the table in front of her. "Take it. Ł100." He smiled, and she knew she had revealed her shock. "Half of what I offered you yesterday."

"Ł100," she murmured. There was not that much money in the cash box now hidden under Maman's bed.

He slid the pile of money toward her with a single finger. "Take it."

"What gave you the idea I need a partner in the salon?" She stood and moved behind the chair, so she would not be tempted to accept this money she needed so much.

He set himself on his feet and leaned one knee on her chair. His hands clamped hers on its back, pinning her in place, although she was unsure if she could have moved anyway when his gaze locked with hers. "I don't have any interest in becoming a partner in your salon. My talents run in a very different direction."

"Undoubtedly!"

"Be sarcastic if you wish. However, the fact remains we are going to be partners. We must recover your vase."

She frowned. "I thought you said you were not going to talk about the vase."

"I said, if you will recall, that I did not plan to buy the vase today. I said nothing of not talking about it." His fingers caressed hers as his voice dropped to a husky whisper. "If I fail to bring my employer that vase by summer, I shall pay with my life."

"You are lying!" She tried to pull away. When he did not release her, she looked into his face. What she saw startled her. Honesty.

He shook his head. "I had not intended for you to know, but I need your help. If that means telling you the truth, I must. I was hired by a gentleman to bring that vase to him. If I do not, he has vowed to make me pay most dearly. He has, I must admit, reasons to mistrust me.''

''I can believe that!'' Slowly she pulled her hands out from beneath his. ''Who is this man? Why does he want the vase?''

''I cannot tell you that. I must keep such information confidential.''

''And you expect me to be honest when you tell me nothing?'' She turned to the door. ''I think you should leave.''

He came around the chair. ''Brienne, I need your help. Did you see the men take the vase? Did you see anything to identify them other than that they were from the docks?''

Evan clenched his teeth as Brienne's face paled and she touched the swollen spots by her eye. Even rice powder could not cover the bruises. If she had an ounce of sense, she would have sold him the vase yesterday. Word would have spread quickly that Evan had it, and he would have been the focus of the hunt.

He wondered how she would react if he told her she was lucky she had not suffered worse. Lagrille had intimated that no crime was too low if it gained him the vase. With a silent curse, Evan forced those thoughts from his head. Once he found the vase, Brienne would be safe.

He was astonished. Why did he care what happened to this woman? In the years he had been involved in the shadowy world of antiquities and art, he had thought only of himself. Yet, since he had seen her dark eyes gazing out at him from the kitchen, he had been able to think of nothing but Brienne LeClerc. Strong and yet fragile, stubborn but tender-hearted, an innocent temptress.

''Why the money, then, Evan?''

He forced himself not to smile when she used his given name. It would seem he was finding a way to captivate Miss LeClerc after all, but captivating her was not the only thing he wanted to do with her. He fought to keep from drawing her into his arms. Such a sweet armful she was.

Keep your mind on the vase. What good will Brienne do you if you are dead? Lagrille would fulfill his threats. Not for the first time, Evan wondered if he had been offered this commission simply as an excuse to kill him. Brienne was right. That vase had no value, save for this family.

"The money is because I need your cooperation. I will buy it if you will not give it any other way." He smiled. "As I told you, everyone has a price. I thought yours might be Ł100."

"How dare you! I—" A bell chimed softly, and she raised her chin. "I must ask you to excuse me, Mr. Somerset. Maman is calling. I assume you can find your own way out as readily as you found your way in." She picked up the money from the table and jammed it into his hand. "Finding a way in and out of a kitchen is a skill all rats have."

He tossed the money on the floor, and astonishment widened her eyes. "Brienne, you are in danger! Tremendous danger! Help me find the vase, so they will leave you alone."

Again she blanched. The insistent sound of the hand bell sent color flying across her cheeks. "Go away, and take your lies with you! That vase is not worth anyone . . ."

"Anyone doing what?" he demanded. "Beating you? They have done that already! Ransacking L'Enfant de la Patrie? That did not work. Who will be attacked next? Your grandmother? Your mother?"

"Go away!"

"My leaving shall not change anything."

"It shall! I shan't have to listen to your lies!" Brienne ran toward her mother's room, trying to compose herself. Maman must have heard their argument. Seeing her mother's dark eyes, which were sunk in the colorless expanse of her face, she asked, "You wanted me, Maman?"

Maman looked past her in amazement. Glancing over her shoulder, Brienne fought the rage boiling through her. Evan Somerset had no manners. How dare he enter Maman's sickroom without waiting for an invitation!

"Maman, this is Evan Somerset," she said in a strained tone. "He is—he is—"

Sweeping past Brienne, Evan bowed to her mother with the grace of a courtier. With the narrow bed and a dresser piled high with clothing and medical powders, there was barely room for him. "How do you do, Madame LeClerc? Forgive this most unseemly intrusion, but Brienne and I were in the midst of a conversation when you rang, and being the devoted daughter she is, she would not wait a moment to hurry to your side." With that beguiling smile Brienne was beginning to despise, he added, "If I may be so bold, madame, may I say I can see that Brienne inherited much of her extraordinary loveliness from you?"

Brienne was not surprised when Maman smiled, even though her mother often had told Brienne how much she resembled her late father. Maman always had had a weakness for handsome men. At least, that was what Grand-mère frequently mumbled. Brienne had seen few signs of that, for Maman had never entertained any gentlemen.

In her reedy voice, Maman answered, "You may be so bold, Monsieur Somerset." She spoke in the thick French accent she took pride in, for she refused to admit they were staying in London. Glancing at Brienne, she smiled. "Are you calling on my daughter?"

"To be honest, I should say I hope I am. Your daughter is incredibly resistant to my attempts to woo her."

"Brienne is innocent in many ways, but, of course,

every mother wishes to see her daughter settled happily and well.''

''I'm quite happy with my life, Maman,'' Brienne said in a chiding voice.

Before Evan could reply, Grand-mère called, ''Brienne! Lucile! Are you about?'' She paused in the bedroom door. ''Monsieur Somerset!'' She held out a slip of paper. Staring at Evan, she flinched and switched to English. ''Brienne, *ma petite*, there are pound notes all over the parlor. I—''

Brienne plucked it from her fingers. ''They belong to Mr. Somerset.''

''Is that so?'' She frowned. ''I am curious why even a man of your apparent means is throwing such a fortune about.''

''It is a long story,'' he said with a smile.

Grand-mère nodded. ''I would very much enjoy hearing it. Tell your coachman that—''

''Coachman?'' His smile vanished.

''Isn't that your carriage out in the street?''

''No!'' Evan rushed to a window overlooking the street. Pound notes crackled beneath his feet, but he ignored them as he drew the drapes aside. When he saw the street was empty, he cursed under his breath. Madame LeClerc must have frightened them away.

He knew he was being followed. That was why he had come through the disgusting alley at the back of the salon. If they—whoever they were—had traced him here, he must not leave immediately. To be seen now would guarantee more trouble for the LeClerc women.

''Do you recognize them? Will we be receiving a call from more of your friends?''

He turned to Brienne. Any man who thought only of her china doll prettiness would discover he was a fool. She possessed sharp wits. Those wits must not fail her now when she had to learn, and learn swiftly, that he might be her only ally.

"Whoever your grandmother saw is gone." Letting the drapes fall back into place, he lifted one foot and peeled off the pound note stuck to his shoe. He smiled and handed it to Brienne. "I believe this is yours."

She pressed it back into his hand. "Take your blood money and get out. If you don't leave, I shall—I shall—"

"What? Call Haviland?" He chuckled. "Mayhap you like having him panting over you."

" 'Twould be better than you!" A flush seared her cheeks as he laughed.

"I shall try to remember that, Brienne." Lessening the distance between them, he smiled again as she inched backward.

When she bumped into a table, he reached past her to steady a lamp. He curved his arm around her waist and pulled her to him. Her softness was everything he had remembered last night as he had stared at his ceiling, unable to sleep. She opened her mouth, but he gave her no chance to protest.

Her lips were as sweet as wine beneath his and just as intoxicating. Seeking within her mouth for more pleasure, he relished the caress of her breath against his tongue. When her fingers swept up his arms, he leaned her back against the table. He wanted to sample every inch of her, tasting each flavor she offered, urging her to be as bold. He deepened his kiss until her breath strained against his mouth.

Something crackled under his foot. The noise made by the money crashed like a fist against his face. With an oath, he pulled away.

Brienne watched in silence as Evan went to stand once again by the window, his hands clasped so tightly behind his back, she could see his bleached knuckles. Looking down at the pound notes scattered on the floor, she took a single step toward him. She froze when he spoke without facing her.

"Now that we have personal matters out of the way, shall we talk business?"

Personal matters? Was that how he dismissed that mind-sapping kiss? She did not dare take another step. Her legs were still atingle with the sensation of his strong limbs against them. What a fool she was to let him sweep her away from her good sense with his well-practiced kisses!

"Is this how you seduce all your business partners into giving you what you want?" Frustration filled her voice.

His laugh was terse. "Of course not, but business must come first."

"Don't you ever think of anything other than this business?"

"I cannot." He turned to look at her, and she wished he had not. His eyes were as dull as the cast-iron stove, and the fire within was as fierce. "And neither, Brienne, can you now. Our enemies will kill to get what they want."

She gasped. "But no one kills someone over something like that silly vase."

"You are innocent, Brienne. Some people need no reason to kill. They do it simply for the pleasure."

Her grandmother walked slowly into the parlor, sparing Brienne from having to answer. "Lucile is resting," Grand-mère said as she sat. "Brienne, *ma petite*, I think we should delay opening the salon one more night."

"But, Grand-mère—"

Shaking her head, she smiled with fatigue. "I know you have toiled so hard to have everything ready, but what are you going to serve?"

"I thought I would serve cold platters tonight."

"No, *ma petite*. Tonight you will serve only your

maman and me and Monsieur Somerset, if he feels inclined to join us for dinner.''

Brienne glanced helplessly from her grandmother's smile to Evan's astonishment. Was Grand-mère so exhausted that she could not see the foolishness of allowing Evan to remain in this apartment even a moment longer?

"After the dinner I had here two nights ago," Evan said, "I look forward to another chance to sample Brienne's cuisine."

Grand-mère's smile broadened. "She is an excellent cook. Even her cold platters are exceptional."

"Then, I gladly accept as long as there is enough . . ." He flashed a grin in Brienne's direction.

Brienne vowed not to give him the satisfaction of forcing her to lose her temper before Grand-mère. Or was it only her temper she feared losing when he was close? So easily she had thrown aside all caution when he fascinated her with his touch. He was even more dangerous than she had guessed.

Quietly she said, "You will find Grand-mère has no intention of allowing you to starve."

"Why doesn't Monsieur Somerset pick up his money," Grand-mère asked as if nothing were amiss, "while you, *ma petite*, get us some tea and biscuits?"

"Grand-mère, I—"

"Go, child." She regarded Evan steadily. "By the time you come back, Monsieur Somerset will have explained to me why he is being so careless with his money."

Irritation pricked Brienne. "I can tell you what—"

"Go, *ma petite*. That cool wind has cut into my bones. I need tea as well as some answers."

Evan sat on the settee. "Tea sounds good to me also." Cocking his head, he flashed her a smile. "Honey, if you have it, instead of sugar."

Brienne opened the door and left before she could

embarrass Grand-mère by speaking her mind. How dare Evan try to seduce her, then order her about as if she were a child! And Grand-mère! She was conspiring with him to shut Brienne out of the conversation. She thought of slamming the door, but did not want to upset Maman.

She coughed and rubbed her nose with the back of her hand as she started down the stairs. The smoke from the chimney pots must be heavier than usual. She put her hands over her mouth. A spasm of coughing paralyzed her. Dear God, she sounded as consumptive as Maman. Tears filled her eyes. She looked up. The stairwell was distorted by wisps of smoke.

She raced to the door at the foot of the stairs. Shoving it open, she cried out in horror. Billows of black smoke erupted through it.

Fire!

The kitchen was on fire!

Chapter Four

"No!" Brienne cried.

She ran into the kitchen. Smoke struck her like a blow. Reaching for the water bucket by the door, she moaned when she realized it was empty. Someone had tipped it over. She grasped her apron from the table and slapped at the flames. The fire leaped up onto it. She threw it away and ran back up the stairs.

Bursting into the parlor, she slammed the door and stared at Grand-mère's and Evan's startled faces. She struggled to speak past the smoke clogging her throat and could only cough.

"Brienne, *ma petite*, what is the matter?" cried her grandmother.

"The k-k-k-kitchen . . ." She pressed her hand over her stomach as she coughed more. "The kitchen is on fire!"

Evan leaped to his feet as spirals of smoke spread ghostly fingers under the door. "Go!"

"Maman—"

"I will get her! Hurry!"

He did not wait to see if they obeyed. Rushing into the bedroom, he called, "Madame LeClerc! We have to leave."

"No," she mumbled, and he realized she was half-asleep, "no, not without Marc-Michel! Marc-Michel, *mon amour*, not without you."

Gently he touched her shoulder. Her bones were as brittle as a bird's. She opened her eyes, and he saw a flash of sorrow. Curiosity pinched him. Was Marc-Michel Brienne's father? That did not matter now. They had to get out of here before the fire cut off their escape.

"Madame LeClerc, there is a fire below!"

She promptly fainted.

"You should not have told her that," Brienne cried as she dashed into the room. "Maman is very fragile."

He scowled at Brienne. Did she have no sense at all? "Why haven't you gotten out?"

"Go! Help Maman!" She knelt by the bed and pulled out a box.

"Is that box worth your life?"

"The only money we have is in here."

"Money won't do you any good if you're dead."

She stood. "Get Maman. We don't have time to argue."

Evan snarled a curse under his breath. Brienne was the one delaying him. But she was right. Now was not the time to quarrel. He bent and lifted Brienne's mother from the bed. She did not weigh more than a child. Following Brienne back into the parlor, he cursed again, this time louder when he saw both Brienne and her grandmother there. This whole family was want-witted.

"Get the door!" he shouted. "Get outside!"

Brienne pushed past her grandmother and touched the latch on the door to the stairs. It was still cool. The fire had not cut them off from escape. "Take a deep breath. The smoke is bad."

She led the way down the stairs, holding her grand-mother's hand. When they reached the bottom, she turned and saw, through the eddies of the smoke, Evan going toward the kitchen.

She grabbed his arm. "Not that way!"

"I can't see where to go!"

Realizing what was wrong, she pulled the collar of her mother's dressing gown away from his face. She grasped his sleeve and steered him through the blinding smoke in the salon.

"Grand-mère," she shouted over the crackling of the flames, "take Evan's arm. Follow me."

"I hope you know which way to go," muttered Evan.

"I do." *I hope*, she added silently as her throat was scraped with the smoke's vicious claws. How many times had she bragged she could cross this salon with her eyes closed? Within a step, she found she had been wrong. She bumped into a chair and swore.

"Go slow," Evan said beneath the roar of the fire as it burst through the pass-through. "You can find the way. You know this salon better than any of us."

She repeated his words under her breath as he continued to urge her forward. She groped for the door, then cried out in relief when her fingers found it. Grasping the knob, she tried to open it. It would not budge.

Desperately, she tugged on the bolt. The door was not locked. Again she tried to turn the knob. It refused to move.

"Brienne, hurry!" Grand-mère gasped. "The fire is closer."

"It's stuck!"

"Step back!" Evan's voice was distorted by the smoke.

"Back?" she cried. She saw fire licking at the frame of the door by the stairs. "We cannot go back."

"Look out!" He pushed past her. "I will kick it out!"

Brienne backed away. Her pain was as vicious as the

smoke. L'Enfant de la Patrie was dying around her. Everything she had worked for . . . everything Grand-mère had worked for . . . all gone. Grand-mère! Grasping for her grandmother's hand, she tensed.

Evan's foot struck the wooden part of the door. It wobbled, but did not open. "You are going to have to do it, Brienne!"

"Me?"

"I cannot carry your mother and kick hard enough."

"The glass—"

"I might cut her."

Brienne grabbed a chair. "Look out!" She flung it through the glass. Shards sprayed everywhere. Fresh air burst into the room. The smoke was pushed back toward the kitchen, then surged toward them once more like a fierce wave.

"Get out!" Evan shouted. "What are you waiting for?"

Taking her grandmother's hand again, Brienne helped her out of the salon. Brienne tripped. In horror, she stared at the stack of heavy cases piled in front of the door. Someone had tried to barricade them within, knowing there would be no escape through the back door.

A bucket was shoved into her hands as she was whirled into a line forming in front of the salon. She handed her bag to her grandmother, telling her to take care that it was not dropped. The vase must not be broken.

Someone called orders to get the bucket brigade under way. Not someone. Evan! Where was Maman? Was she away from the smoke?

"She is safe over there," Evan answered, although she was sure she had not spoken aloud. "Let's get this fire out!"

Brienne pushed her other questions aside as she worked mechanically. The cold wind sliced into her, but she ignored it and her chattering teeth. Water splashed her. She kept the steady rhythm of the buckets swinging back and forth as they were refilled. It no longer mattered that it was her home burning. It no longer mattered that they were fighting a fire that could destroy the whole neighborhood. It did not even matter that the fire must have been deliberately set. The only thing was the tempo of the buckets.

Empty . . . full . . . empty . . . full. . . .

Hands on Brienne's shoulders slowed her aching arms to a stop as the roof collapsed with the rumble of a dying beast. The fire vanished beneath it, then reappeared, weaker. It was almost vanquished. Some men from the watch ran toward the ruins and poured water onto the rims of the fire. If they could keep the flames from spreading, it would die within the ruins of L'Enfant de la Patrie.

An arm went around her shoulders, drawing her back so the watch could get more water. Looking up, she stared at Evan's smoke-streaked face. His fine coat was pocked with holes from embers. He must have stood very close to the fire. That was not a surprise. Evan Somerset would not give up, even when he could not win.

She sagged against him as he turned her to walk across the street that was littered with puddles. Her neighbors milled around, whispering as if they feared the fire would hear and attack them. She closed her eyes in despair. Somehow she would have to find a way to repay them for the furniture and dishes she had borrowed—the furniture and dishes that were now just glowing embers beneath the scorched rafters.

"Where is my bag?" she asked, standing straighter.

"Your grandmother has it." He smoothed her hair back from her face. "Are you all right?"

"How can you ask such a stupid question? I wish this was a nightmare and I could just wake up and have all of this disappear."

"And me? Do you wish I would disappear, too?"

She started to snap an answer back at him, but instead

stared at the smoke of a dying dream. A dream that was as dead as the past, a dream that was as hopeless as her future.

"So now you see the truth, Brienne," Evan continued as he turned her to face him. "The game, as Shakespeare put it so succinctly, is afoot. I warned you the attack on you by those sea-crabs would be just the beginning."

"The beginning?" She shook her head. "It is over. There is nothing left."

"You are still alive." When she choked on her horror, unable to reply, he put his thumbs beneath her chin and tilted it toward him. "Mayhap you will listen to me now when I warn you that they will come back again and again and again until they get the vase or destroy you. Which do you think will happen first?"

Brienne turned away from him and the charred remains of what had once been her lovely salon. She tried to blink away the haze obscuring the edges of her eyes, unsure if it was from tears or the smoke. Her toe hit an uneven cobblestone, and she stumbled. Before she fell, she was scooped up into strong arms. She clutched the front of a linen shirt, and she again looked up at Evan's face.

She almost laughed. Not with amusement, but with the taint of despair. Evan had lost his aristocratic mien. Now he looked like an overgrown chimney sweep. Soot was etched into his skin, shading his face to reveal the strong angles he had hidden while wearing his charming smile.

"What is so funny?" he asked as he placed her on the seat of a carriage she had not noticed before.

Fury struck her like a spark, hot and painful. "I thought you said it was not your coach Grand-mère saw!" She edged over as he climbed in and sat beside her on the red velvet seat.

"It wasn't. I left orders with my driver to come and pick me up at four o'clock." He pulled a gold pocketwatch from his water-spotted vest. Opening it with a click, he tilted it so he could read it in the last hints of light. "Which was more than two hours ago and after the fire started. You can rest assured that I was not lying to you."

"That time."

He grinned as he rested back against the cushions. His mud-encrusted boot pounded on the door in a signal to the coachman. "You are becoming more suspicious, Brienne. That is good, but, unfortunately, you are suspicious of the wrong person."

"Why shouldn't I suspect you of causing me trouble? I have had nothing but trouble since—" She gasped as the carriage lurched, throwing her back into his arms.

When she began to move away, his arms tightened around her. Suddenly she wanted to be held, to be kept from the horror stalking her. Closing her eyes, she rested her face against his damp coat as he stroked her shoulder. For the moment, she did not care that Evan held her. She forgot her anger at his outrageous attempt to try to buy her assistance. All she wanted was to be safe with . . .

"Maman? Grand-mère?" It was easier to whisper when her voice was scratchy from the smoke.

"Don't fret, Brienne. I sent them to my house on Grosvenor Square as soon as the carriage first arrived around four o'clock. They are waiting there for you."

"Your house? You really live on Grosvenor Square?" She drew back. If he had been honest about that, had he been honest about the rest? Seeing the twinkle in his eyes, she knew she would be a fool to swallow his story whole.

He chuckled as his fingers swept aside her tangled hair. "It is temporarily mine. As it shall be temporarily yours, if you are willing to accept my hospitality."

"We have no place else to go."

"Not quite a thank-you, but you are welcome."

Brienne squared her shoulders as she met his gaze steadily. She had never met such a vexing man. "You know that is not what I meant. I am grateful for what you have done today.''

"But you wish I had never come into your well-ordered life.''

"Yes.''

He caught her chin in his hand, so she could not look away. The sparkle vanished from his eyes, and his voice became a low growl. "If it had not been me, it would have been someone else who was not as gentle with you.'' When she winced, he edged his fingers away from the bruises on her face. "As you have seen.''

Lowering her eyes, Brienne said, "We will not intrude on you for long.''

"You are welcome to stay until you decide what you shall do.''

"I know what we will do. After all, there is nothing to keep us here in London with L'Enfant de la Patrie destroyed.'' Her voice cracked on the last word, and she swallowed tears that were clogging her throat.

"You are leaving London?'' He frowned. "Where are you planning to go?''

"Home.''

"Home?''

"Back to France. Maman has been asking me to take her back, because she wants to be buried next to my father. Until now, I have been able to talk her out of it. I was always too busy with the salon, but now it is gone.'' A shudder ached along her stiff shoulders. "It is gone.''

Evan was surprised when Brienne looked out the window. He had guessed that she must be at the end of her strength, but her back was soldier-straight. When he put a consoling hand on her shoulder, a sob erupted from her. She pressed her face into her hands and wept. Gently he turned her against his waistcoat.

He sighed as he slipped his arms around her to discover that her sobs came from deep within her. He did not urge her to stop crying. She needed this. He did not know anyone who could have suffered what she had these past two days and not break. Nothing he could say would comfort her, so he said nothing. How could he tell her that it all would be fine? It would not be.

Someone else wanted that dashed vase. That person had shown that he was not afraid to risk the lives of three women to get the vase.

His hands clenched into frustrated fists against her back. That idiot may have overplayed his hand. If the vase had been in the salon, it would have been destroyed when the roof beams crashed down into the rubble. His lips tilted in a wry grin. Somehow, he was going to have to find a way to explain all of this to Lagrille's men and persuade them not to kill him.

He would rather think about Brienne's ebony hair draping over his arm. It was filled with cinders and had come loose from its chignon. He sifted his fingers through its satin sheen, sending the ashes falling onto his lap.

When she raised her face, he ran a finger along the path of her tears that had cleaned lines through the soot on her face. "We are almost to Grosvenor Square," he murmured.

She put her hands up to her face. "I must look horrible."

"You look like a bedraggled heroine who fought a brave battle to save her home."

"I don't feel brave, just angry and scared."

"You are brave. Don't let anyone tell you differently."

"I want to find the ones who did this!" She sat straighter. "I want to make them pay for hurting Grand-mère and Maman. I want them to rot in prison. I want them to be drawn and quartered. I—"

He chuckled and placed his finger over her lips. "I did not guess you possessed such diabolical thoughts, Brienne. I am very glad that I had nothing to do with this fire."

"Don't laugh at me!" Her obsidian eyes crackled like static in a wool blanket.

"I am not laughing at you." His hand smoothed the soot from her cheek. "I cannot imagine ever laughing at such fervor."

"Evan, I—"

His lips lowered over hers. He thought she might halt him, but she leaned into his kiss. As his arms tightened around her, he explored each contour of her mouth, not asking, but offering pleasure to let them escape from the horror.

Slowly, hesitantly, her hands rose to his shoulders. He smiled as he drew back enough to see the soft expression on her face. She wanted this as much as he did.

He captured her lips again, discovering each hidden secret and savoring it. His fingers tangled in her hair as he tasted her soft cheeks before his mouth sought its way along the smooth column of her throat. Eager need spiraled through him as her fingers twisted in his hair which fell over the back of his high collar. His whole body became a pulse, beating with the rhythm of her eager breath against his cheek.

Evan pulled back. Was he out of his mind? He had no time for this delight. He should be devising his excuses for Lagrille that would keep his own heart beating.

"Evan?"

Her sweet voice tempted him to put aside good sense again, but he said, "I half expected you to slap my face, honey, but you did not."

"No, I did not." She traced his jaw which had become scratchy with a day's growth of beard.

He caught her wrist and drew her hand away. Seeing her eyes widen in the thickening twilight, he chuckled. "You are a confusing woman. Do you hate me as you have asserted you do since I walked into your salon yesterday, or is this''—he brushed her lips with his—''is *this* real passion I taste in your kiss?''

Brienne tore herself out of Evan's arms. Wrapping her own around herself, she said, ''You are taking advantage of my unsettled state. You know I should not be kissing you.''

''You should not?'' He kissed the bare skin above her modestly scooped bodice. When she gasped as a quiver of pleasure raced along her, he smiled. ''And why not?''

She fought to gain control of her errant emotions. ''I do not know you well, Evan, and, what I do know, I must own that I do not like.''

He laughed and claimed her lips once more. Again the surge of ecstasy rippled through her. When his fingers tantalized her nape, she pulled away and slapped his face. He recoiled, striking his head on the carriage.

''I know what you want, Evan Somerset! Don't think you can seduce it from me.''

Rubbing the back of his aching head, he demanded, ''How can I seduce the vase from you if you do not have it? Or do you?''

She slid to the far edge of the seat, wanting to put as much space between them as possible. ''I thought so.'' She hoped her retort covered her wounded dignity. She had been a fool to let him hold her when he cared about only one thing. And he must have guessed how his kisses had sent a thrill through her. She could not let him force her into revealing the truth like this again.

''You thought what? That I wanted to hold you simply because I want that dashed vase? You senseless woman!''

He grasped her shoulders and jerked her to him again. When he drew her mouth under his, the sweet fire was gone. Unfettered desire sought to persuade her to submit to his passions. Fear swelled through her, and her cry echoed in the recesses of his mouth. With a smile, he released her.

"That is an example of the way I do not want to kiss you, Brienne."

"The way you do not want to kiss me? What are you talking about?"

"How silly you are to think that I want you in my arms simply so I can learn where the vase is. After all, if the vase was in the salon, looking for it now would be futile."

"And you would not want to do anything futile, would you?"

"That is better," he said with a warmer smile. "I like it better when you are snarling at me. It offers me a challenge to—"

"Cheat me out of a family heirloom?"

"Arguing is a waste of time, Brienne." He rested back against the cushions, clearly not worried about soot staining the velvet. Folding his arms over his chest, he asked, "You don't know where it is, do you?"

"I do not have it."

"Then, why—?" He glanced out of the window as the coach slowed. "Never mind. Here we are."

She tried to peer past him. When he laughed and drew her closer so she could see out his window, she gasped, "*This* is where you live?"

"I told you I lived on Grosvenor Square."

"I know, but . . ." Her voice trailed off as she looked at the elegant townhouse. Only a wealthy man could own a townhouse like this one.

Who was this man who had invaded her life, bringing such disaster in his wake? Everything he had said came back to haunt her. If he had been as honest about other things as this, was it possible that the vase was truly valuable? Mayhap he truly had a friend who wanted it for some reason.

Again she was caught by how his blue eyes twinkled merrily. He was no more sincere than a suitor whispering court-promises in a lady's ear. Evan Somerset was many men, but she doubted if she had seen the real one yet. She was not sure who he really was, but he was not a legitimate art dealer interested in buying an odd piece of art from her family.

Then, why does someone want that old vase so badly?

She had no answer for that as she gazed at the house while the coachman jumped down and opened the door. She looked up through the dusk at the roof of the structure, four stories above the walkway. Marble edged the door and windows in a simple, classic style. An arch accented the door. Statuary, in fanciful designs, pranced over the arch and on top of the ground-floor windows. Every brick and bit of plaster announced that this house belonged to a member of the *ton*.

Evan said, drawing her gaze back to him, "To answer your question, Brienne—"

"I did not ask you a question."

"Not aloud, but your face reveals what you are thinking, so I will tell you that a friend has been kind enough to allow me to use his house while he is visiting other friends at a country estate. I needed a place to live while I searched London for your vase."

"You want me to believe that a friend of yours owns this?"

"Impressed?"

"Yes." When she saw his eyebrow quirk, she added, "And didn't you expect me to be? Why else would you live here? You must want to impress your—"

"Clients."

"I was thinking victims might be closer to the truth."

He laughed. Stepping out of the carriage, he held up his hand to her. "We can enjoy this quarrel within the comfort of the house. Shall we go inside?"

When he held up his hand, she hesitated, then placed her fingers on it. The unwanted warmth slid along her arm. She did not *like* this man. *But you like his kisses*, taunted a small voice in her head.

With manners as polished as any lord's, he handed her out of the carriage. He reached past her. She whirled, not sure what he planned. Her eyes widened when he picked up the bag containing the box from under Maman's bed.

"I thought you might want this taken care of," he said, "so I put it in the carriage when I sent your mother and grandmother here. They must have forgotten to take it in."

"Thank you," she whispered.

"I saw you give it to your grandmother; but she set it down while we were fighting the fire, and I was afraid it would get stolen if it was left on the walkway."

"Thank you."

"I wish we could have saved more."

"I wish so, too. I—"

"What is it?" he asked, frowning.

"I don't know."

"Brienne?"

"I don't know!" She stared at the front door of the house. "Something is wrong."

"With the house?"

"I don't know!"

"You are making no sense."

"I really don't know what is wrong, but something is." She shivered. "I know it as surely as I know L'Enfant de la Patrie is ashes."

She could not imagine explaining to him about the *feelings* she sometimes experienced. He would laugh at her, and she could not blame him. She knew these sensations often heralded trouble. More trouble. How could she explain when her stomach roiled as if a riot were taking place within it?

"Brienne?" called a voice from the front door.

"Grand-mère!" She ran up the steps to the door that had been thrown open.

Her grandmother threw her arms around her, squeezing her until Brienne could not breathe. "Oh, Brienne, thank heavens you are here!"

Breaking out of the near stranglehold, Brienne said, "I am safe, Grand-mère." She stared at her grandmother's ashen face. "*Mon Dieu*, what is wrong?"

" 'Tis your mother, child. I think Lucile is—" She choked, then whispered, "I fear she is worsening."

"Worsening?" queried Evan as he motioned for Brienne and her grandmother to enter the house.

Grand-mère nodded, but held Brienne's gaze. "I think she is dying."

Chapter Five

"Dying? Maman is dying?" Brienne ran for the stairs, rushing up them.

"Second door to your left!" her grandmother called after her before turning to Evan. "We must send for the priest at the Berwick Street Chapel in Soho."

Evan stared at Madame LeClerc in astonishment. For once, her face showed every year of her life as grief stripped away its laugh lines. "Madame, was she injured in our escape?"

" 'Tis the consumption. The smoke has sapped her, so she cannot breathe. Monsieur Somerset—"

He put his hand on Madame LeClerc's arm. It was the only solace he could offer her.

"I shall send for the priest immediately." When she followed him as he reached for a bellpull, he added, "I shall tend to sending for the priest if you wish to return to your daughter."

"Lucile wished to see Brienne alone." Tears filled her eyes. "She wants to say good-bye to Brienne. I thought

I would find the kitchen here and make some tea for all of us while we wait—''

"For the priest," he hurried to finish for her.

She nodded. "Yes, for the priest. Where is your kitchen?"

"A moment." Evan tugged on the bellpull so hard it almost ripped from the ceiling. A footman and Hitchcock, the butler, nearly collided running toward them. He gave quick instructions to the footman to get the priest. "Be sure to hurry. We need the priest right away."

"Yes, Mr. Somerset." The footman glanced at Madame LeClerc, then ran out of the house.

Hitchcock closed the door in his wake. The butler wore deep gray livery that never was wrinkled or showed a spot. As the butler looked down his nose at him, Evan resisted wiping cinders from his ruined coat. "Yes, sir?"

"Madame LeClerc would like some tea brought upstairs to her daughter's room."

"Yes, sir." He turned and walked toward the back of the house.

"Thank you," Madame LeClerc murmured.

Evan helped her to sit on a backless settee beside the curving stairs. The gold color of the wallcovering added a sallow shadow to Madame LeClerc's cheeks. He knelt on one knee beside her. "The priest will be here soon."

"Thank you," she whispered again, then stared down at her tightly clasped hands.

Evan gripped the side of the settee and looked up the stairs. Brienne must be saying farewell to her mother. How much more could she endure before even her strength was gone? She must stay strong, for, he knew, her greatest trials might still be ahead of her.

Whoever else was seeking that vase might not give up pursuing Brienne simply because the vase had been destroyed. Neither could he.

* * *

In the beautiful bedroom, Brienne ran to the fancy tester bed where her mother was lying. She drew up the steps beside the bed and knelt on them. She did not want to think that this might be the final time she would be able to speak to her mother. No, she must not think of that. Then she would not be able to halt the tears which flooded her eyes.

"Maman?" she whispered in French. "Maman, I am here with you." She got no answer. "Maman, 'tis Brienne."

Her mother opened her eyes with painful slowness. "Brienne, what has happened to your face?"

She almost smiled, for the scold sounded so familiar. Maman insisted that Brienne be the pattern-card of propriety even when she was cooking in a hot kitchen. Reaching up, she touched the soot on her face. "I did not wait to clean away the ashes. I wanted to come right away to see how you fared."

"Am I so close to dying, then?" She raised her fingers off the white coverlet to halt Brienne's answer. "Do not lie to me, Brienne."

"You need not talk, Maman. I will be glad to sit here and hold your hand while you rest." Brienne fought the fear rising within her. Her mother's voice was breathless, even for her, and her chest strained for each breath.

"Brienne, *m'enfante*, tell me that you have not been hurt more."

"I am fine."

"L'Enfant de la Patrie?"

"It can be rebuilt." She guessed that was a lie, but it no longer seemed odd that she protected her mother from the truth, for she had been doing it all her life. "I have the money that was in the box under your bed. We can start again, as we did before. We—"

Maman slid a skeletal hand over Brienne's. "Do not

be so frightened by death. It is something I welcome. For so long, I have been waiting to be with your papa. Tonight I will be with him again. Do not mourn for me, *ma chere*. Promise me that.''

''Maman—''

''Promise me!''

Not wanting her mother to overexert herself, Brienne murmured, ''I promise, Maman.''

''Good.'' She relaxed into the pillows. ''Rejoice that I have found my release from pain.''

''Maman, I cannot rejoice, for I do not want you to die. I love you.''

''I love you, too, Brienne. That is why I must ask you. The vase. Do you have it?''

''Yes, Maman. It is still in the box, as you requested, but do not fret about the vase. It does not matter now.''

Her mother's eyes grew round and bright with zeal. ''It matters more than you can know, child. Take the vase to France. Take it home to where it belongs. Promise me that you will take it home and present it to whoever is living there.''

''There? Where?''

''Home,'' she answered so low that Brienne had to lean forward to hear her.

''But, Maman, I do not know where that is. You and Grand-mère never told me where—''

A spasm of coughs tormented her, but she whispered, ''Go there. Do not let anyone know where you are going, not even your grandmother. You must do this. You must go. Promise me, Brienne.''

''I promise, Maman, but where do you want me to take the vase?''

''Go! It is what your father would have wanted for you. This is why I have guarded you so closely.'' A shudder threatened to shatter her weak body. ''But be wary, Brienne. The door will betray you. Do not forget to watch for the door.''

"Door?" Every word her mother said only confused her more. "Maman, I do not understand."

"You will when you are home. It all, at last, will be yours."

"What is mine? I do not understand!"

"Promise me that you will tell no one that you have the vase until you have claimed what is yours. Not even your grandmother must know."

"Maman—"

"Promise me, Brienne. Promise me please."

"I promise." She could say nothing else.

Her mother closed her eyes. For a fearful moment, Brienne feared she had died. Then she saw the slow rise and fall of her mother's chest. Leaning her head on the edge of the bed, she tried to pray. It was impossible when she wanted so much. To have her mother well, to be safe, to understand why her world was self-destructing around her.

When the door opened, she looked up to see a priest entering the room. She stood and stepped respectfully aside. Her tears blurred Père Jean-Baptiste's familiar face. The balding priest had been the curate at the *émigrés'* church in Soho for as long as she could recall.

He took her hands between his. "Bless you, child, for all you have done for your mother."

"I love her. I could have done no less."

He nodded before moving to the bed to administer last rites to her mother as Grand-mère came into the room. Brienne put her arm around her grandmother, who was weeping. She wished for words to comfort her grandmother, but could not find any.

A hand settled on her arm. She did not need to look away from the bed, because the sharp pulse told her that the hand belonged to Evan. Wanting to lean her head against his strong shoulder, she did not move. She had to be here for her grandmother.

Brienne realized her mother had breathed her last when her grandmother sank to a chair and wept even harder. Going to Père Jean-Baptiste, she whispered, "Thank you."

"Brienne," he said, folding her hands between his, "as far as the memorial service—"

Evan stepped forward. "Father, I will be glad to discuss that with you if Brienne wishes to see to her grandmother."

"Of course," the priest said, clearly startled.

"Thank you," Brienne whispered, drawing her hands out of Père Jean-Baptiste's and putting one on Evan's arm. "I am so sorry that you—"

"Take care of your grandmother," he interrupted gently.

Brienne nodded. She went to help Grand-mère from the room. Now she owed Evan an even greater debt, for he had come to her assistance yet again. How could he be so kind and yet try to twist her into doing as he wished with a cacophony of lies? She had no answer as she brought her grandmother to her feet.

"I thought Madame LeClerc would like the room across the hall," Evan said quietly.

Grand-mère shook off Brienne's hand. Taking Brienne's face between her hands, she whispered, "Weep, if you wish, *ma petite*."

"I will, but . . ."

"In your own time." She walked back toward the bed. "I would like to pray. Père Jean-Baptiste, will you pray with me?"

Brienne hesitated when Evan put his hand on her arm, then let him steer her into the hallway. He led her to a room at the front of the house.

While Evan crossed the wide chamber to draw the

drapes, she looked about. It seemed strange that she could admire the lovely mahogany furniture and overstuffed chairs as well as enjoy the scent of lavender which must be coming from the washstand next to the tester bed. How could she feel anything but grief? As she walked toward a chair, her toes sank into the thick burgundy carpet.

"It is so odd," she murmured.

"What is so odd?" He pressed a glass into her hand. "Drink, honey. You look as if you could use it."

Because she did not want to argue with him, she lifted the goblet to her lips. Even brandy could not cut through her fog of disbelief. A week ago, her only problems had been ordering mushrooms for her meals and how many bottles of wine she needed for the party that would be dining at her salon before a visit to Vauxhall Gardens.

"It is so odd," she repeated.

His finger under her chin tilted her face up so she could see the worry in his expression. "What is so odd?" he asked again with a patience she had not expected.

"One minute Maman was alive. She could see and hear and talk. The next minute she is gone, but I can still see and hear and talk. It is so odd."

Putting his glass on a nearby table, he dipped a cloth in the bowl on the washstand. He squatted in front of her and dabbed at the soot on her face.

"Don't do that!" she moaned, pushing his hand away.

"If you do not wish me to help—"

"Stop being so kind! If you keep on being so kind, you are going to make me cry."

He stood and walked to an armoire. He opened it as he asked, "Why don't you go to bed, honey? I will have a light supper sent up to you after I speak with Père Jean-Baptiste."

"I should—"

"Tomorrow is early enough to face everything you have

to.'' Closing the armoire door, he put a lacy nightgown in her hands. "Don't ask. Our host seems to have entertained his mistress here."

She looked down at the lovely garment. "I am sorry for all of this, Evan. I had no idea that we would repay your hospitality like this."

"I know." Bending, he kissed her lightly on her cheek. "Good night."

"Good night," she whispered. She did not move until she heard the door close.

Rising, she saw a small bolt above the latch on the door. She slid it into place, wondering if Evan's friend wanted to be certain no one disturbed him and his mistress here.

The bag, which Evan had left on the bed, drew her gaze. She lurched to the bed and upended the bag. Ignoring her father's picture, which rolled along the blue coverlet, she picked up the wooden box that had been under her mother's bed and opened it. She pushed aside the money that was all remaining of her hard work at L'Enfant de la Patrie. Her fingers shook as she reached for the ball of unbleached linen.

She carefully unrolled it. As the blue vase appeared, unharmed despite its rough treatment, tears fell from her eyes. She ran her fingernail along the gilded streak of lightning etched across it.

"I promise, Maman. I will take it home. No matter what, I promise you that I will take it home for you."

"I do not understand why you want to come back here," Evan said. He rubbed his nose which was itchy with the pall of smoke. It was thicker on this narrow street than anywhere else in Soho. Although he had become accustomed to the heavy odor of London smoke, this was different. It held the reek of destruction.

"I need to see it in the daylight." Brienne gasped with dismay as the ruins of the salon came into view. "*Mon Dieu!*"

He looked over the top of the straw bonnet that had come as had her black dress from the armoire in her room. He batted away a feather that was the same shade of bright blue as the ribbons beneath her chin. She would need to get a more sedate hat before her mother's funeral.

Swallowing his curse, he stared at the blackened timbers that were piled together like straws. Passersby had paused to stare at the rubble, forming a half circle around it.

When the carriage stopped, Evan opened the door and climbed out. He handed Brienne out, but did not release her fingers. She did not seem to notice as she continued to stare at the reeking remains of the salon. Holding up the hem of her dress, she stepped over the puddles that still gathered among the cobbles.

"It is really gone," she whispered.

"Will you rebuild?"

She raised her shoulders and lowered them slowly. "It will cost more money than I have to clear this away and build a new salon."

When she stepped away from him, Evan did not follow. He watched her in silence, wondering what she would do now. She could not be thinking of going to France any longer. Her mother had died, saving Brienne from the imperial madness Napoleon was spreading across the Continent. His lips straightened as he recalled his last trip to France. This, most definitely, was not the time for a social call on long-lost relatives.

As she threaded her way through the crowd, he heard grumbles from the people who had paused to gawk. He wondered what she hoped to find. Splinters of glass sparkled in the sunshine, but could not brighten the depressing sight. A few spirals of smoke still wisped up into the garishly blue sky.

He followed as she bent and picked up a blackened item by what had been the front door. It was a silver fork, tarnished black by the flames. He guessed scavengers had already picked through the ruins.

"Good morning, Miss LaClerk."

Evan kept an innocuous expression on his face when he turned to see Haviland behind him. The watchman's face was streaked with black. Putting his hand under Brienne's elbow, Evan drew her to her feet and away from the vulture who had swooped down from his usual roost at the pub half a block away as soon as word must have reached him of Brienne's arrival.

"Good morning, Constable," Brienne said with the same lack of emotion that had stained her voice since her mother's death. "You remember Mr. Somerset, don't you?"

Haviland's smile was as frosty as his eyes when he tilted his head slightly in Evan's direction. "I heard that you and your mother and the old lady had escaped. I am glad to see you unharmed. I am sorry about the fire destroying your salon."

"It was, after all, only a building," she said as she walked away to look at another section of the charred boards.

Evan let Haviland stare at her for a long minute before saying, "She is not wearing mourning for her salon, but for her mother. Madame LeClerc succumbed last night."

"I thought they all got out of the fire."

"They did." He smiled coolly. "Luckily for them, I was calling. They could not have gotten out alone." He paused, then added, "Especially because someone had barricaded the front door before setting the fire in the kitchen."

"You have it all figured out, don't you?"

"It was not difficult when I saw the fire and the barricade myself."

Haviland sneered, "It sounds as if it has been lucky for you. I would guess you do not get a chance to play the hero often in the art business."

Evan knocked his boots against a board to loosen the cinders from them. "You are right. I do not have as many opportunities as there are for a watchman who maintains his post so diligently next to a keg of rum." With a sigh, he added, "Of course, my efforts on behalf of Brienne's mother were futile."

"She is dead? How?"

"The smoke was too much for her. The funeral will be tomorrow." He glanced at Brienne. Although he had offered to help, she had handled the arrangements alone and with too much ease. If he had not held Brienne in his arms, he might believe she was unfeeling. But he had held her and kissed her soft lips, and he knew how strong her passions were. He wondered how much longer she would be able to restrain her grief.

The constable's crude voice cut into his thoughts. "I should warn you, Somerset, that a man matching your description was seen creeping along the alley behind the salon yesterday before the fire started."

He smiled. "I am sure that someone saw a man who looked exactly like me back there, for I was there."

"You admit that you were in the alley?"

"Of course, because it is the truth. Ask Miss LeClerc, if you doubt me." He turned. "Good day, Haviland."

The watchman did not reply as Somerset walked away. If Somerset was this willing to own that he had been behind the salon, he must be hiding something else. He did not trust this man who, for some reason, had attached himself to the LeClercs. Despite Miss LeClerc's assertion that Somerset was a favored caller, Haviland could not remember seeing him here before the last few days. He would have noticed anyone who called on Miss LeClerc.

He watched silently as Brienne took Somerset's arm.

She called a pleasant farewell to him, but he watched emotions sweeping like storm clouds across her face as she walked with Somerset to the fancy carriage.

It was Somerset who looked back. Haviland was curious about what he was hoping to see, but Somerset turned to say something to Miss LeClerc as he helped her into the carriage. Haviland was tempted to shout to her to be careful and not trust Somerset.

He did not bother. She had refused to listen to his warnings that Somerset would bring disaster to her. His words had been proven true. If more horrible things happened to her, it was no longer his fault.

He had warned her, he reminded himself as he walked back to the pub. Now whatever happened to her was *her* fault.

Chapter Six

Brienne hunched beneath the black umbrella Evan held as they walked out of the cemetery. Although the wind blew fitful, chilly rain at her, she ignored its sharp slap against her face. Her teeth clenched as she struggled to swallow past the pain in her constricted throat. Next to her, Grand-mère sobbed under another umbrella. Brienne wished she could release her grief, too. Mayhap, she could once she had done as she had promised Maman.

Père Jean-Baptiste comforted her grandmother. When he turned to her, she tried to smile, but it was impossible.

"Thank you, Père," she said softly.

"If you need me, Brienne, do not hesitate to send for me."

"Thank you."

When she added nothing else, the priest looked past her. "It is very generous of you to escort Madame LeClerc's family today, Monsieur Somerset."

"Generous is not the word I would use," Evan answered, keeping the umbrella over Brienne's head as a gust tried to pull it away. "I have an obligation to this family."

"Really?" the priest asked before he could halt himself.

Evan smiled. "Really." Looking at Brienne, he put his hand on her elbow. "I think we should get your grandmother home. She might take ill in this inclement weather."

When Brienne's gaze rose to meet his, he knew he had never seen so much pain in anyone's eyes. That she could hide it while she tried to ease her grandmother's grief astonished him, although he had learned not to judge Brienne LeClerc by the standards he had set for other people. She did what she had to.

His lips tightened at that thought. Her mother's death would not change that single-minded stubbornness. Yesterday, she had admitted that she would not rebuild the salon. So what was she intending to do now? That question plagued him, keeping him from sleeping and forcing him to guard his tongue. He told himself that he should not care, that he had paid his debt for bringing this trouble to her. He had opened Porter's house to Brienne and her family, so now he owed her nothing. Trying to persuade himself of that had been a waste of time. *It is bad for business—your business—to get involved.* How many times had he repeated that to himself during the past few days to no avail?

And he was no closer to guessing what Brienne would do now. She would not accept his charity much longer, even if he had been in a position to offer it. Somehow he had to discover what she planned and halt her before she created more problems for herself. He had failed to convince her that she had enough trouble already. Once the person who had set fire to L'Enfant de la Patrie learned that she had survived, he would be looking for her and the vase again. That man would not believe that she no longer had the vase. Why should he? Evan didn't.

He listened as she spoke to her grandmother. Together they assisted Madame LeClerc to the carriage. Although weakened by grief, the old woman was not feeble. Her voice was clear as she thanked them for helping her.

He turned to aid Brienne into the carriage, but she drew away, saying, "I would like to walk."

"Walk? In the rain? It must be almost a mile from here to Grosvenor Square."

"Evan, I want to walk. I need to be alone for a while."

He nodded. "I agree to the walk, but you should not be alone."

"*Agree?*" Her eyes snapped with ebony fury. "I did not realize I needed your permission."

Before he could answer, Madame LeClerc said through the carriage window, "Heed him, *ma petite*. I think you should have someone with you. I shall order a bath for you, so you do not take a chill."

Brienne bit back her retort. Everyone seemed determined to tell her what she should or should not do. It had not been this way before the fire . . . before Evan Somerset came into their lives. Swallowing her irritation, because she did not want to add to her grandmother's grief, she said, "Very well, Grand-mère."

Brienne stepped back as the carriage pulled away and drove toward Mayfair. Pulling her cloak more tightly over her thin gown, she was grateful for the clothes she had found in the armoire, although she tried not to think that they had belonged to Evan's friend's mistress. She had to have something to wear.

Evan offered his arm, and she put her fingers on his damp wool sleeve. She noticed for the first time how the shade of his coat matched the color of his light brown hair. When he drew her closer, she did not resist. The rain was cold beyond the umbrella.

"I like walking in the rain," he said as they walked in the same direction the carriage had taken.

She looked at him, startled. "So do I. Things are some-how slower when it rains. Mayhap it washes away the hectic parts of life."

"Or it simply keeps most sane people indoors?"

"Mayhap." She was amazed she could smile as she looked at the puddled street. "I like to listen to the rain-drops on the cobbles and to take a deep breath of the hot smell when they strike the dry road." She edged around a puddle. "It has been years since I thought about running about in the rain. I guess I have been too busy with L'Enfant de la Patrie."

"Did you grow up in London?"

"Yes, and you?"

He smiled. "You may not believe me when I tell you that I had the advantages of a country childhood."

"I believe you."

"You do?"

"I do not know what you are now, Evan, but I suspect you were raised in comfort in the country. You seem to fit very well into your life on Grosvenor Square, so I believe your life is now like it should have been."

"What it should have been?" He grinned. "Dammit, I should have known you were an intuitive woman and steered wide of you."

"I told you to leave more than once."

He did not answer as they paused at the curb to wait for a dray to pass with its load of soggy vegetables for Covent Garden. As it bumped over the cobbles, a basket of carrots bounced off and crashed onto the road. Before the teamster's apprentice could retrieve it, another wagon drove over the vegetables, smashing them. Instantly a loud argument erupted.

"Let's go," whispered Brienne. "I am tired of quar-rels."

She expected Evan to answer, but again he remained silent as he led her along the walkway to a spot where they could cross the street. The silence grew uncomfortable between them. She wished for something to say, but she could think of nothing.

When Evan spoke, she flinched, not just with surprise, but with dismay at his question. "What do you remember about your life in France?"

"Very little. I have a few memories, but they are a child's memories of being loved and taken care of. I do not recall coming to London. As I was barely three years old, that is understandable."

"Yes." He swore.

"Evan?"

He chuckled wryly. "Sorry. That rain that just trickled down my back was as cold as a winter Friday."

"Take more of the umbrella." She edged away from him. "I am staying quite dry."

"And you shall stay that way. After all, your grandmother entrusted you to me, and I do not want to break a pledge to her."

She halted in the middle of the street. Hastily, he readjusted the umbrella over her. She reached up and pushed it aside. Instantly the rain matted her borrowed cloak and battered down her bonnet's feathers.

"Get under the umbrella!" Evan ordered.

"No!"

Grasping her arm, he tugged her to the other walkway and under the umbrella. When she tried to step back, he pulled her up against his chest.

"Don't say it!" He swore, before adding, "I shall treat you like a child if you insist on acting like one. Why do you always let your pride get in the way of your common sense?"

"Because I—"

His mouth slanted across hers, silencing her. When she gasped, his tongue brushed hers. Fiery desire exploded through her. She gripped the front of his coat and discovered she wanted to touch him. Her fingers rose to stroke his strong back as he deepened the kiss until she softened against him. All of her senses were overmastered with a sweetness which erased the horror of the past week.

Horror . . . she choked as the dampness on her eyelashes became tears instead of raindrops. She hid her face against his waistcoat and sobbed. His hand caressed her gently as he leaned his cheek against the top of her bonnet. While she grieved for her mother, he simply held her.

"That is better," she heard him say when her weeping eased.

"Better?" she whispered.

Gently, he wiped the pool of tears from beneath her eyes with one crooked finger. "Keeping your sorrow inside you forever is impossible. I learned that a long time ago. Grieving hearts have to grieve before they can be healed."

"I did not realize you were an expert on grief." She flushed when his lips tightened. How could she guess when he was being sincere and when he was trying to twist her into the webs of deceit he spun so well? "I am sorry, Evan. I should not have said that. You were trying to be comforting."

"But not succeeding." His thumbs beneath her chin tilted her face back. "Honey, I know you question everything I tell you, but believe me when I tell you that I am so very sorry that your mother died. I have seen that you will miss her so much."

"More than you know." Her voice broke. "More than I knew."

"You are right, for I cannot imagine being so hurt by the loss of my family that—" His irreverent grin returned. "Can we discuss this somewhere warm and dry? I am getting drenched."

Although she wanted to ask him why he cared so little about his family, Brienne nodded. Asking him would be futile. Evan would converse charmingly on any subject *he* chose, but could close up more quickly than a pickpocket's fingers on a purse when he wished.

As she walked by his side, she sighed. In a way, she knew him better than she knew anyone else in her life, for they had shared so much since she had met him. He was good in a crisis. He was not afraid to speak his mind. He had a kind heart, although he tried to hide it. He had wits honed by his work, and he was handsome enough to draw eyes as they walked along the street.

Yet, in truth, she knew nothing about Evan Somerset, and she could not ignore the temptation to learn more. She was curious if he was actually this kind gentleman or a hard-hearted thief who was treating her with compassion only because he wanted something from her.

But she must ignore that temptation. She had made a vow to Maman. Now she must do as she had promised.

Brienne quietly shut the door to her grandmother's room. Nodding to the maid who would answer Madame LeClerc's call, she hurried along the wide hallway to the graceful curve of the staircase. A cup of tea would be pleasant before she went to sleep, too. She paused at the top of the stairs, and her gaze went, as it did every time she passed this way, to the door of the room where her mother had died.

Through the long, wet afternoon, Brienne had prepared to fulfill her promise to Maman. No one had disturbed her, believing she had secluded herself to mourn. She was ready to leave London, but her plans beyond that were uncertain. There were only a few ways to reach France during this war.

The vase was packed in the very center of the few things she was taking with her. When she returned, she would find a way to repay Evan's friend for the clothing that she had packed in the small bag she had found at the back of the armoire. If she returned. . . . She must, because she could not leave Grand-mère here dependent on Evan forever. She did not want to now, but she was not sure what else to do.

Brienne sighed as she looked at a japanned chest at the end of the hallway. Behind the doors covered with crimson lacquer, there must be treasures far finer than her small, blue vase. So why would anyone want it? That no longer mattered. All that was important was her promise to Maman.

Putting her fingers on the banister, she walked slowly down the stairs. She gazed about in awe, struck anew by the opulence she could not have imagined a few days ago. So proud she had been of her salon, but it could not compare to this splendid house. She recalled how on cold winter evenings she and her family had crowded around the single grate in the parlor, while Grand-mère had spoken of their comfortable home in France.

Had that house been as grand as this one? Silk wallcovering glowed warmly in the candlelight. The delicate furniture lining the long hallway below was as ornate as the house's exterior.

When she heard the clock in the dining room chiming the hour, she counted each stroke with a step down the stairs. It was only nine o'clock, even though she had been sure it was past midnight. Today had been eternally long.

She sighed as she crossed the marble floor of the expansive foyer. The light from the chandelier sparkled through crystal drops into every corner, but could not ease the darkness surrounding her. She wanted to awaken from this nightmare and be back at L'Enfant de la Patrie preparing for the patrons who stopped in before going to the theater. Then she could joke again with Grand-mère and run up the stairs to answer Maman's bell with a tidbit of gossip.

"Miss LeClerc?"

Jerking herself out of her wishful thoughts, she turned to see Hitchcock standing behind her. The butler frowned. He had made it clear that he did not like having her and Grand-mère here.

"Good evening, Hitchcock," she said.

"Mr. Somerset asks for you to join him in the gold parlor." His tone suggested that he liked having Evan here as little as he did her and Grand-mère.

"The gold parlor?" She glanced at the five sets of doors opening off the foyer. "Which one leads to the gold parlor?"

For a moment, she thought he would not answer her. Then he pointed to her left. "There, Miss LeClerc."

"Thank you."

He spun on his heel and walked stiffly away.

Brienne guessed that if the situation had been different, she would have enjoyed a good laugh about the officious butler. As it was, she was too tired to laugh tonight or to talk long with Evan. She hoped she could find a way to put a quick end to this conversation without making him suspicious.

Pushing her feet forward, she opened the door Hitchcock had indicated. She paused in the doorway, leaning her hand against the varnished molding which ended in an arch high above her head. She stared at the grandeur within the room.

By the standards of this house, this chamber was a cozy one, but it could have held the apartment that had been over the salon. A pair of tall windows reached for the ceiling and flanked a floor-to-ceiling mirror that was topped by a pair of rearing, golden lions. Luxurious gold carpet waited beneath the chairs and settees covered in glistening blue brocade. Paintings filled the spaces above the Oriental art set on mahogany tables beside each chair.

A long shadow rose near the fireplace. Evan crossed

the room and held out his hand. When she took it, he
drew her into the sable dusk that was edged with firelight.
She stared at him, realizing that except in the wake of
the fire, she had never seen him before without a coat
and perfectly tied cravat. She admired the smooth motion
of his muscles beneath his lawn shirt. With it open at the
throat, he seemed less arrogant. Her fingers tingled, and
she looked at them in amazement, for they longed to
reach up and explore the rough skin of his neck. She
clasped them in her lap as she sat on a settee.

"I believe that you could use some wine, Brienne,"
Evan said, his hushed voice not disrupting the crackle of
flames from the hearth.

"I believe you are right."

His lips twitched as he poured two glasses of wine and
handed one to her. Sitting in a chair facing her, he asked,
"How is Madame LeClerc?"

"Sleeping. I gave her a pinch of tincture of opium in
some brandy." She took a sip. "She is fond of brandy,
which she has had so seldom since leaving France."

"My friend is an excellent host. He forgot no luxury
when he offered me the use of his house."

"Are you staying in London long?"

Lowering his wine, untasted, he rested his elbows on
the arms of his chair. "As long as I must. And you?"

"I thought I might go to Almack's this week for my
debut into the Polite World."

"No need to be sarcastic."

"At least it is an answer!"

With a laugh, he tilted his wine in her direction. He
took a leisurely sip and leaned back in the chair. With a
smile flirting across his lips, he mused, "Mayhap you
should go to Almack's. You would create quite the sensation among all those misses who aspire to buckling themselves to a titled lord. They flutter about like mindless
moths, spouting French phrases totally out of context."

"You sound very familiar with Almack's."

"Do you doubt that I have spent an occasional evening there?"

"No more than I doubt that I am the Prince Regent's wife!"

Again Evan chuckled. "You are a shrew tonight, Brienne."

Her eyes sparked as brightly as the embers beneath the blue-hot flames. "And you are an ass, my Lord Somerset."

"What did you say?" He stood, putting his glass on the table. Although he wanted to grasp her shoulders and pull her to her feet so he could discover the truth that would be plain on her pretty face, he strode to the window that gave him a view of the square that was nearly swallowed by the fog. He sat on the sill and folded his arms in front of him. Even from this distance, he could see how she recoiled from the anger in his voice.

"Evan, I did not mean to insult you—I mean—"

He waved his hand and grumbled, "Forget it."

Could she heed his advice better than he had? He had spent the past decade trying to forget everything that had happened before. It had been easy until he accepted this commission to find that accursed vase. Surrounded by the LeClercs, he could not help comparing his own family to this one. There was no comparison. Brienne had no idea that the love she received from her mother and grandmother was something unique. He tried to imagine his father turning down a good business opportunity because it might hurt his family. It was impossible, but Brienne had not hesitated to keep the vase to please her mother when the LeClercs could have used the money he offered.

Looking back at Brienne, he saw her forehead ruffled with bafflement. He must not let her guess why her words had infuriated him. As she started to apologize, he interrupted by asking, "So what will you be doing . . . truthfully? Will you be leaving London?"

She stood and refilled her glass. "There does not seem to be much of a reason to do that now, does there?" Her voice was rough as she added, "Maman is buried in Soho instead of beside Papa in France. I guess the only choice I have is to go into service."

"Into service?"

An uncomfortable grin appeared on her pale face. "Do you need a cook, Evan? I am a very good one."

"I know that." He walked to where she sat again on the settee. "However, you need to face the truth."

"Which is?" Before he could answer, she added bitterly, "As if I did not know. Do not bother to warn me about the men who want that vase. If they had really wanted it, they would not have set fire to the salon."

"I would like to agree with you, but I cannot." He sat beside her.

"So you think the fire was an accident?"

"About as accidental as the men coming into the salon to beat you."

As always, when he mentioned that, she put her hand to the bruises on her cheek as if she could belatedly protect herself. "Leave off, Evan. I do not want your help." She flushed. "I did not mean to suggest I am ungrateful—"

"You leave off, Brienne!"

"Is something wrong, sir?" asked a maid, peering into the drawing room.

"Nothing." With a curse, he crossed the room and pulled the doors closed.

In horror, Brienne stared at Evan. He always had governed his emotions, hiding the truth. As he pinned her to the chair with his fearsome gaze, she wanted to say something. But what?

He moved closer without releasing her from his compelling stare. When he leaned forward to place his hands on the back of the settee, she slanted away, astounded. He gripped her face between his fingers.

"Listen to me!" he ordered in a low growl. "You are in more danger than you can conceive. You have been robbed, beaten, and nearly burned alive. How much more will it take to convince you that you need my help?" He sat beside her again and put his hand on her sleeve to keep her from standing. "Honey, you are going to sit here and listen until you admit that is the truth."

"That I am being hunted by a bunch of fools?"

"Mayhap they are fools, but they are determined to see you dead if that is what is necessary to get what they want."

"This is absurd!"

He cupped her chin and brought her face up. "Dammit, Brienne! You are intelligent. Don't be so dashed naïve. If you had not gone downstairs when you did, we might all be cinders now. Not just you. Not just me, but your mother and your grandmother. If you will not heed my warnings for your own sake, listen for your grandmother's. They killed your mother. Are you going to let them take the last member of your family from you?"

"She may not be—" Clamping her lips closed, she realized how easily she might reveal the secrets her mother had told her.

"Not the last of your family?"

"Must you pounce on everything I say?" She tried to pull away; then, with a sigh, she relented. "There must be others who remained in France after Papa died on the guillotine during the Terror."

"He was killed by the guillotine? Then, why did you name your salon after the opening line of *La Marseillaise*?"

"You would have to ask Grand-mère, for she and Maman named the salon when I was just a child."

He released her and sat back. "Your father was named Marc-Michel?"

"Yes," she said, astonished. "Marc-Michel LeClerc, but how did you know?"

"Your mother spoke of him. She clearly loved him very much."

She swirled the wine in her glass. How odd that Maman had spoken of Papa to Evan! Every time Brienne had asked about him, Maman had evaded the questions, telling her it was no longer important. Grand-mère had been as reticent.

"Explain something to me," Evan said quietly.

"Yes?"

"Brienne, look at me." When she did, he asked, "Isn't Madame LeClerc your mother's mother?"

"Yes, but you know that."

"Then, why does she have the same name as your mother and you?"

"What business is that of yours?" Setting herself on her feet, she said in her most frigid tone, "If it is parentage we are discussing, it might be more interesting to explore yours which gave you your beastly manners."

He laughed and stood. "Honey, years ago, my progenitors and I reached an agreement to part ways. They seem pleased with the arrangement, for they made only one attempt to contact me. I think it was after I was involved in a little episode in Bath."

"One I should not ask about?"

"You might regret it if you do." He smiled as if he were remembering a frolic, but she guessed it had more to do with larceny.

"I can only assume it went more successfully than this escapade?"

"You are a cruel woman, Brienne LeClerc, when I am trying to protect you and your family."

"In exchange for finding the vase?"

With a sigh, he drained his glass and put it on a nearby table. "No, for that is useless, isn't it? Although you lied to me after you were attacked, the fire proved the thieves did not get what they wanted. So they wanted to be sure no one did."

She put her glass next to his. "Now I understand why you were so anxious to go back there after the fire. How kind of you to take me when you were eager to sift through the ashes in hopes of finding the vase! I am sick of you and your schemes. Tomorrow I shall look for another place to live!" Silently, as she went to the door, she congratulated herself for steering the conversation in this direction. If Evan thought she was going to find another home tomorrow, he would not suspect what she had planned for just past midnight. "Good night."

"Brienne?"

"Yes?" She glanced over her shoulder and discovered that he stood right behind her.

He put his hands on her shoulders as he moved between her and the door. "Honey, I know you have no reason to trust me."

"You are correct about that!"

"Listen for once!" He frowned. "I am trying to save your pretty neck. I do not know who else is after the vase, but, until I do, I think you and Madame LeClerc should leave London."

She hid her shock. "Where would we go?"

"I have a friend with an estate not far from Brighton."

"Another friend? You have quite a few, don't you?"

"Brienne, I do not know why I care what happens to you. You are determined to get yourself and everyone else around you killed." His hands stroked her shoulders as he drew her closer. "Despite myself, I find I do care about keeping you alive."

When she saw his mouth lowering toward hers, she averted her face. "No," she whispered, "do not do that."

"You did not mind this afternoon." He whispered in her ear, "In fact, you seemed very eager."

Pushing away from him, she opened the door. "That was a mistake. Good night, Evan." She ran across the foyer, then skidded along the slippery floor to avoid bumping into Hitchcock. Grasping the newel post, she careened around it and up the stairs to her room.

She closed the door, sliding the bolt into place, before she dropped into a chair. Hiding her face in her hands, she wondered how she could have ever thought she had control over any conversation with Evan. Or any control over her longing to be in his arms. She could not halt herself from imagining the rapture of his mouth against hers. It was so perfect and all wrong.

She closed her eyes as she leaned her head back against the chair. He shredded all her defenses with his facile, seductive lures which drew her to him even when she knew how dangerous he could be for her and her family.

Her family!

Rising, Brienne went to the armoire and pulled out the bag. After tonight, she doubted if she would ever see Evan again. She would catch a late coach to Dover. There she would find someone willing to take her to France. When she reached France. . . . She had no idea what she would do then, but she must find her way to her father's grave.

She opened the bag and drew out the note she had written to her grandmother. Tilting it, she read:

Dear Grand-mère,

Maman asked me to do one last thing for her. I vowed I would go to France to find Papa's grave. I shall return as soon as I can. With this letter, I have left enough money so you can rent a room and buy food for about two months. If I am gone longer, Père Jean-Baptiste will help you.

I love you.
Do not worry about me. Maman would never ask
anything of me that was dangerous.
Tell Evan thank you for all he has done for us.
I am

> *Your loving granddaughter,*
> *Brienne LeClerc*

Brienne bit her lip as she folded the page over the pound notes she had taken from the box. That left her with far less money than she should have for such a journey, but she could not leave her grandmother to starve. Evan might allow Grand-mère to stay here while he lived in this house. After that, Grand-mère must have money to live on.

Now all she needed to do was wait for everyone in the house to fall asleep. Then she could be on her way, far from London and far from Evan Somerset. Certainly she would forget him once she was in France.

As she clutched the bag holding the small vase, she vowed that in a soft whisper. She would forget him.

She must.

Chapter Seven

In the afternoon sunshine, Dover's docks were worse than Brienne had expected. They stank of things she did not want to identify. Wrapping her cloak closer to her, for the briny breeze was icy, she shivered. If she succeeded in reaching France, she still had to find her family home, then return somehow to England and the security she had taken for granted. Common sense begged her to find a dray and go back to London. No one would admonish her for breaking her vow to her mother when France was at war with the rest of Europe.

No one but herself.

The bales and crates and barrels created a maze along the wooden planks. As she threaded her way through them, she tried to ignore the men watching her. Soon their attention was drawn away by a woman sashaying along the uneven cobbles.

"C'mon 'ere, dearie!" called a man.

Brienne hurried away. She did not want to witness a business transaction between a dockside whore and her customer, who stroked her more boldly than Evan had ever touched Brienne.

Begone! She was furious that Evan continued to invade her mind. She wanted him gone so she could concentrate on her task of finding a way to France instead of thinking how he had tried to buy her with his offer of £200. Clutching her bag close to her chest, she sighed. She could not allow her longings to persuade her to go home to London and his kisses that teased her to believe his lies.

She passed a handcart selling sausages. Her mouth watered, and her stomach growled, reminding her that she had not eaten since dinner last night. She stared at the greasy sausages which had such a delightful spicy scent. She could not waste a single farthing if she wanted to go to France, do as she had promised, and come back to England.

When the man by the cart looked at her, she asked, "Do you know Captain Marksen?" She had heard during the ride from London that Captain Marksen had a reputation as a smuggler who was willing to do anything for the right price.

"Mayhap." He continued to stir onions in a pot. The pungent odor kept him wiping his eyes with the back of a hand covered with thick, black hair.

"I am looking for Captain Marksen."

"Heard ye. Ain't deaf."

"And?"

"And what?"

She understood what she should have before. Opening her bag, she put a coin beside the pot. He glanced at it and away. When she put another coin next to it, he regarded her in silence. Searching for a third coin, she added it to the pile. Easily he made them disappear.

"What d'ye need to know?" he asked quietly.

"Where I can find Captain Marksen."

Hooking a thumb toward a bench where a trio of men sat, he said, "Middle one."

In disbelief, she stared at the man who returned to cooking the food he was hawking. Her money had bought her too little, but at least she knew where to find Captain Marksen.

She walked to the bench which was set next to a tavern door. Raucous sounds burst from the tavern. When a man reeled out, she moved hastily aside, then turned to see the men on the bench appraising her candidly. In her black dress under the long cape, she did not look like the harlots strutting along the quay. She would not let their stares intimidate her.

"Good afternoon, gentlemen," she said. A quick look told her all three men were dressed like the seamen who had invaded her salon. She was glad the curve of her plain bonnet hid her cheek and the bruises.

The man sitting in the middle of the plank balanced on two buckets met her gaze steadily. His narrow face was deeply tanned. Puffing on a pipe, he drew it from his mouth and blew the acrid smoke into her face. As his friends chuckled when she coughed, he said, "Go 'ome to where good little girls should be. We do not need yer preachin' 'ere."

She waved away the smoke and glared at the man whose heart must be as black as his thinning hair. He reeked, and she wondered when he had last washed his clothes. Probably the last time he had bathed, which must have been several fortnights ago.

"I shall be on my way," she returned, "if you are not interested in earning a few extra pounds, Captain Marksen."

"A few extra pounds?" he asked, instantly intrigued.

She smiled as coldly as he had. "Do you always do your business in public?"

He did not speak, but a glower at his companions must

have been some sort of signal. The two men stood. Brienne gasped when one ran his hand along her back and laughed.

"Leave 'er alone," Captain Marksen ordered. "Cain't ye see she be a lady?"

"A lady?" The man laughed again, then reeled down the wooden quay, bouncing good-naturedly off stacked barrels and bales of cloth.

"Sit yerself down, lady." Marksen crossed his legs and leaned back.

Gingerly she did as he ordered. If she let him discover how unsure she was, he would take advantage of her. "Captain Marksen, I need to get to France. If you could arrange passage for me, I will be sure no one knows how I crossed."

"Two 'undred pounds," he announced past his teeth gripping the stem of the pipe.

"Excuse me?"

"Two 'undred pounds, and I'll take ye." He eyed her up and down. "Yer small. Won't take up too much room. Got the money?"

She dampened her lips. "Captain, I cannot pay you such an astronomical fee."

"Astronom—? What the 'ell does ye mean by that?"

"It is too much."

Grasping her arm, he tugged her to her feet. She started to protest, but he growled a warning to her. He led her along the busy pier. No one appeared to notice them, and she guessed if they did, they would forget seeing her with Captain Marksen.

He turned her into a dusky alley, and she cried, "Where are you taking me?"

"I thought ye wanted to go to France."

"But—"

His hand over her mouth silenced her. In terror, she tried to pull away.

"Be quiet, lady. If we're seen 'ere . . ." He did not have to finish his threat.

She peeled his fingers off her mouth. In a whisper, she stated, "I understand the danger."

Brienne's bravado vanished as he faced her. Suddenly she realized how alone they were in this narrow alley. She tried to edge away along a brick wall, but his hand against it halted her. Staring at him, she knew it was useless to try to escape. He wanted the money she could pay him, so she should make him a deal to take her to France.

" 'Ow much can ye pay?" he asked.

"Ł25 is the most I can pay you."

He chuckled. "Ł25? Only Ł25? Ye be bold, girl, to come to me with such a ridiculous offer!"

"Do you want it or no?"

His smile became a frown. "All right. Be at the Fox and Swan at sunset. Ye know where the Fox and Swan tavern be on the marsh road, don't ye?"

"No, but I shall find it and meet you there at sunset."

"If ye ain't, I'll sail without ye."

"So you'll take me for Ł25?"

Again he laughed, the sound slicing through her. "I said be there. What 'appens after that is up to ye. Sunset, lady."

"I understand."

"By the way, darlin', what be yer name?" He put out one hand to the wall, paying no mind to the filth left by many chamberpots dumped in the alley.

"Miss Clark. Miss Bridget Clark."

"Be that so?" At his laugh, she realized she had not fooled him. "Miss Clark, it'll be. Be there at sunset, Miss Clark."

As she watched him lurch away, she realized he was as intoxicated as his comrades. The horrible stench of his pipe had masked the odor of whiskey. She doubted if any of the sailors could afford to drink the fine brandy they smuggled from France. That was all bound for the clubs and homes of the rich.

She followed Captain Marksen out of the alley. Her foot slipped into a pool of some liquid that smelled like the privies edging the docks. She grimaced, wishing she could clean her shoe. Mayhap she could buy some water from the innkeeper at the Fox and Swan. She could spare a few pennies for some water so she could wash before supper.

The thought of food spurred her forward. If she could find this inn right away, she might be able to eat before she met Captain Marksen again. Hurrying along the docks, she ignored the small voice that urged her not to keep the appointment, to go back to London where she belonged.

She wished she could, but a promise must be kept.

Brienne's legs were aching from fatigue by the time she found what she believed was the marsh road. Fearfully she glanced at the sun which was hanging low in the western sky, barely cutting through the fog oozing up from the ground. Sunset came so early this time of year, and she would not have time to retrace her steps if she had chosen the wrong way.

Damp oozed into her bones, and she longed for the comfort of the hearth in Evan's house. She might as well wish for a fancy house of her own, because she would never be going back to that haven. She feared she would never be that safe again.

Evan believed that the men who had set fire to L'Enfant de la Patrie would not be content until they found the vase or killed her. They would hunt her as long as she remained in England, but she doubted they would be able to chase her to France.

Brienne hurried to the side of the road as she heard the

rattle of a wagon. As it materialized out of the mist, she
saw the slow-moving gray horse was almost the same
shade as the fog.

The wagon stopped, and she heard a voice call, "Lost?"

She looked up at the elderly face of the driver. At first
she thought the wizened features belonged to a man. When
the person repeated the question, she realized the voice
was feminine. Bundled in a variety of rags and wearing
a bright handkerchief over her head, the woman smiled
at her.

"I hope I am not lost," Brienne answered. "I am
looking for the Fox and Swan."

"Yer goin' the right way, but what's a fine-looking
lass like ye goin' there fer?"

She was amazed that anyone would think that a mud-
splashed urchin looked fine, but not surprised that the inn
at which Captain Marksen had arranged to meet her had a
poor reputation. Choosing her words carefully, she asked,
"They still have a coach leaving for London from there,
don't they?"

"Aye."

She smiled. "I must hurry if I want to reach there
before it leaves."

"Girl!"

She glanced back.

"Climb 'board, girl." The old woman patted the seat.
"I be goin' past the Fox and Swan. Ye might as well
rest yer feet a bit."

"I—I don't have any money to pay you." Accepting
charity from Evan had bothered her, but not as much as
being offered a ride by a stranger. Only a few days ago,
she would have been grateful, but harsh lessons had taught
her not to trust blindly.

The old woman's eyes almost disappeared in the wrin-
kles of her wide cheeks. "Did I say a word 'bout money?
C'mon, girl. Climb 'board if'n ye want to get there afore

the coach leaves. I likes company other than this old nag and me own voice.''

Brienne climbed up the spokes of the wheel and onto the narrow seat. Rearranging her heavy cloak around her, she sat just as the dray lurched. She clutched her bag to make sure the vase was safe.

"Sorry," mumbled the old woman. "Old George goes when 'e wants.''

"George?''

What Brienne guessed was a chuckle emerged from the collection of rags. It sounded like a metal file rubbed on a dull knife. "Why not? This old nag's as mad as old King George 'isself. I be Granny Wilder. Who be ye, girl?''

"Bridget—Bridget Clark.'' She hated lying to this kind woman.

"Goin' to London? What fer?''

Dampening her lips, she said, "I thought I would find myself a job.''

"Talk right nice, ye do. Like one of them fancified ladies on the arm of a lord. Could get yerself a position like them.'' She slapped the reins on the back of the horse, but the pace continued the same. With another grumble, she cursed, "Damn 'orse! Goin' to sell 'im one of these days if'n I can get a tuppence fer 'im.''

Unsure how to respond, Brienne listened in silence as the old woman rambled on about any subject that struck her fancy. She offered her opinions on the king, the Prince Regent, the state of the weather, and the inevitability of England being invaded by Napoleon's army.

"Not that we won't beat their Frenchie arses right back 'cross the Channel. Almost wish Boney would come.'' She whipped an imaginary staff through the air. "Sure would like to see 'im racin' away like a cur with 'is tail 'tween 'is bandy legs.''

"Yes," she agreed when Granny Wilder seemed to be waiting for an answer.

The old eyes, which once might have been blue but had faded to a gray, regarded Brienne steadily. "Cain't be trustin' none of them Frenchies. They be a bunch of sinners, I 'ear. Bad as old King Louie. Mayhap they'll send Boney to the guillotine, too." Her grin returned. "Chop! No more Boney."

In horror, Brienne pulled away. Sickness roiled in her stomach. Although she heard Granny Wilder asking what was amiss, she could only shake her head as she remembered how Maman had revealed one rainy, winter afternoon that Brienne's father had died on the guillotine.

"Squeamish?" persisted the old woman. She chuckled and drew back on the reins as they drove down a slope toward a house with a barn beyond it. "Well, 'ere ye be, Bridget. Fox and Swan."

Brienne glanced around in dismay. Although the inn was as busy as the one in London, the hostlers here tossed the bags from the waiting coach directly into the mud. Shouts and curses filled the air.

Looking beyond them, she realized the inn was identifiable only by the sign hanging awry on a single hook. Like the barns, it needed a whitewashing. Paint had peeled to hang along the walls. Windows were patched with pieces of oiled paper.

She glanced at Granny Wilder and realized the old woman was waiting for her to say something. With a tentative smile, she murmured, "I guess it could be worse."

"It is. Inside." She leaned forward and put a gnarled hand on Brienne's knee. "Ye sure ye want to be goin' to London, Bridget? Ye don't seem like ye can take care of yerself too well."

"I will find a way." Sliding away from the fingers that were as hard as a tree branch, she eased off the seat, then carefully climbed down. She grimaced as her feet sank into the mud.

"Find yerself a good man. Or a fancy one." She winked and chuckled as she waved a farewell. "Mayhap I be seein' ye soon on the arm of a fancy gent. If ye get a rich one, don't forget old Granny Wilder who did ye a favor today."

When the wagon clattered out of sight in the fog, Brienne picked her way through the mud toward the inn. Captain Marksen had not said where he would meet her, so she would wait in the public room. Even a decrepit inn like this must have the luxury of a fire on the hearth. More than anything she wanted to be warm. No, more than anything she wanted to be safe.

She had no idea what waited on the other side of the Channel, but she knew too well what lurked in the shadows of the English countryside. Her future was in her control. Only by taking the greatest risk of her life could she assure herself of staying alive. There was no turning back.

Brienne held her dress out of the mud as she sidestepped an argument between two men. Now she understood why Captain Marksen had chosen to meet her at the Fox and Swan. With the chaos here, no one would note their negotiations.

She gasped as the men's loud discussion exploded into a fight. She cringed when one man struck the other. She tried to flee, but the press of spectators pushed her toward the melee.

She clawed her way out of the crowd. The spectators stepped aside reluctantly, for their attention was on the fight. Suddenly a broad hand clamped onto her wrist and snatched her through the crowd.

Captain Marksen's grim face offered her neither a smile nor a greeting as he cocked his head to the left. Pulling her hand out of his, she followed him. She knew better than to ask questions, because she risked losing his help.

Rushing to keep up with his longer strides, she jumped aside at a shout from a wagon speeding across the inn's yard. "Look out!" called the driver.

The curse Captain Marksen shouted back heated Brienne's dirt-streaked face. Neither man noticed as they exchanged obscenities. Marksen seized her by the wrist again. When the driver gave her a bawdy wink, she gasped.

"Shut up!" Marksen ordered.

She tightened her hold on her bag as he tugged so sharply she almost tripped.

"Watch where yer goin'," he growled.

"I am! I could walk much better if you did not shove me around."

"I said 'Shut up!', and I meant it." With another oath, he grumbled, "Not only is she cheap, but she chatters like a damned monkey." Before she had a chance to retort, he halted just inside the stable door. "D'ye still plan on givin' me only Ł25?"

"It cannot be more than twenty-five miles across the Channel to France. I think one pound for each mile is fair compensation."

"Compen—by all that's blue, lady, why don't ye speak the king's English?"

"I—oh, never mind. Will you take me to France for Ł25?"

"All right. Come with me. We shall see what me boys 'ave to say about yer offer." He grinned with malicious delight. "Of course, there's a thing or two to do afore we go."

She eyed him suspiciously. "Such as?"

"The money, darlin'."

"On your ship."

"Ye don't understand, Miss Clark. I ain't takin' ye nowheres until I see the pound notes."

Her smile erased his. "Then, I guess we are not doing business any longer. Good evening, Captain Marksen."

When she started to walk away, he caught her arm and spun her to look at him. She did not cower. She had let him see her terror, and he had tried to bully her. She could not afford to be so honest again. Staring at him, it took all her strength not to look away from his glower.

"All right!" he snarled. "I'll be trustin' ye a bit, but . . ."

"But what?"

He pulled some dirty material from a pocket. "Ye can't see where me and me boys meet. If'n ye want to go tonight, ye'll wear this until we get there."

Brienne hesitated, but knew his request, under the circumstances, was reasonable. Nodding, she turned so he could tie it in place. "Go ahead wi—"

He wrapped the cloth around her mouth. She reached for it, but he caught her hands and bound them behind her back. With a laugh, he shoved her to sit on the ground. She moaned as she struck the stable wall. When she pulled her feet under herself to stand, he raised his hand. "Move, darlin', and I'll be introducin' ye to the back of me 'and."

She sank back to the ground. He meant exactly what he said. When he grabbed the bag from where she had dropped it in the scuffle, her protest was muffled by the cloth.

Squatting next to her, he smiled. "One more sound, darlin', and I'll silence ye fer good." When her eyes widened in horror, he nodded. "Yer learnin'. Now, let's see what ye 'ave in 'ere."

He dumped the contents onto the wet ground and pushed aside the few personal items she had packed in the small bag. His smile broadened when he lifted the box, but vanished when he discovered it was locked. ''Give me the key.''

She shook her head.

''I want it, darlin'. Don't make me do ye 'arm, Miss Clark. Ye wouldn't be likin' it a bit if—'' Suddenly he glanced over his shoulder.

Brienne heard what he had. Someone was coming. Marksen stuffed her things back into the bag and lifted her off the ground, holding her under one arm as if she were a barrel on his ship. At an awkward lope, he carried her into the shadows of some trees. He tied a second handkerchief over her eyes, crushing her borrowed bonnet, then placed her in a saddle. When her bag was pressed into her fingers, she held it tightly. The saddle rocked with a squeak of leather as he climbed on behind her.

He gave her no warning when he urged the horse out of the yard. She nearly fell, but his arm encircled her waist. She shrank away from his repulsive touch.

Sometime later—she had no idea how long—Captain Marksen slowed the horse and jumped down. She shrieked when he hauled her to the ground. She fell to her knees.

''C'mon, darlin','' he ordered as he pulled her to her feet. ''Me boys'll be glad to meet a real lady like ye.'' He chortled and steered her across the uneven ground.

When she tripped, he did not catch her. He let her tumble to the ground before he forced her upright again. She heard a set of hinges protest. Knowing there might be a sill on the door, she lifted her feet and managed not to fall. Several men had been talking, but as she entered, they became silent.

Fumbling fingers loosened the handkerchiefs. As soon as her hands were untied, she whirled away, undid the cloth gagging her, and tossed the soiled material at Captain Marksen.

At laughter that echoed Marksen's smile, Brienne looked around her. Unplaned boards along the walls were broken by a single door. The ceiling was low, for the captain's head brushed it. In the middle of the small room was a table with a pair of benches. More than a dozen men crowded around it, and a lone candle burned. She recognized the two men who had been with Marksen this afternoon.

"Sit down!" ordered Marksen.

Gingerly she edged to an empty spot on one bench. She did not expect any of the men to move aside, and none of them did. Their eyes followed every motion she made. She adjusted the broken brim of her bonnet, pulling it forward so she did not have to see their leers.

Captain Marksen began telling his men about what they could expect during this voyage. Not once was she mentioned, and she wondered how often they had passengers on their nameless ship. She folded her hands in her lap, keeping the bag close to her. When the captain paused in mid-word, she saw the men tense.

"What is it?" she whispered.

"Shut up," Marksen growled. He motioned, and several men stood, edging to either side of the door.

Brienne swallowed her gasp when she saw the sailors held guns. Then she heard a horse slowing outside the hut.

The door of the hut opened. When she started to hide beneath the table, a pistol appeared directly in front of her eyes. She followed its glint to Marksen's hand and on up his arm to his rigid face. She froze. Even breathing took more courage than she could muster.

When a man stepped into the hut, the others welcomed him with laughs and rambunctious shouts.

"Evan!" she gasped. Her gaze moved from his elegant riding coat along the dark riding breeches which followed the firm lines of his legs. Polished boots reached to his knees, but did not shine as brightly as the pistol in his hand.

"Ye know 'er, Somerset?" asked Marksen.

Smiling, Evan put out a single finger and lowered Marksen's gun toward the table. "Brienne is not dangerous. Deluded, mayhap, but not dangerous."

"Brienne?" Marksen glared at her. "Told me 'er name be Bridget."

"You know women. They never tell the same story twice."

"Cheap doxy. Offers me Ł25 to take 'er 'cross. Yer type, Somerset. Yer always lookin' fer a cheap one." He grasped Brienne by the arm. Jerking her to her feet, he propelled her toward Evan.

Torn between delight at seeing Evan and outrage that he had followed her, she pulled away. "Don't touch me, Mr. Somerset!"

Evan took her arm again as the men jeered, mocking her words in high-pitched voices. He twirled her, entangling her skirt with his legs. "I shall do whatever the hell I want with you, honey." He caught her other hand as she raised it. When she moaned as he twisted it behind her, he looked past her to Marksen. "I want to talk to her alone."

"Go ahead." Pointing to the corner opposite the door, he said, "Me and the boys will iron out a few things while ye deal with yer doxy."

Brienne refused to be dragged about the hut. She had to get to France. If Evan's intrusion persuaded Marksen to leave her behind. . . . She shook her head when Evan repeated the captain's order.

He caught her face in one hand and said so softly only she could hear, "I do not want to hurt you, honey, so do what I tell you."

"You would not dare. You—" She saw the truth in his crystal blue eyes.

He smiled, but with no humor as she let him lead her to a darkened corner.

Not wanting to be overheard by the others, she spat in a whisper, "I should have guessed you would be involved with smugglers."

"Me? You are the one negotiating with Marksen for passage across the Channel." He laughed. "I must admit that I did not think that you would be so calm when I caught up with you."

"Did you think I would throw myself on you, sobbing out my joy at seeing you?"

"Hardly, but I did anticipate a little curiosity about how I found you."

"You obviously are following me. Is Captain Marksen one of your many friends?"

"We have done business in the past."

"We are doing business now! Why don't you leave?"

He gripped her arm and pushed her against the wall. "Brienne, your sarcasm is tiresome. Keep it up, and I shall give you to Marksen and his crew to deal with as they see fit."

Although she doubted he would do as he threatened, she knew she must not embarrass him before Marksen's crew. She nodded.

"That is better," he said. Leaning forward so his face was close to hers, he added, "How in hell did you get involved with Marksen?"

"On my way from London, I asked for the name of a captain who was interested in making some money. His name was mentioned more than once."

"Dammit, honey, how can you be so stupid?" His hand settled on her shoulder to keep her from edging away, and she glared at him. "Running off like this was crazy. You need protection now, and I am going to give it to you whether you want it or not. Do you understand?"

"But—"

His finger on her lips silenced her. "Do you understand?" When she nodded, he smiled with satisfaction.

"Good. Now, to make *them* understand. Cooperate, Brienne, if you value our lives."

Waiting for him to reveal some great plan, she stiffened when his arm slipped around her and brought her tight to him. His fingers framed her cheeks, keeping her from averting her face as his lips captured hers. The gentle stroke of his mouth belied his angry words. When her arms eased up around his back, his strong sinews moved smoothly beneath his skin. He pressed her to the wall, warning her that his desire for her was very real.

When the tip of his tongue teased the curve of her lips, they softened. Boldly, he sought within her mouth for the pleasure waiting there. The heat of his breath caressed her as it mingled with hers. Her fingers crushed the wool of his coat as she tried not to be swept into the eddy of passion.

He raised his head and whispered, "Very good, honey. Every man in the room is watching. I knew I could depend on you to put on a good act for them."

Rage seared her, but her anger was not aimed at him. She was furious with herself for believing yet again that he was wooing her because he found her enticing. He had never wanted her, as much as he wanted what he thought she could bring him.

With a chuckle, Evan kept his arm around Brienne's stiff waist as he steered her back to the table. He had seen her scowl, but he ignored it. Now was not the time for her ruffled sensibilities. Nor was now the time to imagine holding her much more intimately. The longing to explore every curve that had brushed him sent a tightening through him. He pushed those tempting thoughts from his mind as Marksen stepped in front of him.

"Where're ye goin', Somerset?"

"You are busy, so I shall come back for a call some other time." He glanced at Brienne. "I have what I came for."

Marksen's cadaverous face appeared more skeletal in the candlelight. "Then, get the 'ell out of 'ere. Ye've 'ad yer chance to say farewell to Miss Clark or whatever 'er name be." His cold gaze settled on Brienne, and he licked his lips. "Say goodbye to 'im, darlin'. It be time fer us to be leavin'."

"Leaving?" asked Evan with studied serenity. He would not let Marksen know how the smuggler's leer infuriated him.

"She be payin' me to take 'er to France."

"She is not going to France."

Brienne cried, "Evan—"

"Look, Somerset," Marksen said with a sneer, "she be payin' me fer takin' 'er there." His thin lips stretched as he stared at Evan's clothes. "Of course, if ye've enough gold to make it worth me while to forget m'deal with yer Miss Clark, I be glad to listen to yer offer."

"I am going!" she insisted.

Ignoring her protests—had Brienne lost every bit of sense she had ever had?—Evan said, "You are forgetting that small debt you owe me, Marksen. April of 1807. Or have you forgotten you told me that you would be willing to repay me whenever I wish?" He smiled as Marksen's shoulders sagged. "This is it."

Evan knew Marksen did not want to remember the night when Evan and his partner had saved Marksen's ship, cargo, and life. It was an obligation that had never been mentioned again until tonight.

"Get out," Marksen snapped. "Take 'er, and get out."

"No!" cried Brienne. "Captain Marksen, you promised to take me to France! I shall pay you—"

With a laugh, Evan muffled her by putting his hand over her mouth. He shook his head when Marksen offered him a filthy handkerchief to gag her. Drawing a clean one from his pocket, he released her long enough to move behind her. She could not flee, for Marksen caught her.

She kept her lips closed tightly when he held up the cloth.

Quietly Evan ordered, "Cooperate, honey." When she shook her head vehemently, he bent to whisper, "Marksen will not let you leave alive if he suspects you could find this place again. Either cooperate, or I shall knock you senseless."

"You would not dare!" The rest of her objection was silenced by the cloth.

Brienne relented, knowing it was useless, as Marksen bound her hands behind her again. When a second handkerchief was held in front of her eyes, she saw Evan's smile. He was enjoying this! If he thought he had gotten the better of her, he would learn he was wrong. She was not sure how she would best this man who had too many connections throughout England, but she would.

Soon, she promised herself. Soon Evan Somerset would watch her exult in triumph. Soon.

Chapter Eight

Evan slowed the horse as he reached the marsh road and settled Brienne more securely on his lap. When her face turned toward him, she radiated rage. She could not see anything. He swallowed his chuckle. If she discovered his amusement with her circumstances, she would be even more impossible to deal with.

And she usually was incredibly difficult! Never had he met anyone who was so eager to disbelieve him when he was telling the truth and accept his lies as fact. He had no one to blame for that but himself. If he had gone to L'Enfant de la Patrie with a story of a wife or lover who desired the vase, Brienne's generous heart would have been touched, and she would have sold the vase to him.

Instead he had allowed her impoverished gentility to touch *his* heart, and he had made her suspicious with his ridiculous offer for the vase. He gazed down into her face which was nearly hidden by the two handkerchiefs and asked himself, yet again, what it was about Brienne that had made him forget his well-whetted instincts.

Holding her with one arm, he untied the cloth gagging her. He tossed it into the underbrush edging the road. "Be quiet," he warned.

"I shall do what I want, Evan Somerset! I shall—"

He silenced her by capturing her mouth. The soft promise of untapped passion on her lips maddened him with a desire he found hard to control. He sighed when she jerked away. He loosened the cloth covering her eyes.

"How about my hands?" she demanded, but in a whisper.

In the darkness which was broken only by the cold fog concealing the countryside, he could see the glitter of fury in her eyes. "Can you be better behaved?"

"Can you be less insulting?"

"Honey, we are not going to get anywhere tonight if you are a shrew."

"*I* was going somewhere until you interfered!"

From beneath his coat, he pulled a knife. Her eyes widened as she drew back. He cursed as he slit the bonds on her wrists and made the blade disappear. "Did you think I was going to slay you?"

Hating the breathlessness in her voice, Brienne whispered, "I never know what you will do."

His hand on her shoulders tilted her beneath his lips. She wanted to pull away, but any motion could cause her to lose her precarious balance on his lap.

As his mouth descended toward hers, he murmured, "You can trust me on one thing. I will never hurt you, honey."

When he kissed her again, she wanted to pretend she was as angry as she had been moments ago. It was useless, because she clutched his upper arms while sweet desire resonated through her. Her mind shouted for her to push him away, but her hands refused to heed the inner voice as his tongue blazed a searing path through the dark cavern of her mouth, setting her afire. Her breasts caressed his iron-hard chest with each swift breath she took.

Her fingers rose to comb through his thick hair as he brushed his lips along her throat. His face's sandy texture rubbed against her, augmenting her craving as he found her mouth again.

The tender kiss lasted only a single heartbeat before the horse shifted beneath them. With a shriek, Brienne grabbed Evan's sleeves. He laughed as his arms closed around her, keeping her from falling.

"Did I not tell you I would not let you get hurt?" he asked, laughing.

"You should not expect me to be too trusting of you too quickly."

He smiled and drew her nearer. " 'Tis getting damned cold out here, and the horse wants to get back to its stable. I think we should think about doing the same."

"A stable?" She sat straighter, but bounced back against him as the horse picked up speed along the road which was empty except for the cloying mist. "If you think I will spend the night with you in a hayloft, you are a fool!"

His laugh rumbled through his chest. She was glad the darkness hid the telltale heat climbing her cheeks as he leaned her head on his shoulder and murmured, "You suggest the most charming fantasies, but I have already arranged for rooms at the inn where I rented this beast."

"The Fox and Swan?"

"Hardly. How did you know about that horrible place?" He chuckled and answered his own question, "That is where you met Marksen, isn't it? Brienne, you have to be more leery of the ones you so unwisely choose for allies."

"Like you?"

Tightening his arm around her, he asked, "So am I

your ally at last? 'Tis about time you realized we are both on the same side.''

"Of what?"

"That is a question I think would be best answered inside, where it is warm.''

On that, Brienne could agree. As she relaxed against him, she found sleep oozing over her like the fog. Relentlessly she fought it. Each time her head rested against Evan's chest, she forced herself awake. Her eyes watered with fatigue, and she did not dare to blink, for she found it more and more difficult to open her eyes again.

She did not realize she had lost the battle to stay awake until she heard Evan call softly, "Wake up, honey. We are here.''

Bright light came from a lantern in a stableman's hand. In his other hand, he held the horse's bridle. When Evan helped her out of the saddle, she swayed with exhaustion.

His arm curved around her shoulders after he had unhooked her bag and handed it to her. "Let's go inside. I think you could use something to eat and a good night's rest.''

"Yes," she mumbled. Letting him guide her toward the inn, she stumbled beside him as she fought off sleep. Something to eat might wake her up and ease the cramp in her stomach.

Her curious gaze swept across the entrance of the inn. Except for a small desk with a lamp glowing on top of it, the hallway was bare. A rough staircase led up to the left, and several doorways opened on the opposite wall.

A round woman appeared, her apple red cheeks as full as her shelf of bosom. Folding her arms in front of her, she planted herself firmly between them and the doorway to the public dining room. The aromas wafting from inside made Brienne's mouth water.

"We allow no vagabonds here," the woman said.

"There be other places fer ye if ye want her with ye, sir."

Brienne was startled until she looked down at her filthy gown. No wonder the woman thought she was a beggar.

She sensed Evan's irritation, but his voice was filled with his most endearing tone as he answered, "I stopped earlier to arrange for a room for a friend of mine. Unfortunately, as you can see, her carriage was upset when it was rammed by another vehicle on this devilish night."

Instantly the woman cooed, "Poor lamb. Take her up, sir. I will send some water to ye so she can clean herself. Will ye be needing some bandaging, miss?"

"No, I am fine." Brienne wished Evan had not made her the focus of his lies.

"Brave, isn't she?" Evan asked with a smile. "Hungry, too. Could you have some food brought upstairs for us? I am sure you can understand that she does not want to be seen in such a state."

"Of course, of course." The woman's smile was as broad as his.

Brienne could not decide if she abhorred the woman's fawning or Evan's lies more. "May we go up now?"

The innkeeper opened a drawer in the desk and pulled out a pair of keys. "As you requested, sir. Two rooms with an adjoining door."

Brienne whirled to look at Evan. "Adjoining—?"

"Thank you." Evan took the keys and swung Brienne toward the stairs at the same time. Pushing her ahead of him, he said lowly, "Behave yourself, or I shall give her back the key to the second room. Of course, I will be glad to give her back the key if you want me with you all night."

Silence was the only answer that would not cause more trouble. Brienne let him hold her elbow as they walked to her room. He opened the door and motioned for her to enter the chamber which was lit only by a fire on the hearth.

"My key?" she asked, holding out her hand.

"Go in. We can discuss this and everything else inside."

"I have no intentions of discussing anything with you in a room of an inn!"

"Then, you can listen to me." A gentle shove propelled her into the room. After closing the door, he lit a candle and placed it on the table by the window on the other side of the broad bed. "Having you listen to me would be novel. Why don't you take off your damp cloak and relax?"

Wondering how she could relax when she stood with him in this rented room, she put her bag on the table and struggled with her trembling fingers to undo the ties at her throat. Folding the muddy cape over the room's only chair, she shivered. The night's dampness had gnawed into her bones. She went to stand by the hearth. When a blanket was draped over her shoulders, she glanced back at Evan.

"Thank you," she murmured.

Gently he untied her ruined bonnet. Her hair cascaded atop the blanket in a sable shadow. His fingertip grazed her bruised cheek. "This looks better already."

"It does not hurt as much, if that is what you mean."

"If I could find the ones who did this to you, it would take them a lot longer to heal."

"Evan!"

His grim expression became a smile. "You do not want me to be your friend or your hero, and I cannot be your enemy. It makes for a very peculiar relationship, *duchesse*."

"What did you call me?"

A knock kept him from answering. When he opened the door, a maid brought in steaming water. She poured it into the ewer on the washstand next to the bed. The young girl stared at them as she dipped in a curtsy and rushed out of the room.

Evan grimaced at Brienne, and she began to laugh. Something about the servant's silent awe struck her as hilarious. Hungry and tired, she was too weak to control her own laughter. When a second knock announced the arrival of their meal, she wiped tears from her eyes and fought the quakes of laughter.

Evan took the tray and carried it to the table. "You need not wait to be invited to eat, Brienne." He held out a spoon and a dish.

She savored the beefy scent of the soup. Steam billowed into her face as she took an eager sip. "Wonderful."

"Your soup is better."

"But I have never been so hungry when I ate mine."

His hand on her wrist halted her from taking a second spoonful. "When did you eat last?"

"Dinner at your house."

"You mean you have not eaten all day?"

Easing her hand from beneath his, she gulped another mouthful of soup before saying, "I need my money to get to France."

His eyes became a deeper blue as they narrowed with the fury she had come to recognize. "Don't you know how upset Madame LeClerc is?"

"I left her a note explaining I would be back as soon as I could."

"Along with enough money to pay rent on a room and buy food and fuel for the rest of the winter." He grumbled a curse as he put his hands on her shoulders and pushed her to sit on the bed. "You thought of everything."

She tried to shrug off his hands, but it was impossible. "If you know all that, then you know that I promised Maman that I would go to France and find Papa's grave."

"Why would she ask you to do something so addle-witted?"

"I do not know."

"Didn't she realize the danger she was sending you into?"

Brienne sighed. "I am not sure. She was not completely lucid at the very end, I fear. She warned me to be careful of a door."

"A door? What did she mean by that?" Another knock sounded, and he frowned. "Who the blazes can that be?" He went to the door.

Peering past him, Brienne saw the woman who had greeted them downstairs. They spoke lowly, but Brienne heard the woman ask if the rooms were suitable. Evan's voice was calm, instead of heated as when he argued with her. She was awed by how easily he governed his emotions. No wonder she could not tell when he was being honest and when he was lying.

After he had assured the innkeeper that all was well, he closed the door and pulled out the key and locked it. He put the iron key beneath his coat, then took his soup bowl from the tray. Pushing her cloak onto the floor, he sat on the chair and ate as he regarded her with a strange expression she could not decipher.

"You should eat," he said as if there were nothing unusual about them sitting together in the room of a wayside inn.

"I shall do what I want when I want!"

With a snort, he chuckled. "You sound like a *duchesse* already."

"What are you talking about?"

He did not answer as he dipped his spoon into the chipped bowl. He reached for the bottle of wine on the tray and poured a glass for each of them. As he handed her one, he mused, "They could use your cooking skills here, *duchesse*."

Putting her bowl on the table, she rose. "Evan, why are you calling me that?"

He stood and put his arm around her waist. Drawing her to sit on the bed, he laughed. "If I am going to tell you a fairy tale, it might as well be a bedtime story."

"If you think I would—" His mouth grazed hers, but she pushed him away. "You are making a mistake, Mr. Somerset. This is my room and my bed."

"Paid for by me."

"I will be glad to repay you if you would leave." *Before I let your kisses seduce every bit of sense from my head.* She started to stand, but his arm around her kept her on the bed.

"I do not want your money. I want you to listen to me while you eat before you faint from hunger." He pressed her bowl in her hands.

"Evan, you should leave."

"After you finish your supper and listen to me."

Brienne nodded, knowing that he would not go and let her sleep until she agreed to listen to whatever he had to say. She hoped it was interesting because the weight of exhaustion was heavy on her eyelashes again.

"That is better," he said, leaning his elbow on the curved footboard. "Once upon a time—"

She frowned. "I am too tired for this skimble-skamble."

"It is not silliness. It is something you need to hear."

With a sigh, she said, "All right, but make it a short story."

"Once upon a time," he repeated with a taut smile, "not too long ago, a little girl was hidden away by two fairy godmothers so she would not be found by the ogre who wanted to steal her father's castle. For years, the little girl lived in a cramped cottage in a distant city, but the ogre never forgot her. He knew the godmothers' magic would not protect her forever. He waited and planned and waited some more while the little girl grew up into a beautiful woman, not knowing about the ogre.

"The ogre became tired of waiting. Using sorcery, he convinced a good-hearted lad to go on a quest for him. In exchange for finding what he sought, he would give the lad a casket of gold. If the lad failed, he would be given a casket of wood in the earth. Not trusting the lad, the ogre sent his evil henchmen to seek out the little girl who was not so little any longer. They—"

"Enough!" Brienne cried, carrying her empty bowl to the tray. "Why don't you just say what you are trying to say?"

His eyes twinkled. "All right, honey. To begin with, your name is not Brienne LeClerc."

"No? And what is it?"

"Brienne Levesque."

She shrugged. "Many of the *émigrés* changed their names when they fled France. LeClerc and Levesque are common names. Whether my name is Brienne LeClerc or Brienne Levesque makes no difference."

"It makes a great difference when your father was not Marc-Michel LeClerc, but Marc-Michel Levesque, the *Duc* of Château Tonnere du Grêlon."

"A *duc?*"

He stood and seized her shoulders. "Don't you realize the truth, Brienne? You are the *duc's* heir, mayhap his only living heir. Your grandmother told me there was a son—your brother—but he was killed when your father was taken to die on the guillotine."

She stared at him. If only she could be sure he was not lying, but it was impossible to discern that with Evan. He lied so easily. "And if I am the *duchesse* as you say, how do I prove it? I cannot go to the château, knock on the door, and say, 'This is mine.' "

"The vase taken from the château by Madame LeClerc when you fled would identify you. If you still have it, honey, we can turn it into a château and a magnificent title for you.''

''Ah, the vase,'' she said with a cold smile. ''Now I understand. It always comes back to that vase, doesn't it? And, if I do not swallow the clunkers you told me with this story, Evan, what lies will you devise next time? Mayhap, you should tell me I am the lost daughter of King George. I could be Princess Brienne!''

He glared at her. ''I am sick of your sarcasm.''

''Good, because I am sick of your lies!''

Taking a deep breath, he unclenched his hands and put them on her shoulders. ''I am not going to convince you, am I?''

''No.'' She brushed his hands away and pointed toward the door that must lead to the other room. ''Why don't you go to bed so I can?''

''I will as soon as you listen to me.''

''I have listened to your nonsense.'' She yawned widely. As she had before, she told herself that if letting him spin his cock-and-bull story would allow her to get to sleep, it was worth listening to it. ''All right, but first I want you to explain a few things to me. Maman hated London. Why didn't we return to France after the Terror was over?''

His hands framed her face. ''Before I answer anything, you need to know the truth. Lucile LeClerc was not your mother. Yvonne LeClerc is not your grandmother.''

''Are you mad?'' Pulling away again, she folded her trembling arms in front of her as she went to the hearth. Not even the fire could ease the icy hurt left by his deception. ''I could have almost believed you, Evan, but I should have known you are just embroidering a story to try to get what you want.''

He moved toward her in a silence that was suddenly threatening. When she started to edge away, he caught her arm and refused to release her. A smile twisted his lips as he shoved her to sit on the bed again. "Believe it or not, as you wish, *duchesse*. I found the tale unbelievable when your grandmother told it to me before I left to find you."

"And you expect me to believe it?"

"I do not care what you believe! The truth is Lucile LeClerc was your nurse at Château Tonnere du Grêlon. Madame LeClerc told me that her daughter adored your father, but the *duc* was very devoted to his wife and, after their marriage, never noticed any other woman."

"Are you done with your story yet?" she asked when he paused.

"I do not know why I am bothering to tell you this."

"Because you cannot resist the chance to lie to me?" She jumped to her feet again. Going to the door leading to the other room, she flung it open. She ignored the crash as it struck the wall. "Get out!"

"This is not L'Enfant de la Patrie, honey. You cannot throw me out."

"Then, take this room! I shall use the other one." She scooped up her cape and bag. "I have heard all I want to."

"You do not want to know that you may have a sister alive somewhere?"

Brienne whirled to stare at him. She wanted to accuse him of lying, but his face was lined with strain. Sweet heavens, he believed what he was telling her! Grand-mère had no reason to lie to him. She shuddered as she realized that if she accepted Evan's story, then she had to own that her grandmother had been lying to her all her life.

"Evan, it is cruel to jest with me like this."

" 'Tis no jest. You may have a sister alive somewhere on the Continent." He hesitated, then added, "Mayhap even your real mother is still alive."

She let the cloak drop to the floor and the box fall atop it. "My real mother?" The words brought only one image into her head. Dear Maman. "Evan, if you are lying to me—"

"I am telling you the truth. Madame LeClerc was horrified to learn what her daughter had asked of you. She sent me to stop you from going to France without knowing the truth." He crossed the room and took her hands in his. "Mayhap I should have taken you directly back to London and let her tell you. Then you might believe it."

"It all sounds impossible. My father was a *duc?*"

"Your grandmother told me that he went to serve with the Estates-General, but was arrested as many moderates were. Your mother did not know that when she left for Paris to visit him. She took your baby sister, but left you behind because you were recovering from a light fever. When word came of your father's execution, the LeClercs wanted to protect you, so they fled to London."

"Where Maman was always miserable." She smiled sadly. "I cannot believe what you are telling me, because my heart tells me that Maman was my mother."

When she yawned again, he led her to the bed and sat beside her. "Lucile LeClerc and her mother raised you, but you have another family somewhere that may be looking for you. Didn't Lucile LeClerc explain any of this to you?"

"No."

"Then, why did she want you to find your father's grave at Château Tonnere du Grêlon?"

"Château Tonnere du Grêlon? Castle Thunderstone?" Her eyes widened. "The design on the vase! Lightning cutting through a rock!"

He nodded. "I thought of that also. I was hired to find a vase with that design. The man who contacted me described it exactly."

"But the vase is—was useless."

"I realize that now. It is you he seeks. He is the ogre

of my tale, and he knows where the thunderstone vase is found, you may also be found.''

Pressing her hands to her chest, she gasped, ''Me? Why would anyone want me? Who is this man?''

''I know him only as Lagrille.'' His brow rutted as he concentrated deeply. ''He is French, and he may live in Paris or somewhere else on the Continent. I have met him only once face-to-face, and that room in Paris was kept dark, so I could not identify him later. Usually I deal with one of his men who brings me my instructions. That does not explain why he is seeking you.''

''Mayhap he is a shy admirer who has seen my beauty and grace and—''

''Be realistic, Brienne!''

She shook her head. ''You tell me a tale like this, and you expect *me* to be realistic?''

''It is true. The vase proves it.''

''I am sorry, Evan. I wish I could believe you, but I cannot.''

He slanted toward her until his nose brushed hers. She leaned away, gasping as she fell back onto the bed. Softly he asked, ''Do you believe this?''

Unable to evade his lips, she knew fighting him was foolish as the familiar thrill raced through her when she lifted one hand to curve along his nape. His body pressed her into the bed. He might be a rogue or a liar and a thief, but his kisses and gentle caresses were beguiling.

As she answered his fevered lips with her own desire, she stroked his back. His firm thighs against her teased her to be bolder. Her fingers slipped beneath his coat to touch him with only a thin layer of lawn between his skin and hers.

She pulled away when she discovered a crease along his ribs. ''You were hurt?''

''Shot.''

''Shot?'' she repeated in horror.

"Not by a jealous husband, if that is what you are thinking." The tip of his tongue teased her earlobe. "I try to stay clear of romantic complications. That has been easy until now."

"But what happened?"

"It was many years ago, honey. Another job. I try not to think about the past. I would rather think of right now."

She moaned softly as his fingers glided over her breast. Drawing his mouth down to hers, she melted against him. As her breath came faster and shallower, she surrendered her mind to the ecstasy.

The sound of her name took several seconds to invade the rapture surrounding her. Slowly she opened her eyes as the bed moved beneath her. When she was about to scold him for being so forward, she realized he was standing. Knowing that she was being absurd when he was doing as he should, she sat up and asked, "Evan, where are you going?"

"To bed . . . in my room." He smiled and stroked her unbruised cheek with the back of his hand. "Unless you want me to stay with you. I must own that I have never had the pleasure of sleeping with a *duchesse*."

"So you believe all of this?"

"I believe that I need to go now before I give in to the craving to make love with you." He grasped her chin and kissed her hard. "Good night, honey. Get some rest. In the morning, we need to start back toward London."

She watched as he walked to the hall door, tested the latch to be sure it was locked, then went to the door to his room. "Don't you trust me?"

"Trust you?" He laughed. "Brienne, I would trust a she-tiger before I trusted you. You have claws as sharp and a killer's wit as vicious and a beauty as wild. Good night, honey."

When she heard no latch slide on the adjoining door, Brienne jumped up to lock it. As easily as Evan stripped her of all sense with his kisses, she must keep him far from her.

There was no lock.

With a curse, she kicked the door. Hearing laughter from the other room, she muttered the oath again. She was so tired of Evan flaunting his control over her. That she had been a willing participant in his triumph this time added to her fear of the strong passions he aroused in her. They allowed him to govern her as nothing else could.

A soft sound encroached, easing her vexation. When a second pebble struck her window, she scrambled around the bed to peer out. It was so foggy she could not see anything. She threw open the window, hoping that would be better.

She gasped as she stared at Captain Marksen, who was crouched on the low roof. "C'mon, darlin'. 'Tis time to sail."

"But, Evan—"

"If'n ye don't want to be goin', goodbye."

"No! I want to go, but I am locked in here!"

"Not if'n ye climb atop the roof." He held out his hand.

Brienne did not hesitate. It did not matter if she was the daughter of a *duc* or a cook. She had made a promise to Maman to take the vase to her father's homeland.

She tiptoed across the room. Grabbing her cape, she tied it around her neck. She clutched her bag as she went back to the window and flung one stockinged leg over the windowsill.

She glanced back at the door leading to Evan's room. "Goodbye," she whispered. "I wish it could have been different."

But it was not, she reminded herself as she slipped through the window. When she put her foot on the roof shingles, she heard a threatening creak.

"C'mon!" called Marksen as he edged down to the ground.

Sitting, she slid down the roof as if it were a snow-covered hill. When her feet dangled off the edge, Marksen held up his hands. She turned over to lie on her stomach and lowered her feet. She tried not to think about the immodest view of her limbs that she was offering him.

"Let go!" He grabbed her ankles.

Breathing a quick prayer, she obeyed. He caught her before she hit the ground, but the impact against him jarred her teeth. He set her on her feet and grasped her hand, tugging her to where a horse was tied by the road. When he had flung her in the saddle and mounted behind her, he turned the horse's head toward the shore road. They exploded out of the stableyard.

Brienne did not look back. Her future waited in a country she could not remember.

Chapter Nine

In dismay, Brienne stared at the small ship rocking with the waves in the deserted cove. She should be excited to be on her way to France. Instead she tried to figure out why Captain Marksen had sought her out in the inn. Not for the money, because he had considered £25 far too little for her passage. She suspected he was helping her to spite Evan. He had repaid his favor to Evan by allowing her to leave the hut, but had not promised not to come back to take her to France with him.

She stood on the strand and listened to the hushed song of the waves. Each gentle caress of the foam on her shoes reminded her of how sweetly Evan had held her. She shook her head. She must not think of his kisses now. Evan Somerset belonged to her past, not her future.

"Let's go, darlin'," mumbled Captain Marksen as he gestured toward the plank leading to his ship.

Climbing it, she discovered the darkness had played her false. The ship's deck could have held L'Enfant de la Patrie twice over. The craft shifted beneath her feet, and she fought to keep her balance. Marksen walked as easily as he did on land. He assisted her around dark piles of rope and crates lashed to the two masts which stretched up into the starless sky.

One of his men approached.

"What d'ye want?" Marksen asked. "Let's get 'er out into the Channel."

"Cap'n, the cargo—"

Marksen waved him to silence. With a glare at Brienne, he ordered, "Sit 'ere. If'n ye get in m'way, I'll toss ye over the side."

She nodded and sat against cases she knew contained contraband. A shiver cut across her rigid shoulders. For the first time since she had left London, she had a chance to contemplate what she was doing. France was a foreign country where she knew no one.

She leaned her chin on her arms crossed on her drawn-up knees and stared at the railing. Evan's story continued to haunt her. He had acted hurt when she had not believed it. Yet, if she accepted his story as true, her mother was not her mother, and her beloved grand-mère had spent a lifetime lying to her. She sought in her memory, but could find no nebulous hints of another family.

Through the bag, she ran her fingers along the box that held the vase. She was going home. It might be to Maison LeClerc or to Château Tonnere du Grêlon. She wanted to do as her mother had asked.

She gritted her teeth. Evan Somerset must be lying. He must be! If he had told her the truth, she was sailing blithely into danger. The man Evan had called Lagrille was French. How much easier it would be to hunt her in France than in England!

Mayhap she should go back. Go back to the shore and to London. Grand-mère would tell her the truth.

Brienne started to rise, but fell back to the deck as the ship lurched. Overhead, the sails filled with wind. It was too late. Captain Marksen would not turn back because of a passenger.

She tried to make herself small as the men raced past her, intent on tasks which were as mysterious as a magician's tricks. Staring up at the sky, she watched as the fog was left ashore. Overhead the moon glowed. When a shadow crossed over her, she lowered her gaze to see a strange man's smile.

"Well, well, so the cap'n did get ye!" He chuckled as he squatted in front of her. "What ye be goin' to France fer, dearie? Want yerself some of that Frenchie lovin'?"

She pulled her feet closer to her. She did not want to let even her hem touch this disgusting man. Not answering, she waited for him to leave.

"Cain't talk, dearie?" When she did not answer, his dirty hand patted her cheek. She turned away. He pinched her face between his fingers as he forced her to look at him. "Don't worry, dearie. We be takin' good care of ye. Ye'll enjoy yerself, mark me words."

Although fear flashed through her, she did not reply. The sailor was called away by a gusty shout, and she sagged against the crates. Again her innocence of the world beyond L'Enfant de la Patrie had betrayed her into trouble. She should have stayed ashore instead of running off without thinking.

As she huddled against the crates, time passed slowly. Her head drooped, but she stayed awake. When the water became choppy, she fought nausea. If the voyage lasted much longer, she would be sick. Closing her eyes, she swayed with the ship, hoping it would relieve the stress in her center.

A shout came from across the deck.

Brienne woke, shocked that she could have fallen asleep. Jumping to her feet, she tried to run to where Marksen was standing over a man struggling to stand.

Even in the moonlight, she recognized the man who fell back to the deck.

She lurched to where Evan was fighting to sit. She understood why when she saw his arms were bound. Kneeling beside him, she gasped, "Evan! What are you doing here?"

"M'question exactly." Marksen motioned to his men.

Two of them grasped Evan's arms, hauling him to his feet. Brienne stood as they herded him to the cabin at the stern. Fearing what they might do, she tried to follow. Marksen grabbed her arm. When she struggled to pull away, he laughed and shoved her ahead of him into the cabin. She tripped over Evan's legs and moaned as she landed on her knees.

Evan snarled an oath before saying, "There is no need to abuse her, Marksen."

The smuggler rested his shoulder against the door frame. In the flickering light of a lantern, his sunken cheeks became a death mask. "Ye need to be worryin' 'bout yerself. Ye know what I do with stowaways, Somerset."

"I am not a stowaway. Miss LeClerc is paying my way."

"Me?" she squeaked.

"Didn't you tell the good captain, honey, about the plans we made at the inn?" His voice was teasing, but his eyes narrowed with fury. A line of blood dropped from the left corner of his mouth, and red marks on his face would become bruises to match hers.

Quietly, Brienne said, "I must have forgotten to mention that, Captain."

"When? When ye be climbin' out on the roof to escape Somerset? Or when ye snuck through the marsh down to the ship?"

"It must have slipped my mind," she answered with an innocence that no one would believe.

"Slipped yer mind?" Marksen laughed. "She be nearly as dumb as ye be, Somerset, if'n ye be thinkin' I believe such a tale."

"I am stupid," Evan answered evenly. "Damn stupid, for I believed you, Marksen, when you agreed not to take her to France."

"Nay, I agreed only to give 'er back to ye. She be comin' of 'er own free will with me." His eyes raked along her, and she edged closer to Evan. "Ye got yerself a looker this time, Somerset. Don't know when I've seen a better set of legs danglin' in front of me eyes."

She shrieked when he tugged her to her feet and to him. She fought, but he was too strong. Hearing Evan's curses, she moaned again when Marksen fondled her. She repeated Evan's oath as she plucked a pistol from Marksen's belt and pressed it to his chest.

Marksen swore as Evan laughed. Stepping back, Brienne stared at the smuggler.

"Let Evan go!" she ordered.

"Ye won't be shootin' me, darlin'. M'boys will see ye and Somerset dead if'n ye do."

"Mayhap, but you shall be dead by then, so you will not be able to enjoy seeing us die." She held the long pistol with both hands, keeping her finger on the hammer. "Untie him."

Marksen pulled a blade from under his shirt. She drew in her breath as he raised it.

Brienne screamed when she was struck behind the knees. She collapsed to the deck. Evan pressed her to the uneven boards. The cabin door crashed closed as the knife clattered, left behind as Marksen raced out.

"Evan Somerset," she cried, "what—?"

"Don't move!"

Something struck the side of the ship. The window burst with the force of the impact. Glass sprayed over them.

"What was that?" she cried, realizing Evan had been trying to protect her.

"Cannonball!" He raised his head enough to smile at her. "Welcome to the world of smugglers, honey."

"Cannon? It could sink us!"

"That is the idea."

She struggled beneath him. "We have to get out of here!" Grabbing the knife, she cut the ropes on his wrists. "We have to—"

"What? There is no place to go. If Marksen does not repel this attack, we shall be killed trying to swim to shore."

She moaned and hid her eyes against his coat as she heard a second dull thud in the distance. The ship shivered with the impact.

Evan leaped to his feet. "Get between those crates, Brienne. Go!"

"What are you going to do?"

"Find us a way to get out of this alive, if I can. Get down between those crates." Taking the pistol from her, he opened the door, and she heard Marksen shouting orders. The ship bucked as its cannon returned fire.

She knew Marksen would never surrender to the authorities. To do so meant jail or worse for the crew. Marksen had a reputation as a wily smuggler. He would not allow his ship to be taken or sunk.

Evan was back before Brienne had a chance to slip between the heavy boxes. "Dammit, you have done it this time, honey."

"Me?"

"Word on deck is the ship firing on us is after you. Marksen will do anything to save his ship. This attack may make him forget why he brought you aboard."

"What do you mean?"

"You asked about Marksen's help, but never bothered

to investigate rumors about certain women who approached Marksen and were never heard of again.''

''Never?'' She blanched.

''Brienne, why do you think I risked Marksen's fury by going to his meeting place? Why do you think I stowed away on this ship?'' He pulled her against him as the ship was struck again. ''If I had not, Marksen would have reneged on his offer to take you to France until you paid a much higher price.''

''Why didn't you tell me when we were at the inn?''

With a wry smile, he said, ''I thought you had seen enough of Marksen to realize the truth.''

The ship's cannon fired, knocking them against the wall.

''Let's go,'' Evan ordered.

''Where?'' She rubbed her sore elbow.

His answer was drowned out by an ear-wrenching explosion as another cannonball was fired from Marksen's ship. As the sound faded into silence, he said, ''Your friend Marksen—''

''Not my friend!''

''In order to save his ship, Marksen will hand us over to whoever has been shooting at us. Of course, the captain of the other ship may be trying to protect you from your own idiocy by keeping you from going to France.''

''I thought protecting me was your job!''

He grinned. ''How romantic.'' He kissed her, then nibbled on her earlobe.

''Evan Somerset, you are a fool!'' she gasped. ''We need to get off this ship.''

''You are right, Brienne. I am a fool. I was foolish to believe that you would not run off to France and to think I could stop you without any trouble.'' His smile faded as he took her hand to draw her closer again. ''But I was most foolish when I thought I could keep this purely professional.'' His lips brushed hers with swift fire.

She tasted desperation in his kiss and feared he was telling her goodbye. "Is it that dangerous?"

"Yes."

His simple response terrified her. She picked up her bag and held it against her chest.

"Stay close," he ordered.

She nodded. "What are we going to do?"

"Don't ask. We shall have to improvise as we go. Come on! Before Marksen notices we are gone."

When he pulled her out of the cabin, she stayed close to him. He motioned for her to remain in the cabin's shadow as he inched forward. She tried to slow her breathing that sounded as loud as a tempest while he skulked up behind the unsuspecting sailor. Another quick downswing left the man in a senseless mound on the deck.

As he pulled the man's gun from his belt, he tossed it to her. "Do you really know how to fire it?"

"Yes."

"And reload?"

"I think so."

"That will have to be good enough." Taking her arm, he drew her toward the stern.

She pulled her gaze from the men who were waving to another ship that was coming alongside. She glanced over her shoulder and groaned when she saw Evan tearing the canvas off a small boat. In it, they would be an easy target for the gunners of both ships. She wondered if they could reach the shore in a rowboat because she had no idea how far they were from either England or France.

When her feet slipped on the deck, she glanced down. Her stomach roiled. The dark liquid staining her shoes was blood.

"Are you all right?" Evan asked, drawing her behind the small boat.

"I hope I will be."

"You will be. Trust me."

"I hope I can."

A strange expression crossed his face, but he held out his clasped hands and told her to step onto them. As she gripped the railing, he hefted her into the boat.

She struck a seat and moaned when her breath exploded out of her. With her hand against her ribs, she sat. "Evan, hurry!"

"Be quiet!" She heard a soft clanking, then he ordered, "Hold on tight, honey."

Brienne fell back against the side of the boat as it began to drop past the side of the ship. No! He could not be saving her by sacrificing his life! She would not let him do that. She tried to stand, but hit the bottom of the boat again as it struck the waves.

Water sprayed her. Wiping wet hair out of her eyes, she looked up and smiled. Like a squirrel racing along a tree, Evan was scrambling nimbly down a rope dropped over the side.

"Push the boat over here!" he ordered in a whisper.

She groped through the dark for the oars. She found only one. When Evan called to her more urgently, she put one oar against Marksen's ship and shoved. The boat drifted farther away.

She heard a curse, then a splash. A hand reached over the side of the boat, which tilted wildly, and she clutched the opposite oarlock.

When Evan heaved himself into the boat, she exclaimed, "Thank God, you are safe. I thought—"

"Honey, we are far from safe."

As if in echo of his words, shouts came from above as Marksen's crew discovered they had escaped. Evan found the other oar and began to press them into the waves. A gun fired, hitting the water just beyond the boat.

"Brienne, your gun!" he shouted.

She raised it. Although her fingers shook, she pulled the trigger. The explosion seemed as loud as cannon fire.

She rocked back off the seat and heard a sound from Evan that was suspiciously close to laughter. As she climbed onto the narrow plank, she glared at Evan.

She shrieked as a cannonball sailed over their heads. It sprayed the boat as it struck the waves. When another cannon fired, she ducked with her hands over her head. Only when she heard a crash behind them did she realize that the other ship was firing on Marksen's.

Across the waves, a voice echoed eerily. "Give her to us, Marksen, and we will let you and your men go."

Evan cursed as he pressed the oars to take them farther from the ships. "Get the damned gun reloaded, Brienne."

She bent her head over the barrel as she tried to keep the gunpowder from spilling. The dark grit cascaded over her fingers.

"Take mine!" He paused in rowing to shove the gun into her hands. "Be prepared to fire it while you are reloading yours. Hurry, Brienne!"

"I am doing the best I can."

"Then, do better." As she bent to her task again, he added more quietly, "I am sorry, honey. Just hurry."

Blinking back tears which made her task even more difficult, she gulped, "It is all right."

Brienne concentrated on readying the pistol as he stroked the oars against the water. Finishing, she put the gun on her lap. She looked up in horror as she heard the disembodied voice repeat its demand to turn Brienne LeClerc over. They were so close to the ships. One well-aimed shot by the cannon would sink them.

She watched Evan's muscles strain against the oars as he panted in their rhythm. Moving carefully in the unsteady boat to sit next to him, she put her hands over his on the right oar.

"Let me help," she whispered.

"Can you?"

"Yes."

He did not waste energy thanking her. "Watch me and work at the same pace. We do not want to end up going around in circles."

She nodded as they rowed in silence while the captains of the two ships shouted to each other. She learned to dip only the very end of the heavy oar into the water. Up and down the waves they went as she stared at the two ships.

She was shocked when she realized they were not headed for the shore but around the stern of Marksen's ship. She understood why when the small boat slipped into the shadows beyond the ship. Now they were hidden from the pursuing vessel as well as the crew on Marksen's. Only the soft splash from the oars could betray them.

When a cannon blasted, she shrieked. Marksen's ship rocked before turning away from the other. She feared it would run them down, but headed away from them. More cannon fire raged through the night.

"Just row," Evan muttered. "As long as they pay attention to each other, they may not pay attention to us."

Brienne nodded, too tired to talk. An ache started in the center of her left shoulder and ran like a fiery thread across her back and into her right one. Inching down her spine, it settled in both shoulder blades as she wrestled with the water to extract the oar and push it through the wave again and again and again.

"How—much—farther?" she gasped.

"We are nearly there."

"Nearly there?" She glanced over her shoulder to see the dark silhouette of the land rising past the soft foam of the waves.

"Don't stop!"

She continued to match his strokes until the small boat grated on the sand. He leaped out into the pulsating water and reached for Brienne's hand.

Helping her out of the boat, Evan grimaced. He waved

aside her questions as he ordered, "Hurry, honey. Get ashore while I confuse your friends." His foot shoved the boat out into the waves. The sea would play with it until it was dashed into tinder. With luck, the debris would wash ashore far from them.

She watched it bounce on the waves as they stood in the shadow of the hills edging the shore. In the distance, the low lights from the two ships were like two stars hugging the horizon.

"My pistol!" she cried.

"Where is it?"

"In the boat."

"It is too late to worry about it now." Evan tugged on her hand.

She turned and followed him up from the water. He did not need to tell her that they needed to disappear . . . fast.

Chapter Ten

Evan kept his arm around Brienne's waist as they climbed the hill that seemed as steep as the cliffs near Dover. She leaned against him, and he knew that two nights without sleep were weighing every step she took. She was not accustomed to this life. When his breath banged against his throbbing ribs, he realized he had gotten soft in the past few years, too.

"Evan," she whispered, "will you tell me one thing?"

"What?" He fought to keep his pain out of his voice.

"Where are we?"

He paused and chuckled. That hurt his ribs, too. Marksen's men played rough, and several of them had been waiting a long time for this opportunity. "You really don't know?"

"I would not ask if I knew."

"England. Marksen has been paralleling the coast all night."

"Good."

He had not guessed she could surprise him more, but she had. "Good?"

"I think I should talk with Grand-mère before I continue on to France."

"Mayhap you should have thought of that before you ran away."

When she stumbled against him, he glanced down at her again. Even in the dim light, she did not resemble the tidy woman he first had seen at her salon. The night shadowed her bruises, but with her hair hanging around her shoulders and the white of her chemise visible through the tears in her black dress, she wore the scars of every hour of her ordeal.

"What happened to your forehead, Brienne?"

She touched it and winced. "I don't know. I must have bumped it somewhere. It is not as bad as it must look. I will be a sight by the time I get back to London."

"Can you keep going?"

"Do I have any choice?"

Evan smiled. She would not admit to exhaustion until she fell right where she stood. Looking ahead, he saw a copse that clung to the top of the hill. That would give them shelter until the sun rose and he could determine exactly where they were.

"You were as clumsy as a three-legged cat on Marksen's ship," he said with a laugh, "and not much better now."

"I don't think I was meant to be a sailor." She walked beside him, depending on his support more with every step.

When she wobbled, he tightened his arm around her. She rested her head on his shoulder, even though his coat still dripped sea water. He had to smile as he enjoyed having her so close. At what sounded like distant thunder, she stiffened.

" 'Tis fine, honey." He glanced back. "That they are

still firing on each other means they are not sure where we are. They will trade insults for a while, then leave.''

"Leave? Just like that?''

"Night beasts hate sunlight.'' He grinned. "You really do look terrible. I have seen dead men with more color in their faces than you have.''

"You do not look so great yourself.'' Brienne pushed herself away, wondering how she could be so selfish when he must be as exhausted and aching as she was. "I should not be leaning on you.''

He drew her back. "You are still my responsibility. I got you into this bumblebath, and I guess I am going to have to get you out of it.''

"Evan Somerset, you give incredible service to your victims,'' she murmured as she relaxed against his muscular chest.

She heard his frown in his voice. "Victim?''

"Didn't you intend to steal the vase from my salon? Now you act like a dashing knight rushing to my rescue.''

His terse laugh rustled her hair. "Not all my clients, which is the term I prefer, rate my favorite services. Only very special ones.'' When she did not shoot back a quick retort, he went on, "Don't worry, honey. With that lump on your head and me aching in every bone from chasing you halfway across England, I do not think either of us is ready for a night of passion as you seem to be suggesting.''

"Me suggesting? I never suggested anything of the sort!''

"No?'' He looked up at the starlight sifting through the fog which still clung to the shore. "The night is nearly over, but we should sleep before the sunrise. I do mean sleep!''

"I hope you do, Evan.'' She quivered and drew her cloak closer around her. She hoped he thought she was shivering from the damp, not because she could not keep from thinking of how splendid it was to be in his arms, his mouth on hers, her body craving his. Wanting this scoundrel proved she was witless.

"You do not trust me," he murmured.

"Is that a surprise?" she returned to cover her true thoughts.

Instead of answering, Evan whistled an uneven tune Brienne did not recognize as he led her up a grassy knoll to the copse. Under a tree which was twisted from years of strong winds from the sea, he helped her gently to the ground. He dropped next to her and groaned as he hung his head over his knees.

"Are you all right?" she asked.

"I will be as soon as we are on the coach back to London." He raised his head and smiled. "You do have enough money for that, don't you?"

"You don't have any money with you?"

"Not much." He chuckled, then winced as he put his hand to his left side. "I rushed out the door after you so quickly that I forgot a few small details."

Brienne rolled her eyes as she set her bag on her lap. "That is not a small detail. Fortunately, I have—" She gasped when she opened her bag. "My money is gone!" Pushing aside her clothes, she shook her head. "It is gone!"

Taking the bag from her, he peered into it. "Didn't you have your money in this box?"

"No!" She tore the bag out of his hands. When he stared at her in amazement, she hastened to add, "It was here with my clothes."

He arched a brow. "I assume you took your eyes off your bag for a moment."

"I kept it beside me." She choked on another gasp. "They stole it when I fell asleep!"

"On Marksen's ship?" He crowed with laughter, then grimaced as he touched his left side again. "You are either the bravest or most foolish woman I have ever met. At least Marksen got the Ł25 you offered him to take you to France.''

"He stole twice that much from me." Wanting to check the box to be certain the smuggler had not made off with the vase, too, she knew she must wait until Evan was asleep.

"Consider it a cheap lesson, honey. It could have cost you a lot more." He pulled off his drenched coat and rolled it into a ball. "Now, how about that sleep? I could use a week or two of it myself." He drew her down next to him on the cold ground.

She sat. "Evan, I cannot sleep here with you."

Pulling her to lean over him, he gave her a leer. "Would you rather *not* sleep?"

When she pushed him away, he winced. "Evan?" she asked, her irritation becoming concern.

"One of Marksen's boys gave me a bunch of fives right in the ribs." He curled his fingers into a fist and smiled. "Then I gave him a bunch of fives in the nose."

"Thank you for coming after me," she whispered.

"You're welcome, although next time I think I will put on that knight's shining armor before I give chase."

His arm around her shoulders drew her back into the mat of grass, and she nestled her head again on his chest. The muscles which had been so rock hard when he pressed her to the deck became a lush pillow. The combination of his potent, masculine scent and the barely perceptible stroke of his fingers on her bare arm beneath her cloak enticed her to make her dreams of savoring his kisses come true.

When her hand drifted across his chest, he groaned. She started to ask him if she had hurt him, but he rose over her. Even in the dim light, she could see his smile. She stared up into his eyes which had become dark pools. Whispering her name, he found her mouth with the ease of craving. He took her hands and wrapped them around his shoulder as his fingers began a tender tour of her.

Swiftly she was caught up in the whirlpool of his passion. His lips' caress against hers mirrored the stroke of his fingers along her neck. When they swept lightly over her breast, she could not silence her fired moan of rapture. A pulse swelled through her, as powerful as the waves beating on the shore. She surrendered herself to the desire that ached in her very center. She moaned softly as his mouth moved down her neck while he loosened her cloak. His heated, moist kisses followed the neckline of her gown. Her breath burned hot and fast.

"Brienne?" he whispered in her ear.

She trembled as his breath grazed her fevered skin. "What did you say?"

"Go to sleep."

"Sleep?"

He laughed with regret as he kissed her parted lips lightly. "At least try. It will not be easy to hold you in my arms when I would rather have you beneath me."

"Evan—"

He placed his finger to her lips. "No, say only good night. To tell you the truth, right now, I believe sleeping is the best thing to do."

"You would rather sleep than—"

"If you insist, honey, I can be convinced." He pressed her back into the grass again. "Very, very easily."

Brienne did not need more than the faint starlight sifting through the fog to know that he was being honest, for she could feel his need all along his body. With a strained laugh, she ordered, "Then, go to sleep!" She shoved his hands away and chuckled as he collapsed on the ground, being careful not to land on his left side. His joking covered other, far stronger emotions, she knew, for hers did. She longed to succumb to the luscious love he offered.

"Good idea." When she nestled beside him, he murmured, "I don't know why I did not think of it myself."

Already half-asleep and warmer as she savored the happiness he offered her, she glided into dreams of being in his arms as he discovered every bit of desire within her. It was the sweetest dream she had ever had . . . and one she wanted to come true soon.

Lips against her nape brought Brienne instantly awake. In confusion, she rolled over to see Evan smiling down at her. Before she could move, his mouth slid across hers to bring forth the rapture they had sampled last night. Luscious sensation spread along her with his eager touch.

"Good morning, honey," he whispered as he teased her with ethereal kisses. "I wondered if you were ever going to wake."

"Have you been awake long?" It seemed ludicrous to have this commonplace conversation while he was giving life to her frenzied dreams.

He chuckled. "To be honest—"

"And that would be a pleasant change."

"I see you are going to be as vexing as ever." He smoothed her hair back from her cheek. "To be honest, I just woke. It must be near midday. With you in my arms, I was able to sleep so well."

Her face flushed. A week ago, she had not even met him. Now she was lying in his arms, although she did not trust him. "Do you know where we are?"

"Other than on the English shore, no. I would guess we might be closer to Norfolk than London."

"It will be a long walk home."

"Yes."

Brienne sighed as she sat and braided her hair. Pushing herself away from him, she rose to gaze across the pulsating azure water. The waves were empty to the horizon.

Evan had been right. Smugglers despised the bright light of day. She wondered if it had been prearranged for Marksen to meet the other ship. No, the smuggler would not have risked his ship for Ł25. Even though he had stolen closer to Ł50 from her, he would have had no idea how much money she had until he took it from her bag. He had not had enough time to count it at the Fox and Swan.

Evan stood also. Facing him, she saw rage twisting his rigid lips and guessed his thoughts matched hers.

She put her fingers on his arm. "Evan, I am so sorry. I should have listened to you about Marksen."

"You were doing what you had promised your *maman*." He smiled ruefully and drew her back to him, propping his chin on her head. "You told me that you do not have the vase. I believe you."

She was glad that he was not looking at her, for she did not want him to see her shame at lying to him. But she had vowed to Maman that she would not reveal the truth to anyone. Guilt taunted her, for how could she expect Evan to be honest with her when she was false with him?

"What are you going to do now?" she asked.

"You have gone on with your life after losing L'Enfant de la Patrie. I need to get on with mine after this setback in my dubious fortunes." He shrugged with a nonchalance she could not believe. "Even Evan Somerset cannot be successful on every job. Lagrille cannot kill me if he does not catch me. All I need to do is stay hidden for a while, and he will not find me."

"Come and call on us when you can. Grand-mère would be glad to see you." She bent to pick up her bag. "I must be going, Evan, if I want to start the trip back to London. Thank you again for your help."

He spun her to face him. "Do you think your pursuers will give up so easily, Brienne?"

Fear stabbed her. Again she could see he was being honest. "But why?" she whispered.

"I have no idea other than the daughter of a *duc*, a daughter who has a strong claim on Château Tonnere du Grêlon, is a great prize."

"A prize?" She stepped back. "Is that why you are still here with me, Evan? For the prize?"

His eyes burned like bright brands in a dark room as he closed the distance between them again. "Yes, I am still with you for the prize I would like to win, but it is not the blasted château." His finger glided from her chin down along the front of her gown. When she trembled, unable to dampen the longing within her, he whispered, "I want a very special prize, honey."

Brienne looked away before his gaze could captivate her in his spell. She was glad he had no idea that while she slept in his arms, her dreams had been of just what he wished.

In the same low voice, he said, "And I think you could use an ally or two on your way to London."

"Two? Do you have another friend who might help me?"

"No one who would acknowledge me in the daylight, I'm afraid." He patted the pistol under his coat. "I was thinking of this."

Her laugh was genuine. "Two centuries ago, you could have been burned as a witch for speaking like that of something that is not alive."

"You are trying to avoid giving me an answer."

Yes, I am. I do not want to tell you how much I want you as my lover. She silenced that mutinous thought. "I cannot ask you to risk yourself further for me." She stood on tiptoe to kiss his cheek which was rough with whiskers. "When I get back to London, I will send you money to pay for your ruined coat."

"Honey, I do not want your money." He slipped his

arm around her waist. "Heroes do great deeds for the honor, not the monetary reward."

"Are you volunteering to be a hero?"

"I find it hard to resist damsels in distress, especially when they are covered with dirt and sand." His smile faded. "Honey, you have to realize how much danger you still may be facing."

"Some things are more important than doing what is safe."

"I know."

When he bent to kiss her, she drew away. She could not let him seduce her into his arms again. Today, she might not be able to resist. "Goodbye."

In silence, Brienne walked out from beneath the trees and toward a path that should lead to a village. Evan had become too involved in her disasters. Now he could hide from Lagrille's vengeance.

She turned as she heard footsteps behind her. As she paused on the rutted road, she smiled when Evan hurried to catch up with her. "You are insane, Evan, but I am glad you are coming with me."

"I just did not want to miss all the fun, honey." He put his arm around her shoulders and squeezed her gently.

"I hope you think it is fun by the time we get back to London."

"I am certain the fun is just beginning."

She put her hand over his on her arm. It did not matter why he really was staying with her. What was important was that she was not alone. And even more important, Evan was with her. As he walked beside her, whistling the same light tune he had when they came ashore, she began to believe they might succeed at whatever they faced in the bright sunlight.

Chapter Eleven

Curious about the crowd gathering in the center of the small village, Brienne left Evan negotiating with an old man who was selling freshly baked bread. This coastal village was named North Seaside, but that still did not tell her where they were. Along the North Sea, or mayhap the name meant no more than another village was called South Seaside.

There was nothing unique about the village, which was a cluster of thatched cottages set around a green with a church at one end. It appeared to be a market or festival day, because the whole population must be gathered on the green.

She smiled as she glanced back at Evan. He was still busy bargaining for the bread. Although he had told her that he had no money, he either had a few coins or was using other skills to get the bread. He could get the best of anyone in a bargain and leave them remembering his smile. As her stomach growled, she wished she was not so eager for him to be successful in getting them some bread.

Moving toward the people gathered in front of a stone church that was more ornate than the plain cottages surrounding the green, Brienne listened to the excited children. She eased through the fringes of the crowd. Her eyes widened when she saw what was drawing the villagers like a lodestone.

Set up on the dusty lawn of the church were the props of a traveling theater company. A single man stood in front of the patched curtain which was a brilliant crimson. With a rumbling voice, he called, "Come and watch the Teatro Caparelli perform for your enjoyment and erudition."

She chuckled as children rushed past her to get the best view of the stage. The man's accent and the name of the theater troupe told her they were from Italy. With the war raging throughout Europe, the actors must have decided that England was the safest place to practice their craft.

Leaning against a tree whose bare branches sifted the late winter sunshine, she watched as he disappeared behind the fluttering curtain. A set of cymbals and the *rat-tat-tat* of a drum announced the beginning of the play. She listened to the awed murmur as the curtain was pulled back to reveal a painted backdrop of a castle.

A slim woman came on stage in a garishly bright gown. As she introduced the play, Brienne realized they planned to perform a story very close to the one she knew as *Cinderella*.

When the woman disappeared behind the scenery, the play began. Brienne was surrounded by the excited children. She cheered with them for the poor heroine and laughed when they jeered the evil villain.

Maman had told her this story for the first time many years ago. As a child, Brienne could not have guessed that Maman's persistent cough would become stronger as she weakened or that, one day, she would oversee L'Enfant de la Patrie. Her life had been so simple . . . then. But, if she were to believe Evan, that life had all been a lie.

"What is this?" Evan asked as he came to stand next to her. He carried two loaves of bread.

Moving so he could lean against the tree also, she murmured, "A traveling show. They have just finished the first act."

"Are they any good?"

"The audience thinks so."

His finger played with the heavy braid draped over her shoulder. "What is wrong, honey?"

"How do you know anything is wrong?"

Sorrow tainted his smile. "Reading people's feelings is something I have learned to be good at."

"So you can cheat them?" She tapped a loaf of bread. "It might be interesting to hear how you got these without any money."

"Not very interesting at all. I traded the buttons off my coat." He pointed to the front of his ruined coat. "What is wrong?" he repeated as he put both loaves under his left arm and slipped his right arm around her waist.

Trying to shrug it off, she found she could not without making a spectacle of herself. She sighed deeply. "Can't you just leave me alone?"

"I would like to when you are petulant, but I cannot. I promised your grandmother I would bring you back to her."

"You did?"

He gave her a wry smile. "One of the stupider things I have ever promised." He looked at the closed curtain. "What is wrong?"

Blinking rapidly to keep the weak tears dammed in her

eyes, she whispered, "They are performing *Cinderella*. Maman used to tell me that story before I went to sleep."

"You loved her, didn't you?"

"Of course! She was my mother. I cannot imagine not loving my mother."

His lips became as tight as his fingers on her. "I can."

Brienne stared at him in disbelief. Never had Evan revealed so much to her. She stroked his wool sleeve. "I am sorry."

"It is not important. Don't let it bother you."

"You do!"

"Brienne, I said 'tis unimportant. 'Tis . . ." His voice trailed away as the curtain opened to reveal the next act of the play. When he chuckled, his smile was genuine. "Well, by cock and pie!"

Evan knew a stroke of luck when it was right in front of him. Although he had spent the afternoon lambasting himself for staying with Brienne, it might all work out. He had promised Madame LeClerc to watch over her and bring her home safely. Now that might actually be possible and without walking all the way to Grosvenor Square. Then he would be rid of her and this absurd commission.

That would give him a chance to find a place where Lagrille would not look for him and stay there. In six months, he would be back to work again, worrying only about whether he could stay one step ahead of his past.

In spite of himself, he looked at Brienne, who was as bedraggled and ragged as a street urchin. But there was nothing childlike about her enticing body that beseeched him to forget everything but finding satiation of his gnawing need by being deep within her. Six months from now, if he abandoned her here, he would be wondering how she had fared in the hands of her foes, for without his expertise, she would become easy prey. Six months from now, he would be wondering if he would ever have a woman like her in his life again. She fascinated him with her little-girl naïveté and world-weary sophistication as well as with her response to his touch when he had held her in his arms last night.

Last night. . . . He winced as he moved and his ribs complained again with a sharp pain. If Marksen's men had not broken one, they had come close. He did not want Brienne to guess the truth of why he had let her sleep last night instead of making love with her as he wanted. Having her hover over him, scolding him for being so foolish, would be beyond vexing. Especially when he ached for her soft lips.

As the second act began, Evan noticed that Brienne remained as stiff as the tree behind them. He could not fault her. The problems of Cinderella and her prince seemed insignificant compared to the ones shadowing her. Again and again, he saw her glance at him when he laughed and booed along with the rest of the audience.

He asked, amid the clapping, as the actors bowed for a final time, "Did you enjoy that?" He readjusted the loaves and offered his arm to her as he led her away from the stage.

"Yes."

"That does not sound too enthusiastic."

When she put her fingers on his sleeve, she sighed. "I am not like you, Evan. I cannot push aside my emotions on demand. What I feel, I feel."

"And now you feel confused?"

"You need not make that a question." She smiled. "You can guess what I feel like inside, can't you?"

"I would like to discover what you feel like inside," he whispered.

Scarlet flashed up her face, but he was not tempted to laugh. Every temptation burning within him was to find a private place and prove to her how much she wanted to discover that, too.

Her voice was as prim as a governess's as she said, "I was speaking of emotions."

"Not sensation?" This time he laughed when her cheeks deepened to crimson, hiding those horrendous bruises that were a constant reminder of how he had made a shocking mull of this job. As he drew her farther away from the stage, he said, "You are not difficult to understand, honey, for you react strongly to everything. Like now. You are embarrassed because you think I am avoiding the lad who is passing the hat to collect money for the actors."

"It is normal to pay for entertainment, but I forget that Evan Somerset does not play by the rules of others."

"Nasty today, aren't you? Mayhap I can find a way to cheer you up a little. How about meeting some friends of mine?"

"Friends? Do you mean the Caparellis?"

He let her hand slide off his arm. Taking it, he squeezed her fingers. "You are catching on quickly, honey. I am going to have to keep on my toes to prevent you from discerning everything I think."

"And why shouldn't I know what you are thinking?" she retorted. "Aren't we allies?"

"We are, and we have some more here."

"Do you know everyone in England?"

"Not yet." He smiled as he tugged on her hand. "Pietro and Sal are—"

"I know. Old friends."

Nodding, he chuckled at her sarcasm. "C'mon. Let's go and enjoy some company unlike you have ever met."

Brienne walked with Evan toward the shadowed side of the church. There, a trio of brightly painted wagons was parked. Gypsy wagons, she thought until they got nearer. These green and red wagons were different. Instead of obscure designs painted on their sides, the vehicles had been decorated with drawings of various scenes on a stage. The largest one had Teatro Caparelli lettered in broad script across it.

She tripped over something. Bending, she picked up a mask to discover it was the evil stepmother's face with its hideous grin.

A spurt of angry words in a language she did not understand froze her. A dark-haired man who wore nothing but a pair of baggy breeches burst out from among the wagons to snatch away the mask. He continued to shout at her, then paused in midword and cried, "Evan! Evan Somerset!" The rest was gibberish.

Beside her, Evan chuckled. "In English, my friend. I cannot understand Italian at that speed!"

"Evan!" he shouted again. Calling something over his shoulder, he leaped toward them.

Brienne cowered, but arms swept her into the middle of hugs and kisses and greetings in a mixture of English and Italian. She could not understand any of it, for her head was pressed to a male chest that was sticky with sweat. When she put up her hands to escape, she flinched as she touched naked skin.

Someone whirled her away and kissed her soundly on both cheeks. As she tried to catch her breath, a woman grabbed her and did the same. All the time, voices tried to outshout each other with what might be greetings. When another man took her by the shoulders, he swiftly pressed his lips to her cheeks. Then, with some comment she did not understand, he caught her face between his hands and kissed her on the lips.

Brienne tried to squirm away. When he released her, she backpedaled a pair of steps and bumped into Evan. She grasped his arm as she stared at the man who was now laughing. Behind her, Evan was laughing, too.

The man made a motion with his broad hand toward the largest wagon. As he climbed the trio of wooden steps to the low door, the others began to follow, their voices raised in excitement.

Evan gestured for Brienne to precede him. She shook her head. "I am not going in there. Who knows what might happen?"

"Come on, honey," he said as he steered her toward the wagon. "The Caparellis will not do you any harm."

"He—you saw what he did!"

"I saw what he did. It seems like a good idea to me."

His mouth over hers wiped away any thoughts but the overpowering longing. As her arms moved along his shoulders, she savored the firm strength of his body beneath her fingers. He smiled gently and stroked her cheek with a single fingertip.

"Give them a chance," he whispered. "The Caparellis are good people, like you and your family."

"Not like you?"

He wrapped his arm around her again. "Not at all like me. Shall we?"

"Where is the bread you bought?" Brienne asked, astonished.

"Come with me, and you shall see."

As soon as Brienne stood in the doorway of the wagon, a sinewy arm herded her inside the crowded room. Renewed shouts met Evan as he entered. The Caparellis clearly liked him. She wondered if there was anyone in the world he could not beguile.

When Evan took Brienne's hand, he winked and shouted, "Do you want me to tell you who this lovely lady with me is?"

A male voice called, "She is a very good friend of yours. We saw that."

Brienne flushed as she heard enthusiastic laughter. She should have guessed their kiss would not go unnoticed.

"Pietro Caparelli," Evan announced, gesturing toward the tall man who had played the prince on stage. Pointing to the man who had kissed her so exuberantly, he said, "That is Salvatore Carbone, but you can call him Sal as everyone does."

Pietro motioned to an older couple. "Evan, I do not think you have met Guido and Constanzia Benedetto. They and their daughter Angiola joined us since we last saw you." He glanced at a corner. "Angiola, come and greet our friends."

Brienne recognized the blonde as Cinderella. When she eased past her parents, the sloe-eyed beauty smiled seductively at Evan, who bent over her proffered hand. Brienne bit her lip as his gaze swept along Angiola's curvaceous body that was barely covered by a wrapper.

"I commend your parents on choosing the perfect name for you," he said. "You are as pretty as an angel."

"You are most kind to say that, Evan," she murmured, her breathless voice unlike the one she had used on stage. She glanced with disdain at Brienne before smiling again at Evan. "I hope you do not object to the familiarity of using your given name. We are so intimate among the Teatro Caparelli."

Before he could answer, a plump woman pushed Angiola aside. "Let an old friend greet him!"

Evan smiled as he put his arms around the buxom woman. "This is my *cara mia*, Giovanna Caparelli Carbone." Kissing her as eagerly as Salvatore had Brienne, he patted her on the back of her full skirts. He put one arm around Giovanna, and the other encircled Brienne's waist. "My friends, I want you to meet my dear friend Brienne LeClerc."

Sal, who was nearly as round as he was tall, made some comment she could not understand except for a single word. If it meant the same in Italian as it did in French. . . . She flushed again.

Evan answered in halting Italian, then grinned and winked at her.

Slowly she relaxed as she waited for the conversation to return to English. If Evan thought they were safe, she had to trust him. After all, he would do nothing to risk his skin.

Signore Benedetto motioned for his wife and daughter to leave. When Angiola started to pout, he took her arm and led her past the others. Angiola glared at Brienne as she walked out.

"How long has she—have the Benedettos been with you?" Evan asked, his gaze following Angiola's swaying skirts.

"After Rosina and Vito left last year, we had no one to play the princess." Pietro patted Giovanna playfully. "My sister is too round for the role. The Benedettos joined us in the summer. Signore Benedetto helps with the stage, and his wife is a skilled seamstress. As for Angiola—" He grinned. "You yourself saw her talent."

As the men laughed, Giovanna reached for a bottle and glasses on the overflowing shelves. "Brienne, correct?" she asked in English. "Such a pretty name. For a pretty lady. I never thought Evan would hobble himself with just one woman, but I can understand why with—"

"Evan is not hobbled by me." She wished she had stayed outside, so she had not witnessed Evan staring at Angiola Benedetto. "I am traveling to London, and so is he."

Giovanna motioned for her to sit on a bench beneath the one window. Easing between a stack of clothes and pillows, Brienne sat. The bench must be used as a bed because she saw no other in the tiny space. The men now sat at a small table which was bolted to the floor so it would not shift. At the front of the wagon, a curtain was open to reveal storage shelves.

Grabbing two of the glasses Pietro was filling with wine, Giovanna ignored his complaints. She handed one to Brienne. "Why are you going to London?"

"It is where I live. My grandmother is there."

Laughing, Evan said, "She is not telling you the whole story. She was trying to get to France when I convinced her to turn back."

"France?" Sal frowned. "A fool's destination now."

"Exactly, but if Brienne could reach Château Tonnere du Grêlon, it would be hers. Her father was the *duc*. She is his lost heir and the next *duchesse*."

The Caparellis stared at her in awe as Sal rubbed his cheeks with pudgy fingers. "Château Tonnere du Grêlon? That sounds familiar. Pietro, did we play there last winter?"

"No, that was Château de Villandry." Grinning at Brienne, he added, "The name does sound familiar, though. Where is Château Tonnere du Grêlon?"

She gestured toward Evan. "Ask him. He is the one who keeps repeating this fairy tale."

"Brienne does not believe she is the daughter of a *duc*." He gave them a sheepish smile. "Why won't she believe me?"

Giovanna slapped him over the head with a small pillow. "She is a smart girl. The one who believes you, my friend, soon finds his or her pockets much lighter."

"I do not want her money."

"No?"

"Ask her," he retorted as Brienne had.

When the Caparellis turned toward her, she fought the temptation to snarl an answer at him. She was tired and hungry, and the wine was making her light-headed. "You did mention that you were not interested in my money when . . ." She did not want to reveal how they had discussed that after she had slept in his arms.

Evan stood and eased past Sal to sit beside her. Tapping her on the nose, he said, "You can be honest. You are among friends here."

"Among family," corrected Giovanna.

Take A Trip Into A Timeless World of Passion and Adventure with Kensington Choice Historical Romances!
—Absolutely FREE!

Let your spirits fly away and enjoy the passion and adventure of another time. With Kensington Choice Historical Romances you'll be transported to a world where proud men and spirited women share the mysteries of love and let the power of passion catapult them into adventures that take place in distant lands of another age. Kensington Choice Historical Romances are the finest novels of their kind, written by today's bestselling romance authors.

4 BOOKS WORTH UP TO $24.96— Absolutely FREE!

Take **4 FREE** Books!

We created our convenient Home Subscription Service so you'll be sure to have the hottest new romances delivered each month right to your doorstep — usually before they are available in book stores. Just to show you how convenient Zebra Home Subscription Service is, we would like to send you 4 Kensington Choice Historical Romances as a FREE gift. You receive a gift worth up to $24.96 — absolutely FREE. There's no extra charge for shipping and handling. There's no obligation to buy anything - ever!

Save Up To 32% On Home Delivery!

Accept your FREE gift and each month we'll deliver 4 brand new titles as soon as they are published. They'll be yours to examine FREE for 10 days. Then if you decide to keep the books, you'll pay the preferred subscriber's price of just $4.20 per title. That's $16.80 for all 4 books for a savings of up to 32% off the publisher's price! Just add $1.50 to offset the cost of shipping and handling. Remember, you are under no obligation to buy any of these books at any time! If you are not delighted with them, simply return them and owe nothing. But if you enjoy Kensington Choice Historical Romances as much as we think you will, pay the special preferred subscriber rate of only $16.80 each month and save over $8.00 off the bookstore price!

Illiliillimillililiilililiillilillliliilliilliilliilliilliilliilliliiliilliilliilliilliil

KENSINGTON CHOICE
Zebra Home Subscription Service, Inc.
P.O. Box 5214
Clifton NJ 07015-5214

PLACE
STAMP
HERE

"Among family," he amended with a smile in her direction. "You do not have to guard every word."

Listening as Evan chatted with his friends, Brienne wished she could share his sense of camaraderie and security. She could not put aside a tremor of foreboding. The same foreboding she had experienced just before Maman died. What it was she did not know, but its lurking presence was like a stench in the tidal marshes. There was trouble ahead.

Brienne tried to keep her head from nodding with fatigue, and she struggled to stay awake through the meal. Even the boisterous conversation and the spicy sauces on the vegetables and bread could not help to keep her awake. Over and over, she found herself blinking, not sure how long she had lost track of the conversation.

"Evan, you should take that girl to bed before she falls asleep in the pasta." Sal laughed at his own jest.

Coming to his feet, Evan helped her to stand. "Too much wine and too little sleep has caught up with her."

"I am fine," Brienne argued, but wove on her feet. She rested her cheek against Evan's shoulder and let the words drift around her.

"Come with me," he said softly as he guided her toward the door and down the steps.

She shivered as a chilly breeze blew up from the sea, carrying a misty curtain of rain with it. Only then did she realize that she had left her cloak in the wagon.

"No, no," Evan said, drawing off his coat and putting it over her shoulders. "No going back. You need to get some sleep."

"Where?"

"I will show you."

She smiled as she imagined sleeping in his arms again. Having the long line of his legs against her had been splendid. Then she had been in his arms with his mouth on her as she listened to the accelerated pulse of his breath matching hers.

As if he could hear her thoughts, he kissed her lightly when he paused in front of another wagon. When he lifted his lips from hers, she whispered, "No, Evan! Kiss me. Really kiss me."

She saw the flare in his sapphire eyes before he recaptured her lips. With his arm around her, he cradled her against him, but there was nothing gentle about his fiery kisses that left scintillating sparks across her skin. He drew her into the shadows between the wagons and held her against the wall of one. The cold mist vanished as she delighted in the escalating desire spiraling through her.

Her fingers entangled in his hair as he bent to nibble along her neck. A moan escaped her lips when she rediscovered the passions that came to life when he caressed her breast. She could not be still, moving against him with a rhythm deep within her.

Singing intruded into her pleasure. The voice, heavy with a dolorous melody, warned her of the danger she was courting. She could not bridle her longing for Evan, but she must. When she opened her eyes, she saw his grin. A flush climbed her cheeks, for she knew he had guessed her exact thoughts. He stepped back and held out a hand. She hesitated as she looked from his fingers to his face.

"I think you can trust me enough," Evan whispered, "to let me help you to the wagon, honey."

Anything she might have said would sound ridiculous. Silently, she placed her hand on his. Before she could speak, he pulled her back into his embrace.

"Honey," he whispered, "I think we should travel toward London with the Caparellis. They have room for us here in the extra wagon."

"Evan, I don't think—"

His mouth over hers interrupted her. His arms held her in the sweet prison from which she did not want to escape. When he looked down at her, he grinned. "You do not think too clearly when I hold you."

"Have you noticed that?"

"I have, and I wondered if it might be because you can think only of the love we could share."

She started to slip her arms around him, then pulled back as he moaned. Not with pleasure, but with pain. Stepping back, she pressed her fingers over her mouth as he put his hand to his left side and his face twisted.

"You *are* hurt!" she cried.

"I shall be fine."

"But you are not fine now." Being careful not to touch his side, she guided him toward the front of the wagon.

"Not this one. The next one." He gave her a cockeyed grin. "Unless you want me to sleep with Angiola and her parents."

"That would be very interesting for all of you." She kept her arm around him as they went to the third wagon.

Ignoring her exhaustion, she hurried ahead of him to open the door as rain began to fall in a downpour. She smiled when she saw a lantern was lit within and clean linens lay on the benches on either side of the wagon. Guessing from the scrapes along the floor that this wagon held the backdrops, she went back down the stairs to help him climb up.

"I am not an invalid, Brienne."

"It must hurt bad if you are showing it. You did not wince once when you were burned while fighting the fire at L'Enfant de la Patrie."

He grinned as he dropped to the bench. "You do not miss much, do you?"

"Take off your waistcoat and shirt." She helped him shrug off his coat, tossing it onto the floor. It was so ruined nothing else could damage it.

"I was wondering when you would ask." He laughed, then groaned.

"I am going to strap your ribs. Do not think about anything else."

As she pulled the sheet off the other bench and ripped it, he slowly drew off his waistcoat and shirt. "Why not? You do."

Turning, she feared she had forgotten how to breathe as she stared at the breadth of his bare chest. Bruises were already forming along his left side, but they only emphasized the shadowed planes of his muscles. Her fingers tingled with the longing to stroke the naked skin from his shoulder to his waist.

"Sit still," she whispered. Although it would have been easier to wrap the strips around him if he were standing, she did not trust herself to be so close to such brawny temptation.

"Are you sure?"

"Very." She handed him one end of the strip. "Hold that over your breastbone while I put this in place."

Brienne expected him to throw some jest at her, but he complied as she wound the strips around him, giving him enough room to breathe. He lifted his arms as she asked and then lowered them so she could reach behind him. When she tried to tie the last piece in place, she knelt beside him to make certain she did not hurt him by pulling the strip tight.

"Is that all right?" she asked, slipping her fingers beneath the topmost layer to be sure there was enough room to draw a breath.

"It is fine. Thank you."

"You are welcome." She smiled up at him.

His hands caught her face between them. Tilting her mouth under his, he drew her between his knees. His fingers loosened her braid as he slowly raised her up along him. Her hands slid along his legs when he pulled her to his chest.

She drew back. "Evan, you are asking too much."

"I want only what you want to give me." He leaned forward and tantalized her ear with his tongue. As a shiver raced along her, he whispered, "I want this pleasure you have for me."

Pushing herself out of his arms, she tried to slow her frantic breathing. "What makes you think I want you to make love to me?"

"The way your eyes threw knives at Angiola when she was speaking to me. I never expected to see you act jealous when I simply greeted another woman."

"I am not jealous!" she lied. When he arched a light brown eyebrow, she retorted, "I just do not like her!"

"Why not? You barely spoke to each other."

"I do not have to explain my reasons to you."

He stood and pushed the cushions from the benches onto the floor. Dropping pillows and a single blanket on top of them, he sighed as he dimmed the lamplight. "No, you do not need to explain. You need to—"

With a laugh, he pulled her into his arms and down onto the thin cushions. His lips clamped over hers, silencing her before she could speak. The pungent aroma of wine flooded into her mouth as his tongue caressed hers. Heated by his breath, the taste was delightful. Her fingers clenched helplessly against the blanket as he explored her mouth eagerly. All the dreams she had been chasing through her restless sleep last night coalesced into this moment when she was in his arms.

He released her wrists and swept his arm beneath her shoulders. Holding her to the cushions with the length of his strong body, he tasted the soft down of her cheek. She moaned with need as he teased her earlobe, and heat spiraled through her as his breath grazed her ear.

Her hands rose along his back. "If I hurt you—"

"You cannot when all I feel is pleasure."

As his lips roved along her face, she sighed with wordless rapture. This must be a dream. Only in her dreams could she be in his arms and have him touch her so lovingly.

In the dim light glinting off the raindrops clinging to the window, she looked up into his face as he drew her to sit amid the crumpled blanket. A grin stripped away the unyielding fervor on his face as he laced his fingers through her hair.

"You are so beautiful," he whispered.

"I am bruised and scratched and torn."

"And beautiful."

"Are you drunk?" She traced the curve of his jaw with her fingertip.

"Somewhat, but not so drunk that I do not want to hear you tell me that you want to make love with me."

Through her mind flitted a score of reasons why she should tell him no. Even as they paraded in her head, she whispered, "Make love with me until both of us have had our fill."

He laughed. "That might take forever."

"Is that a problem?"

"Not at the moment."

She stroked his chest above the strapping to find it surprisingly warm. Her gaze settled on his lips, and she knew she wanted his mouth on her again. Reaching for the hem of her ripped gown, she lifted it over her head and tossed it aside.

She reached to undo the laces of her chemise, but he pushed her fingers away and untied them. She moaned when, as the chemise opened, he bent to press his mouth in the hollow between her breasts. Pushing aside the last of her clothes, he led her to the buttons on his breeches. Her fingers quivered with anticipation as she loosened each one. He kicked the garment away to leave nothing to separate their heated skin.

As he leaned her back against the pallet, myriad sensations exploded along her skin as it touched his for the first time. His hand cradled her head as he bent to taste the curves which had known no other man's caress. Blazing liquid pleasure across her skin, he sampled the dusky valley between her breasts. The rough texture of his whiskers burnished her skin, heightening the fiery yearning in her. As his tongue climbed her breast's curve to draw its very tip into his mouth, she breathed his name.

He laughed as his lips continued to explore her. As she writhed with the passion he incited, she sought to discover every pleasure along him. His eager moans matched hers as he entwined his legs with hers and leaned over her. When her hungry mouth met his, she urged him closer. She wanted to touch every inch of him.

Her cry of rapture raced from her throat to his when he began to caress deep within her. Dissolving into the sweet pleasure, she became the rhythm he was teaching with his probing stroke. Her body arched toward his, craving the ultimate enchantment he could offer her.

When he moved over her again, she wrapped her arms around him. His lips covered hers as he brought them together. She gasped, opening her eyes to see his face wondrously near to her. The hard lines were softened slightly by the desire glazing his eyes.

She cried out in delight as he moved deeper within her, creating a storm of rapture whirling around her. As his mouth covered hers, she strained closer to him. Clutching his shoulders, she gave herself to the escalating need. Faster, more urgently, adding to the tantalizing torment, he sought each bit of passion within her.

She became lost in their combined need. Its potency erupted through her, splintering her into shimmering droplets of joy. Through the storm of her ecstasy, she knew that they were one for that perfect second. For that moment, it was enough.

Brienne woke with a start. She sat and searched the darkness. Where was she? Something cold dropped on her. Rain! Where *was* she?

When a gentle hand stroked her bare back, she drew in her breath to shriek. She let the air back out in a soft sigh as Evan's touch reached through her terror.

He draped the blanket over her shoulders and pulled her away from the drip coming through the wagon roof. "What is wrong, honey?" He kissed her bare shoulder. "Are you all atremble at the prospect of sharing more of this?"

"I wish that was it."

"Then, what is wrong?" he whispered, his voice abruptly serious.

"Can't you feel it?" She wrapped her arms around herself. "It is out there. Waiting, eager, sure of victory over me . . . over us."

"What are you talking about?"

"I thought you would know."

His hands on her shoulders leaned her back against him. She closed her eyes and welcomed the comfort of his strong body. "I know, honey," he answered as he placed his arms over hers. "I am just surprised that you believe me."

"I have believed part of it from the beginning." She laughed before correcting herself, "Almost from the beginning."

He sighed so deeply that she could hear it from within his chest beneath the strapping. "Neither of us doubt that someone may still be following you. I hope they will not look for us with an Italian theater troupe." He tilted her so she could see his smile. "Besides, I would like to be an actor for a while."

"When aren't you acting, Evan?"

"Now, honey." The gentle pressure of his mouth against hers increased steadily as he wrapped his arms around her. "I want you more now than ever. I want to feel the silken texture of your skin against my mouth. Not just your lips, although they are sweet as honey. All of you."

She sighed as he placed his lips in the curve of her neck which was still damp from the drip. The water boiled away beneath the heat of his kiss.

"Do you know how crazy I have been with longing," he whispered, "to loosen your clothes and discover the loveliness underneath?"

"I know." Her fingers quivered as they smoothed his hair back from his face. An answering hunger twisted within her as she wanted to melt against him like late snow warmed by a spring morning.

"When I think of tasting the curve of your breast"— he brushed his lips against her as his fingers glided along her thigh—"or the length of your slender legs, I fear I will explode with the craving for you. To dream of satisfying that yearning deep within you, to feel you all around me while your breath is warm against my mouth . . ."

He seared the rest of his longing into her lips. As he leaned her back into the soft cocoon of the cushions, she pushed aside her fear. All she wanted now was rapture.

Chapter Twelve

Brienne washed her face in the icy water of a brook. Fumbling for the bit of toweling she had brought from the wagon, she gasped as her fingers touched a leather boot. She wiped water from her eyes and looked up. "Evan!"

He tossed her the stockings that were hanging on the bush. "You shall catch your death of cold out here. Why didn't you have Giovanna warm you some water so you could wash in the wagon?"

"I considered it, but when I went to the door of their wagon, I think—that is, they were . . . busy."

When he chuckled, she had to smile, too. In the week they had been traveling with the Teatro Caparelli, she had found it easier every day to smile. They were almost to London, and there was no sign of anyone pursuing them. Even Evan had admitted to that last night while they helped take down the backstage after a performance.

"You are a good guest," he teased.

When she pulled on her stockings, he ran his finger

along her leg. She batted away his hand. "How are your ribs after all that work yesterday?"

"You should have asked me that last night." He nuzzled her neck.

"I did not want to halt you from doing what you were doing just then." She laughed. "That is why I am asking now."

"I am trying to do the same thing now."

Standing, Brienne tapped the frozen grass with her toe. "Not out here."

When he came to his feet, she could not miss the wince that dimmed his smile. He waved aside her sympathy before she could speak it. "I am getting better."

"You would be getting better more quickly if you told Sal the truth. Then he would not have you carrying those heavy backdrops."

"Don't dress me down, honey." He gave her that roguish grin that always sent delight sparkling through her. "Dress down . . . now that sounds like a good idea."

"Can you think of nothing else but making love?"

"Why should I when thinking of you is so much fun?" He draped his arm over her shoulder as she slipped her feet into her shoes. "How about some breakfast? Signora Benedetto was preparing it when I passed their wagon."

Her nose wrinkled. "I think I would rather skip breakfast."

"Now you are thinking as you should." He took her hand and led her back to their wagon. "Shall we work up an appetite first?"

Laughing, she went with him into the wagon. She wanted to hold on to this joy—and to him—for as long as she could.

The days fell into an easy pattern. Each morning, while the men set up the scenery for the afternoon's performance, Brienne shopped with Giovanna for the day's food. Angiola offered no help, preferring to loiter near Evan.

"Do not concern yourself about her," mused Giovanna as they wandered along the single street of the small town where they had arrived after midnight. "Angiola tried to put her claws in Pietro, but my brother was too smart to fall for her ploys. Evan is as wise."

Selecting eggs for the soufflé they would eat between the two performances they did each day, Brienne said, "I am not concerned about Evan."

"Good. I am glad to see him happy at last."

"At last?" She hesitated, not sure what she wanted to ask.

"Has he not told you how he and his family had a huge argument years ago? He has cut himself off from them, making for himself the life he wants." Giovanna smiled. "A life with you."

"I am not so certain of that."

Giovanna put her hand on Brienne's, stopping her from picking up a chunk of cheese. "Didn't your mother teach you the signs that show a man is in love with you?"

"Evan? In love with me?" Her laughter did not need to be feigned. Picking up the cheese, she handed it to the woman selling it to have it weighed. "A pound, please."

"Mayhap you do not see the truth because you do not see how he looks at you when he thinks no one is watching," Giovanna argued, clearly unwilling to change the subject. "It makes my heart sing. I never thought Evan would find a woman he loved more than his freedom, but I believe he has."

"That is absurd!"

"Possibly, but 'tis true."

Brienne decided the best answer was none. After paying for the food with the coins Sal gave her out of the money collected after each show, she walked toward where children were watching the men prepare the stage. She listened as the youngsters peppered the men with questions, but did not stay. She did not want to talk with Evan or have him draw her into his arms until she could think over Giovanna's words.

As she hurried to where a portable stove sat outside the wagons, she shivered. The cold wind had not cut through her while they had been sheltered by the village's buildings. This village could not be more than another week from London. Then she would get the truth—all of it—from Grand-mère. Then Evan would be gone, hiding from a man who would kill him because he had failed to steal the vase from her.

Her fingers curled as she looked at their wagon. She trusted Evan with her body, but not with the secrets in her heart. How she wished she could believe Giovanna was right!

"Brienne?" Sal's voice cut through her disquiet.

Turning, she smiled and waved to him. "I am right here."

He walked to her side. "Put away the dishes, Brienne. You do not have any time to cook today."

"That is right," Giovanna said, grinning. "I shall have to cook today."

"I hope Angiola gets better quickly." He rolled his eyes, then tweaked Giovanna's cheek and chuckled. "*Cara mia*, we thank heaven any day you are too busy to cook."

"Be quiet!" she retorted with mock fury. "A woman cannot be good at everything. You never complain about my other skills."

Knowing they could go on like this for a while longer, Brienne interjected, "What are you talking about? I was going to make a soufflé for today's meal."

"It will have to wait," Evan said as he joined them.

"Today, you make your acting debut in the production of *The Golden Lion*."

"What?"

"Angiola is not feeling well. You have seen the play performed enough to know it."

"Not all the lines!" She looked from one smiling face to another. "I am not an actress. Giovanna—"

Giovanna chuckled. "Did you never tell a tale to your *maman?* Have you never sung a song and pretended that you were dancing at a ball with a prince?"

"Yes. Years ago when I was a child."

"Then, you shall do fine."

Nothing Brienne said would change their minds. When Giovanna handed her the costume, Brienne sighed. She had seen the play, and it was close to a story she had listened to when she was young. As Giovanna herded her to the wagon to try on the costume, she reassured Brienne that the exact words of each line were not as important as telling the story.

Brienne saw Evan's grin as she went into the wagon. She knew this was his idea. She simply wished she knew why.

She had no chance to ask him as Giovanna worked with her to get the story of *The Golden Lion* straight. Repeating back the entrances and exits, Brienne tried to concentrate as she basted the costume to fit her. She was more slender than Angiola, so she had to take in the waist. When Giovanna left to prepare their meal and help with the stage, Brienne hurried to finish the dress.

Shaking it out, she realized a button was missing in the very center of the corsetlike bodice. She had to get it repaired. Rushing out of her wagon, she hurried across the frozen ground. She knocked on the door of the Benedettos' wagon; then she tightened her cloak around her. Winter cold slapped her face. Glancing about, she saw the trees rocking in the thinning light. She hoped there would not be a storm. She did not want rain blown between the cracks in the wagon's wall to pelt her.

When she got no response, she rapped again, louder. She had thought Angiola would be resting inside.

She lifted the latch. "Is anyone here? Signore Benedetto? Signora? Angiola? Are you in?"

When she got no answer, she scurried in and looked about in confusion. The wagon was divided by a curtain. Only a chair was on this side of the curtain. She hated to sneak through the wagon, but she needed the button. The show would be starting within the hour. Taking a deep breath, she pushed the curtain aside.

She smiled when she saw a sewing basket on a tiny table. Quickly she found a button to match the one on the princess's costume. She scooped it up.

As she turned to leave, she heard the unmistakable sound of the latch rising. In horror, she froze. How could she explain being back in this private area?

Her pounding heartbeat dimmed as a familiar laugh sifted through the curtain. "You are looking better than I expected when I heard you were sick," she heard Evan say.

Angiola's laugh was throaty and inviting. "How kind of you to say that!"

"There is no kindness in the truth." A pause, then he asked, "Shall I put this box here on the chair?"

"Wherever you wish. Thank you so much for helping with it, Evan."

"You are welcome. Rest so you can be back on stage tomorrow. Sal is pleased with the money collected when you perform."

"I like to please my friends."

"I am sure you do."

Brienne heard the rumble of amusement in his voice, but was not sure if he was laughing at Angiola or what she said.

"And I am sure you need your rest to get better."

"Evan, stay just a moment. I want to talk to you."

"Yes?"

"About Brienne."

Behind the curtain, Brienne pressed her hand over her mouth to silence her gasp of astonishment. She had not thought Angiola would speak of her when she had lured Evan into her wagon. Peeking through the tattered curtain, she wished she was anywhere but there. Too late, she realized that if she simply had been honest and admitted straightaway that she had come into the wagon for a button, she could have avoided this embarrassment.

"What about Brienne?" Evan stood in profile so Brienne could see his smile as he looked at the blonde.

"She and you came to the Teatro Caparelli together." Angiola stepped closer and walked her fingers along his arm. "Have you been traveling together long?"

"Not long."

"Then, I find it very, very, very strange," she purred, "that you have failed to notice how I have been watching you in the short time *we* have been together."

"I have noticed you."

"I thought you might have." Angiola slithered her arm around his shoulders and rubbed her leg against his. "An Englishwoman does not understand what we Italians do. Men and women need each other."

When his arm settled on Angiola's waist, Brienne's eyes filled with tears. How he had teased her about being jealous of Angiola! Now here he stood in what he thought was an empty wagon and welcomed Angiola's attentions.

"That is very true," he murmured.

"I could satisfy that need for you, Evan."

He chuckled and put his fingers under her chin. "There is no doubt about that, angel."

"Then, let me." Angiola's hand on the back of his

head brought his mouth to hers. The leisurely kiss seemed to last an eternity.

Brienne drew back from the curtain as tears ran along her face. She ignored them. Could anything be more ridiculous than having to admit that she was falling in love with Evan at the very moment he was holding another woman? Leaning her head against the wall, she swallowed her sobs.

The voices beyond the curtain ripped her out of her grief. When she heard Evan suggesting a walk beyond the wagons, she wondered if someone had struck her in the stomach. She could not catch her breath, for pain ached as if she had suffered Evan's bruised ribs. The door closed behind Evan and Angiola, and Brienne shoved the curtain aside.

She ran to the door and opened it enough to be sure no one would see her leave. If she met Evan when he had his arm around Angiola, she would not know what to say. The clouds darkened the day, but her heart was lost in a void of a deeper ebony. Running to her wagon, she was not shocked that it was empty. Pietro would be working with his sister and Sal. Angiola would be with Evan. Only Brienne was alone.

"Good evening, *principessa*!"

Brienne tensed as Giovanna continued to lather thick makeup on her cheeks. Trying not to let her pain filter into her voice, she asked, "What are you doing here, Evan? I thought you would be helping with the scenery."

"We are done. The storm has passed, and the show will open as soon as the leading lady is ready."

Putting her hand over her stomach, she silently ordered the quaking to cease.

Evan edged around Giovanna. When he smiled, she tried not to think how he had worn a similar expression in the moment before he kissed Angiola. She wanted to shriek at him, telling him to leave the wagon and her life, but she could not. The Caparellis were depending on her.

"No need to stare," she said coolly. "I know I look funny with all these cosmetics, but—"

"You do not look funny." His gaze moved along her. "You look like a princess, honey."

"Not a *duchesse?*"

"Nasty, nasty," he admonished as Giovanna chuckled her throaty laugh. "Shall I excuse your lack of manners as stage nerves?"

"If you wish." *Or we both could be honest, and I could tell you how you have broken my heart.*

"All finished," announced Giovanna. She motioned for Brienne to stand. "Turn around. Let me be sure the tucks in the waist do not show."

As Giovanna bent to check the hastily altered dress, Brienne kept her smile in place. She would not let Evan know how he had hurt her. Not in front of Giovanna. Any sympathy would crush her totally.

Giovanna smiled. "Perfect. Five minutes before the curtain, Brienne. You shall do wonderfully. Shall I come for you?"

"I shall be sure she is there for her entrance," Evan said lightly, but his gaze remained on Brienne.

The door closed. An uneasy silence smothered her while Brienne tried to think of something to say. Finally she mumbled, "I feel like a painted doxy."

"No angel could aspire to your beauty."

Angel! That was what he had called Angiola. Had Angiola fallen for his seduction as readily as Brienne had? She could not ask that. Instead she said, "I hope I do not make a fool of myself when I step out on the stage."

Evan's hands settled on her shoulders which were bared by the dress's deep neckline. As his gaze moved again along her, she shrugged them off and turned away.

To her back, he said, "You need only go out on that stage and smile. That will thrill every man watching."

"I am not Angiola."

"That is something I have to agree with."

She bit her lip. She had given him every chance to admit to the truth, but yet he continued to act as if nothing had changed. Mayhap he had not changed, but he had changed her.

She heard Sal calling her name. "I have to go. Sal will be furious if the curtain is late."

"Go, honey." When she spun toward the door, he caught her arm. He smiled. "Good luck."

"Thank you."

"And have fun."

"Like you always do?" She rushed out, leaving him with a puzzled frown. Mayhap, at last, he understood her terse answers.

Giovanna met Brienne behind the stage. "The audience is a good one. They were delighted with Pietro's juggling. We thought you would like a few extra minutes to compose yourself, so he and Sal arranged a few tricks to entertain the audience." She smiled. "You shall do well. Evan is right. You look like a *principessa*. Far more than Angiola ever has."

She did not want to hear that woman's name, but said only, "I hope I do not make too many mistakes." *Beyond being behind the curtain while Evan kissed Angiola this afternoon.*

Adjusting the layers of cloth which were meant to be an old woman's rags, Giovanna chuckled softly. "The audience will love you."

Her answer was halted by the drumbeat which announced the beginning of the play. Stepping into the wings, she watched the others take their places. Evan drew the curtain, and the play began. As she stood silently, she repeated her lines in her head. Suddenly she gasped.

"What is wrong?" Evan asked.

"My sash! I left it in the wagon."

"Wait here! I'll get it for you."

Anxiously she looked from the actors on the stage to Evan rushing toward the wagons. Her cue would come soon. She could not miss it. Caught up in her fear, she realized the actors were waiting for the curtain to close to end the first act. Quickly she grasped the rope. It burned her hands as the curtain closed with a loud swish.

"Ready?" asked Sal as he rubbed his cold hands together. Giovanna pressed one end of his fake beard back into place, and he grinned.

"As soon as Evan—"

"Here it is," Evan interrupted as he shoved the white sash into her hands. "My life is much more hectic with all of you on the stage. I am the only one to run errands today." When she started to thank him, he smiled and gestured toward the stage. "Go and show them what a true princess looks like, honey."

Brienne twisted the cloth around her wrist nervously. As Sal took his place on stage, she prepared for her entrance. The curtain opened. The candles at the edge of the stage were far brighter than she had expected. As she heard Sal repeat his line to hide the fact that she had missed her cue, she forced her feet forward.

Her voice wobbled like her knees as she said, "Father, I tire of being shut away."

"I must find the wisest, bravest man to rule my kingdom and win my daughter. Only a man who can solve in eight days the puzzle of where I have hidden my daughter."

"Yet, I wish to see the sun, smell the flowers, feel the breezes on my face."

Sal motioned to his left. In the guise of the golden lion, Pietro inched onto the stage. "See, my daughter, I bring you a gift. A statue of a golden lion which will brighten your day."

"Thank you, Father." She pretended to kiss his cheek, being careful not to loosen the beard.

"Enjoy it, my daughter," he said as he exited.

Looking at the audience, she pressed her hands to her chest and bemoaned the fate of a lonely princess. "What is the use of a fine castle when I have no one but my eleven attendants to share it with me? Where is the man who will be brave enough to lead my father's men and wise enough to unravel this puzzle and handsome enough to win my heart? Can there be such a man?"

"There is one."

"Who spoke?" She glanced about the stage as if searching for the speaker.

When the voice answered, she froze as she realized who was within the papier-mâché lion. A whisper from the edge of the stage ordered her to answer. Somehow she did. Again she heard Evan speak the lines Pietro should have been speaking. She glanced toward the wings where Giovanna stood. When she saw Pietro standing there with a broad grin on his face, she knew that everyone had known of the switch in players. Everyone but her.

Why had they done this? She was not going to get an answer until the play was over. Giving herself to the rôle of the princess, she watched Evan leave along with her promise to assist him by wearing the white sash when he returned. She waited while he and Sal pretended to be searching for the missing princess. Silently she sat on her stool with the white sash in her hand.

They halted in front of her and discussed the eleven maidens who were painted on the backdrop. Slowly she withdrew the sash and tied it around her waist.

"There is my princess!" crowed Evan. He dropped to his knee in front of her. "Be mine, beloved princess."

"You have found my daughter in the eight days granted you," Sal announced. "I give you her and my kingdom. Tonight my daughter marries."

"Will you be mine, princess?" Evan asked.

She fought not to scowl. That was not what Evan was supposed to say next. He was supposed to bow to the king, take her hand and together they would bow to the audience. End of the play.

Hearing eager whispers sweep through the crowd beyond the lights, she knew she had to say something. "You have proven yourself brave enough to lead my father's men and wise enough to solve his puzzle."

"And handsome enough to win your heart?"

Her eyes widened as he lifted her from the stool to stand before him. She wanted this over with. Now! Raising her chin, she knew she could be as insincere as he was. Coolly, she said, "Far more handsome than even my dreams promised. You, brave sir, have won my heart for all time."

She offered her cheek, but he caught her face between his hands. Blue sparks burned in his eyes. When his finger moved to tilt her chin toward him, his other arm slipped around her waist to pull her against him. The audience drew in a collective breath as he pressed her to the hard lines of his body.

"Tonight you will be mine, princess," he said.

Her reply vanished as his mouth covered hers. His arm tightened to surround her with his heated touch. A quiver raced through her. She wanted this, but she must not. Yet, resisting was impossible as, deeper and deeper, she sank into the heated pool of his touch.

A finger tapped her shoulder. With glazed eyes, she saw Pietro grinning. "Curtain," he said, nodding toward where the patched material hung between them and the audience.

Brienne pulled away from Evan, but he smiled and took her hand. She started to protest, then let him lead her to take their bows. The score of people in the audience cheered wildly. She dipped in a curtsy, hoping that the heavy cosmetics hid the icy pallor of her face. How could she be so foolish?

While Pietro collected coins from the audience, the actors hurried to the wagons. It was too cold to linger in the flimsy costumes.

Brienne quickly washed her face and took off the wondrous gown behind a curtain in Sal and Giovanna's wagon. Dressed in a wrapper borrowed from Giovanna, she was amazed when more applause met her as she stepped past the curtain to see Evan sitting with his friends. The men rose, and Evan offered her his place on the bench. She pretended not to see.

"Look at this!" Sal announced as he poured coins on the table. "The audience was only half the size of the last village, but we have collected almost twice as much." He leaned his elbows on the table. "Thanks to you, Brienne. You were born to this rôle . . ."

Giovanna continued for him, ". . . as if you were born to the title. Are you sure you are only a *duchesse?* And Evan!" She chuckled. "Such fire and fervor! I never knew you had such skills as an actor."

"That is because he was not acting!"

"Sal!" she admonished. "Be quiet."

Brienne said softly, "I am very tired. I think I should get some sleep."

"Are you feeling all right?" asked Giovanna with sudden concern. "I hope you are not sickening with what Angiola has had."

She choked out some answer and slipped past the others to the door.

"Let me walk with you, Brienne," Evan said.

Although she had hoped he would stay with his friends to celebrate how well the play had gone, she nodded. She pretended not to see his arm offered to her. He said nothing as he closed the door to their wagon behind them. The distinctive click of the latch sounded very loud in the small space.

"They are correct, you know," he whispered. "You were perfect as the lonely princess waiting for a man to come to win her heart."

"I am a better actress than I thought."

When he bent to kiss her nape, she pulled away. She reached for her plain nightgown. Mayhap Evan could act as if nothing had happened, but she could not. He lit the lantern, and she gasped as his fingers stroked her cheek.

"Leave me alone!" she cried.

"No, listen to me, Brienne."

"Why?"

"Because I know why you are so upset."

"Do you? That is right. You know how to read people's feelings so you can cheat them better. If there is somewhere else you would rather be, Mr. Somerset, do not let me delay you."

His hand cupped her chin and forced her eyes to look at his. "I know why you are so upset. You were hiding behind the curtain in the Benedettos' wagon when I came in with Angiola earlier this afternoon."

"How—?" Trying to pull away, she cried, "Leave me alone!"

"Not until you listen to me. I knew you were there. Your toes were peeking out from under the curtain. Even if I had not seen them, Giovanna told me that she had seen you going in. That was why I walked Angiola there. I did not want you to have to deal with her when you were already anxious about performing on the stage."

"So you thought you would soothe my anxiety by kissing her!" She turned away and hid her face in her hands, wanting to be alone with her sorrow and her shame. "I did not mean to eavesdrop on you and Angiola, Evan."

"And make yourself miserable?"

"Yes." Glancing over her shoulder, she asked, "Does that make you feel better?"

He turned her into his arms and kissed her cheek. When she sighed with the longing she could not deny, his tongue probed into her mouth, refusing to allow any of it to miss his eager touch. Raising his head, he murmured, "This is what makes me feel better. Brienne, I kissed her only because I knew you were watching. I knew only drastic measures would convince you to acknowledge the truth."

"And what truth is that?" she asked, not willing to admit to the truth of the desire pulsing through her.

"That I could never be satisfied with Angiola when you are the one who lures me to madness."

She knew she should tell him to leave, but his lips silenced her. When he leaned her back on the bench, her arms rose to keep him close. Her breath vanished into the depths of his mouth as she stroked his back. Discovering a spot where his shirt had loosened, she slipped her fingers beneath to discover the warmth of his skin, taking care not to touch his left ribs.

Caught in the magic of his fingers, she swayed with the sweet motion of his touch. Along her leg, his fingertips moved, teasing, tickling, tantalizing her into rapture. She gasped against his mouth when he boldly caressed her inner leg.

With a laugh, he reached for the few buttons closing her wrapper. His lips moved along the skin revealed by each opened button, slowly drawing the fabric aside. Fire seared her as his tongue flicked along the skin which ached for his touch.

"Honey, forget—"

A scream ruptured the night.

Chapter Thirteen

Brienne clenched Evan's shirt. He stared at her. When the woman screamed again, he jumped to his feet.

The door crashed open.

Pietro called, "Evan! Is Brienne with you?"

He ran to where Pietro was trying to see into the dark wagon. "She is here. Who is in trouble?"

"If it is not Brienne or Giovanna, it must be—!"

Another scream riveted them. Brienne cried, "Angiola!"

Evan raced with Pietro out of the wagon. Closing her wrapper, Brienne ran after them. She paused on the steps as Giovanna hurried toward her.

"Come with me." Giovanna took her hand and pulled her down the steps.

Brienne stopped between the wagons. "We must help her!"

"Do you have a weapon to protect yourself and her?"

"No." She glanced toward the sea. If she had not left the pistol in the boat. . . .

"Then, let the men handle this! You would be in the way."

Brienne stole one more look through the deepening twilight as Giovanna shoved her through the other wagon's door. Evan was out there where anything could be lurking. Giovanna sat, her face glum. More than once, Brienne started to speak, but nothing came from her confused brain.

What was going on? She shivered as she tried not to think why Angiola would scream like that.

When the door crashed open, Evan lurched in, carrying a crumpled form. Brienne pressed her hands over her mouth as she stared at the senseless Angiola. Then, backing away, she gathered together the pillows on one end of the bench.

"Put her here," she choked, staring at Angiola's bloody face.

He nodded grimly. He placed Angiola on the cushion with care. When her hand dropped toward the floor, he put it across her chest. "She is alive."

Hearing a moan, Brienne turned. Giovanna had her arm around Signora Benedetto, supporting her. Angiola's father's face was long with fear. Neither approached the bench where their daughter did not move.

"Water," Brienne said quietly, "and some clean cloths."

Giovanna repeated the order to Pietro. He pushed past the Benedettos and got what she needed from the storage shelves. Giving the rags to Brienne, he ran out to get some clean water.

Another quiver iced Brienne's spine. When Evan shoved a bucket toward her, she frowned. "You should sit. You look almost as bad as she does."

"Later."

"Now!" she snapped. "Do what I tell you so I can

see to Angiola. I do not need you swooning. Then I would have to step over you while I tended to her.''

Evan smiled weakly as he sank to a seat by the table. He touched the tender spot on the back of his head. He had been a fool not to expect there was more than one man waiting in the bushes beyond the village. If Sal had not arrived when he did, he might be as dead as the man lying in the shadow of the trees.

As Brienne competently cleaned the wounds on Angiola's face, he wondered what Angiola had done to incite such violence against her. He had last seen her by the stage when she had been talking with a young man after this afternoon's performance.

That man was now a corpse. Killed by a jealous lover? He dismissed that idea. Angiola had not been in the village long enough to create trouble.

At a groan, he pushed himself to his feet to peer over Brienne's shoulder. Angiola was regaining her senses.

Angiola screamed as her eyes opened.

Brienne bent to calm her.

''You are safe now.'' She put a cloth on Angiola's lacerated forehead and smiled her thanks to Giovanna, who held out a small bottle. ''Just lie still. I am going to put some salve on your wounds.''

''Get away from me, witch! He cut my face, and it is all your fault!''

When Brienne's fingers clenched on the cloth, Evan said quietly, ''Angiola, you do not know what you are saying.''

''I know exactly what I am saying! This is all her fault!'' she snarled. ''He called me by her name.''

''He? Who?''

She glared at Evan, then at Brienne as she sat up against the pillows. ''I don't know, but he called me Brienne and insisted that I come with him.''

''Was that when he struck you?'' Evan gritted his teeth.

Why hadn't he considered this? Instead of losing himself in the pleasure of loving Brienne, he should have been watching for an attack like this.

"No," Angiola said with obvious reluctance. "He hit me after I had convinced him that he had the wrong woman. He was as tender as a lover before that."

"How about the man with you?"

A malevolent smile twisted her lips. "The cur killed him after calling him Somerset."

Brienne clutched onto his arm, but Evan ignored her as he demanded, "The murderer used my name? Are you sure?"

"How could I be mistaken?" She pressed her hand over her heart as if she were on the stage. "I shall always remember his exact words. 'That is what happens to those who betray us. Lagrille has paid you in full, Somerset.' "

Brienne's knees folded beneath her, and she dropped onto the opposite bench. "Lagrille? Could it be him?"

"Not him, but one of his men." He grasped Angiola's shoulders. "Did you see clearly the man who hit you? Can you describe him?"

Her eyes narrowed as she looked from him to Brienne again. "Why should I? What do I care if something happens to her?"

"Angiola!" cried Giovanna. "He knows you have seen him. If he comes back, he may kill you to keep you quiet."

Angiola flinched, then whispered, "Yes, I saw him clearly. Dark hair, not very tall."

"And the other man?" Evan asked.

She shrugged. "I did not see him during the attack, but he probably was the man with the dark-haired man in the audience during the play."

"During the play?" Brienne's whisper was as loud as a shout in the silent wagon.

Evan turned to look at the others. "We shall leave tonight. We cannot put you in more danger."

"*Sì*, go!"

Brienne gasped as Signore Benedetto raised a trembling finger toward the door. When he shouted in Italian, Evan's face tightened. At a word that if it were close to a similar word in French was an appalling insult, she stepped between Signore Benedetto and Evan, who had not retorted.

"Stop this!" she ordered. "Evan saved your daughter's life. Doesn't that count for something?"

"If it were not for you and him," the old man snarled, "my child would not be mutilated."

Ignoring Angiola's emoted groan, Brienne shook her head. "Angiola is not hurt badly. I was struck as badly during—" When Evan grabbed her arm, she realized he did not want her to speak about the attack on her at L'Enfant de la Patrie. "By the end of the week, with a little extra makeup, she can go on stage again."

"You have no compassion, you whore!"

"Whore? I was not the one having a tryst with a stranger. I—"

Signore Benedetto struck her across the face.

Reeling back, she saw Evan catch Signore Benedetto's hand before he could hit her again. "No, Evan, don't hurt him!"

Shoving Signore Benedetto away, Evan put his arm around her. She nodded when he asked her if she was all right. It was a lie, for her head spun.

"My friends, we will—" he began.

"No, Evan," Sal said, fury squeezing through each word, "you do not need to leave." Black fire burned in his eyes. "Take Angiola to your wagon, signore. In the morning, I want you and your family gone. You do not treat the members of my family so. You have insulted Evan and Brienne. You have insulted me."

"You cannot send us away, Salvatore Carbone. You need me." Angiola stood, looking much better than she had acted. Her face was scratched, but the blood had been washed away.

"No, we have no need for you. Giovanna knows your parts."

Cruelly she laughed. "You are going to have an old sow be a princess? You will starve."

"Then, we shall starve," Giovanna said with quiet dignity. "My husband is the master of Teatro Caparelli. He has told you to leave."

Cursing, she elbowed past Sal to where her deflated father and silent mother waited. Angiola paused at the door. As her gaze settled on Brienne, she said in a superior tone, "I hope they come back for you."

"Begone!" shouted Pietro. When Sal put a hand on his arm, he subsided as the Benedettos filed out of the wagon.

Giovanna smiled. "I am glad she is gone! Evan, Brienne, you shall stay here tonight. If those brigands return, they shall have to deal with the Caparellis."

"What about tonight's show?" Brienne asked.

Sal patted her shoulder. "So the thrill of performing has heated your blood, too, has it?"

"I know you count on the money."

"We made enough money this afternoon to cancel tonight's show."

"We appreciate what you are doing for us," Evan said.

"You are family." Pietro slapped Evan on the back. "We stay together during the good times and the bad. No one will force you to leave until you wish to go."

"I hope you will not come to rue those words."

"I will not."

Although he nodded, Evan was not so sure his friends understood the magnitude of the danger they were calling down upon themselves. He saw fear on Brienne's face.

Finally, she was learning what Lagrille would do to possess the daughter of Marc-Michel Levesque.

"I think it would be for the best if Brienne and I go to the other wagon," he said, hoping none of the Caparellis guessed he was lying. "That way, we have eyes to watch both sides, so that no one might sneak up on us."

Sal held up his hand as Pietro started to argue. "That might be wise, Evan. Do you want me to send this young pup with you? He could help you watch."

"That is not necessary."

"You were hit very hard, my friend. Are you thinking wisely?"

Paying Brienne's gasp of dismay no mind, he smiled. "Mayhap it is the lump that was raised on my head that is allowing me to consider what we should do now." He held out his hand. "Brienne?"

He thought she would pelt him with questions as soon as they stepped out of the wagon. Instead, she showed good sense and remained silent as they skulked through the shadows back to the other wagon. Closing the door behind them, he went to the bench. He shoved her bag into her hands.

"Get dressed and pack whatever you want to take with you, honey. We are getting the hell out of here."

She sat on the bench, holding the bag in her lap. "Mayhap Angiola was telling us a lie so her parents would not be furious at her."

"You cannot truly believe what you are saying." He scowled. "How would she know Lagrille's name?"

"Did you speak it before when she might have heard?"

Shaking his head, he said, "I could have, but she was attacked and a man was killed. Have you forgotten that?"

She quivered so hard, he feared she would splinter into dozens of pieces. "No," she whispered, "I have not forgotten that, although I wish I could. Do you think the man who attacked Angiola saw me on stage?"

"Your innocence is so sweet, but it will betray you." He stroked her cheek with the back of his hand. "These men are desperate to find you, so desperate that they would confront Angiola in hopes she was you."

"Then, they are stupid. She is taller than I am, and her hair is blond."

"Not stupid, desperate to find you. This man who calls himself Lagrille has waited almost two decades to find you. The wealth of your father's estate must be worth the wait. Château Tonnere du Grêlon obviously is far grander than even your grandmother suggested."

"Evan, if we leave here now and go to France and Château Tonnere du Grêlon—"

"That may be what they would like you to do. They would like to have you head right into the lion's den." He tilted her face up so he could see her eyes which were almost lost to the darkness. "Honey, we have to disappear."

"No!" She stood and folded her arms in front of her. "If we do that, they might turn their attention to Grandmère in hopes of finding where I am. I cannot let them hurt her as they have Angiola."

"And you."

"Yes, and me. Evan, I must return to London and speak to my grandmother."

"So she can confirm all I have told you?" He sighed. "I thought you had come to believe me."

"I have tried."

"But you do not trust me?"

It was as if the murderer had struck him again when Brienne turned away and looked out the window. She did not have to answer his question. Any trust that she might have begun to have for him had vanished when he had not pushed Angiola out of his arms.

He stroked her shoulders. For a moment, she softened, but then her shoulders became rigid again. Again he could guess her thoughts as easily as if she had shouted them at him. She had welcomed him into her arms before Angiola's screams had intruded, but now she was certain that had been a mistake.

You will never care for anyone but yourself. Someday you will meet someone who shall care for another more than you. Then you will understand how you have hurt others.

He could not recall who had said that to him. His father, most likely, when Evan had left for the last time.

You find leaving so easy, son. Staying is much harder, but you always look for the easy fun, don't you?

That voice from his memory was unquestionably his father's, spoken on more occasions than he cared to recall. The man could repeat himself endlessly, not seeming to notice that Evan was no longer listening.

Reaching past her, he picked up his ragged coat and drew it on. He would have to leave Brienne, too, if he wanted to keep breathing. But he would not abandon her now. He could not be sure if her enemies were lurking out there, even now, watching for him to leave, so they could snatch her from this wagon.

"Brienne, I am sorry."

"That is easy for you to say now that you have satisfied your curiosity about Angiola's kisses."

He twisted her to face him. "Honey, I should not have teased you that way. All I can say is that I am sorry."

"You never think of anything but finding something funny about everything." She crossed her arms in front of her to keep him away. "So do you think *this* is funny?"

"No."

"Good."

Evan stared at her in disbelief when a smile quirked on her lips. She was giving him a dose of his own bitter medicine. With a grumble, he tapped her nose. "You are impossible, honey!"

"No more than you."

"So do you forgive me?"

She arched a brow. "I will let you know when I do."

"Do that." He kissed her swiftly, wishing there was time for more. Now he must think only of keeping her safe.

Evan smiled as he wondered if Pietro was interested in going for a walk this evening. Lagrille's men would not be watching for three of them to leave the wagons.

Brienne yelped with astonishment when he grabbed her bag and emptied it onto the bench. She caught the small box that had been at the bottom. "Be careful!"

"Is there something breakable in it?"

"The miniature of my father." She stuffed the box back into the bag. "Give me my other things."

"Put them on."

"What?"

He smiled. "If someone is watching these wagons, they will not be watching for Giovanna and her family. Giovanna is much rounder than you, so Lagrille's men should pay no mind to anyone dressed like her. I think Giovanna needs to go with her family to the local tavern now."

"Where we can get the coach to London?"

"Now you understand me."

"No," she said, her smile fading, "I do not understand you, Evan. I fear I never will, but I will go with you. You promised Grand-mère that you would bring me back to her."

"That sounds very trusting, honey."

She pulled another layer of clothes over her tattered gown. "I believe that you will not break a pledge that you have made."

"I never have." He reached for a pillow to slip under his coat. "No matter how difficult the situation has been, I have always done what I vowed to do."

"Until you did not take Maman's vase to Lagrille."

"There is that." He gave her a lopsided grin. "Are you trying to talk yourself out of going with me?"

"I have no choice, Evan."

When she went to the door, he followed. Again she was right. She had no choice but to do what she must.

Neither did he.

Chapter Fourteen

The last of the day's light was slipping behind the buildings on the other side of Grosvenor Square. The trees along the edge of the square were budded, something Brienne had not noticed when she left almost a fortnight ago. Around her, the fog reeked of chimney soot and clung to her face, damp and dirty.

She was home!

Only the need to keep from drawing attention to herself and Evan kept her from twirling about in a merry dance on the grass in the square. Mayhap he had been honest about the tale of Château Tonnere du Grêlon, but that could never be home as London was. She loved every filthy, exciting corner of this city.

Hearing a hushed chuckle as he drew her around to the back of the house, she glanced at Evan. He was smiling broadly, the first time she had seen anything but a scowl on his face since they left the Caparellis.

"You are as glad to be back here as I am!" She kept her voice low.

"Why not? By now, the Season should be keeping the *ton* busy with all their calls and their entertainments. I can think of no better place to make myself scarce than in the midst of all that madness."

"Are you planning to attend the assemblies and teas?"

He cocked an eyebrow. "I shall have to see what invitations await me before I decide." With another laugh, he said, "You are looking at me as if you believe me. Why do you always take me at my word when I am hoaxing you?"

"It is so hard to tell the difference."

"Mayhap you should just assume that whenever you accept my story, it is a joke. Whenever you do not, it is the truth."

"I would be want-witted to do that."

He chuckled as he led her to the back door. Opening it, he peeked in. "No one is about, so let's go."

"Why are we sneaking in?"

"Because it is fun." He laughed again and tugged on her hand, pulling her into the laundry.

Brienne smiled. The more treacherous their circumstances became, the more Evan joked. She suspected he would even find something amusing about the hangman putting a noose around his neck.

"No, not that way," he said when she turned to the left. "That leads down into the cellars, and Porter warned me when I first came here that they are pretty disgusting, a place you would not want to visit."

Although she wanted to remind him how many disgusting places she had been in since he burst into her life, she nodded. He put his arm around her waist to steer her through the maze of sheets hung from lines in the laundry room.

When she pushed away a cloying sheet, he chuckled softly and whispered, "I knew tonight I would be grateful for Porter's fastidious order that the bed linens be changed daily whether he was here or not. I had not guessed how easy that dictate makes slipping in and out of the house.''

She followed him in silence. She hoped he was right about coming back to London. At least, now she could get verification of his story from Grand-mère, and then. . . . She was not sure what she would do next.

Nothing had changed on the main floor of the house. She was not sure why she expected that it had. Mayhap because she had been changed so much.

Hitchcock whirled as he heard their footsteps. The butler's face washed out to gray, then reddened to an unhealthy shade. ''I did not see . . . How did you . . .'' He squared his shoulders, his normal scowl returning. ''Good afternoon, sir, miss.''

''Good afternoon, Hitchcock. 'Tis a pleasure to see your welcoming face, as always,'' Evan said, not a hint of amusement in his voice. ''Will you let Madame LeClerc know we have returned?''

''Right away, sir.'' His nose wrinkled. ''May I ring for a bath for you and Miss LeClerc?''

''You may, although I believe Miss LeClerc would prefer to have hers in her room while I have mine in mine.''

The butler's face became ruddy again as he turned to follow the orders.

Brienne waited until he was out of earshot before she laughed. ''You should not taunt him like that.''

''Give me one reason why not. His officious airs are the one bad thing about using Porter's house.''

''Because,'' she said, curving her hand around his nape, ''you lied to him when you said I would prefer my bath in my room and yours in yours.''

He drew her closer. ''What happened to the Brienne who would have slapped my face for such a suggestion when we last stood here?''

''She has discovered how much—'' A motion past him

caught her eye. Whirling out of his arms, she ran to the stairs. "Grand-mère!"

Her grandmother came down the last steps at a reckless speed. She pulled Brienne to her and hugged her until Brienne feared she would be smothered. She did not pull away, because she wanted to comfort her grandmother.

"My child, my child," Grand-mère whispered over and over again in French. "I have feared for your safety." She put out her hand to Evan as she added in English, "Thank you for bringing Brienne back to me."

"I would not have gone if I had not promised Maman," she whispered.

"Lucile should not have asked that of you." Grand-mère framed Brienne's face in her hands. "She knew the danger may be as great to you now as ever, child."

"Grand-mère, what Evan told me about my father—"

"What is all this?" asked a man's voice from near the front door. "Who are you?"

Brienne kept her hand on her grandmother's arm and turned to see a stranger. He was not as tall as Evan, but had an air of arrogance that dominated the foyer. His short, black hair was brushed forward in a classic style. As he drew off leather gloves, she could not keep from noting that his clothes were as fine as anything worn by the patrons of L'Enfant de la Patrie. His knee-high boots glistened as brightly as the street lamps.

She was about to ask him who he was and what he was doing in the house when Hitchcock took the gloves and the man's hat with a bow and a broad smile. The man must be welcome here. Why hadn't Evan said anything about a friend calling?

A woman came into the house, her eyes becoming as wide as Brienne's. A pattern-card of elegance, the brown-haired woman wore a dress of the palest pink. The ribbons on the high bodice matched the ones on her bonnet and on her silk slippers which peeked from beneath her skirt.

She carried a parasol, although the fog was dense on the square, now hiding the buildings on the far side.

Evan stepped forward. "Porter, what are you doing here? I thought you disdained the Season's beginnings."

"Somerset!" The man laughed. "What to-do are you creating in my house now?"

Turning, Evan took Brienne's hand and drew her forward. She did not release her hold on her grandmother's arm, so Grand-mère stood on her other side.

"Brienne, Madame LeClerc, allow me to introduce our up-until-now absent host, Armistead Porter," Evan said with a chuckle. "Porter, Madame LeClerc and her granddaughter, Brienne LeClerc."

Mr. Porter bowed over Grand-mère's hand, then plucked Brienne's hand out of Evan's and raised it to his lips. "What a pleasurable and most lovely surprise to find awaiting me when I return home." Taking the hand of the young woman who had entered when he did, he said, "Allow me to introduce my dear friend Louisa Woods."

Evan greeted Miss Woods as graciously as Mr. Porter had welcomed Brienne and her grandmother. Brienne was not certain if she was more astonished by Louisa's accent that identified her as French or that Evan spoke all the proper commonplaces as if he were enjoying himself. He never had had patience with such things before.

"If you will excuse us, Monsieur Porter," Grand-mère said in a tone that suggested arguing would be worthless, "Brienne needs to clean up. A bath is waiting for you, child."

"Yes, do excuse us," she added. "I am afraid our journey has left me a dashed shabrag."

"Journey?" asked Mr. Porter, his eyes bright with interest.

Evan slapped his friend on the shoulder. "Brienne went to pay a call in the country. I escorted her back."

"You? You hate daisyville." Mr. Porter chuckled. "I

suspect you would be glad to wash away those memories with some brandy.'' He smiled at Miss Woods. ''I trust you would like to refresh yourself, too.''

''Yes,'' Miss Woods said in her breathy voice that was barely above a whisper. ''This fog is so filthy. It is what I hate most about London.''

''Now, now, Louisa,'' Mr. Porter replied with a strained chuckle. ''It will be gone with the arrival of the sunshine. In the meantime, will you ladies join us when you have finished your ablutions?''

Brienne glanced at her grandmother. She had so many questions to ask her, but she did not want to offend their host. Nodding, she said, ''Thank you.''

When Brienne hurried up the stairs with her grandmother in tow and Miss Woods following at a more decorous pace, Evan noticed his friend watching with obvious interest. Not Miss Woods, but Brienne. He smiled. Porter never had been able to resist a pretty lass, and Brienne must be one of the prettiest his friend had ever seen.

''So why are you in Town so early?'' Evan asked as they walked more slowly up the steps to the book-room where Porter kept his best brandy. ''There cannot be much to interest you now, unless you have your eye on a special lady. Miss Woods, I assume.''

''Louisa is a friend, not someone I would consider for more.''

Evan glanced at where Miss Woods was vanishing around the top of the stairs. She must be the mistress whose clothes Brienne had borrowed during her last stay here in this house. It seemed that Porter had finally tired of his previous convenient. . . . What had been her name? Evan could not recall. Not that it mattered. He doubted if Porter could. His friend enjoyed *à suivie* affairs, what Porter judged to be the proper fare for a bachelor during the Season. It was unfortunate that Porter had selected a French mistress just now.

"So there must be another you are considering, Porter, if you are here so early."

"I cannot fool you, can I?" Porter opened the door to a musty smell, and Evan guessed the room had not been used since the end of the past Season.

"So who is this paragon of femininity?"

Porter frowned when he realized no brandy awaited on the table. Ringing for a bottle to be brought posthaste, he sat in a leather chair and stretched his legs out onto a low stool. "Her identity should remain private at the moment, for she does not yet know of my interest in her."

Evan sighed as he let a thickly padded chair embrace him. Although he would rather have been in Brienne's soapy arms as he helped her wash herself and him, he had not enjoyed such comfort as this chair since he had left here weeks ago. He might have reconsidered his plan to bring Brienne here if he had guessed that Porter would be arriving to take up residence on Grosvenor Square now. Mayhap it would all work out well. If Porter was intent on the pursuit of some young miss, that would keep the eyes of the *ton* on him, so they might not take note of Brienne.

"You are quiet, my friend," Porter said.

Standing to collect the tray from the maid who came to the door, Evan set it on a table between them. "I am trying to imagine which young woman has touched your heart enough to steal your attention from Miss Woods."

"You are thinking of Miss Woods?" Porter chuckled. "I had thought you might have been thinking of the one who has clearly caught your interest."

With an off-hand laugh, he said, "If you mean Brienne, do not conjecture anything by the fact that I retrieved her from the country. It was as a favor for her grandmother."

"Then, you are a beef-head. She is lovely even with mud and dirt on her face." He took the glass Evan handed him. "I assumed because she is living in my house that you brought her here."

"I did. She and her grandmother were made homeless after a fire, so I offered to let them stay here until they could find another place to live."

"Are you endeavoring to be granted sainthood?" Porter laughed again, this time more heartily. "A change in occupation for you, isn't it?"

"I was getting bored with my old one." Sitting again, Evan listened as his friend spoke about his own journey from the country. He replied when Porter seemed to expect him to, but his thoughts were on Brienne.

He *was* a beef-head. Porter was right about that. If Brienne could catch Porter's attention when she was as dirty as a fusty lugs sitting near the gutter, she would garner the gaze of every man in the Polite World when her hair was not hanging limply by her muddy face. Bringing her back to London might have been a mistake. But where else could she go? She was no longer safe with Teatro Caparelli. Going to Château Tonnere du Grêlon was out of the question, for she would be walking into a war.

You could have sent her to your family. He silenced that thought with a curse. He would rather send her into Napoleon's war than inflict his family's battles on her.

"Ah, how stunning you look," Porter said, drawing Evan's gaze to the door.

Evan came to his feet as he delighted in the sight of Brienne standing in the doorway. Her ebony hair was damp, so wiry curls dropped out of her chignon to edge her face. She must have scrubbed her face hard, because her cheeks were a luscious pink. In her simple gown, she was more beautiful than any befeathered and jeweled lady of the *ton*.

Going to the door, he offered his arm. He smiled as he offered the other one to Madame LeClerc. "You must admit, Porter, that I am a fortunate man to have two such wondrous ladies upon my arms."

"The luckiest man in London, I would aver." Porter bowed his head toward them.

"Miss Woods shall be down shortly, Mr. Porter," Madame LeClerc said.

"You do not need to feel obligated to deliver messages," he replied. "You are my friend's guests. Therefore, you are my guests."

Brienne smiled when her grandmother did. Grand-mère had been fearful that Mr. Porter would ask them to take their leave. In fact, Grand-mère had spoken of little else. Brienne had understood why when a maid came out of the dressing room to help her change. Grand-mère had wanted no one else in the house to have an inkling of the truth of where Brienne had been and why.

Did that mean that the tale Evan had told her was the truth? She wished she knew, but that conversation would have to wait until they endured this polite one.

While Evan sat her and her grandmother on a lush settee, Mr. Porter rang for tea for them. Mr. Porter returned to his chair and began prattling with Grand-mère as if they had known each other for years. Grand-mère told entertaining tales of their life at L'Enfant de la Patrie, never hinting that any other sort of life should have been Brienne's, not even pausing when the tea tray was brought.

Brienne glanced at Evan, who wore an innocuous expression. When his gaze met hers, she saw his amusement with Grand-mère's deft handling of Mr. Porter's questions. She noticed wariness in his eyes as well. Although Mr. Porter was his friend, she guessed Evan did not trust him completely. She wondered if he trusted anyone.

Or if she did any longer. That lesson he had taught her well . . . as he had taught her to fall in love with him.

Out of sight of the others, she slipped her hand over his. Again he glanced at her. The amusement had vanished, replaced by the glow of fierce desire that set her heart beating against her chest like a bird on a window.

He drew his hand out of hers as he stood when Miss Woods came to the door. Brienne could not keep from staring, for Miss Woods looked even more elegant in her tea gown of cream bedecked with gold lace. Her cap accented her hair that was nearly the same shade as the lace. When she smiled, the room seemed to get brighter.

"Oh, I am so pleased that you did not wait for me." She took the cup that Grand-mère held out to her. "Thank you, Mrs. LeClerc." She dimpled. "I would prefer, as I guess you would, to say *merci*. My English is very poor, so I hope you will not make note of it." She ran her hand along Mr. Porter's shoulder as she chose a chair next to him. "Armistead wishes me to use only English, so I will learn to speak it with more skill."

"So you are the one who has brought the French style into this house," Grand-mère said. "The touches of the decorating as well as some of the excellent dishes I have sampled have had a definitive Gallic touch." She smiled. "Although yours remain superior, Brienne. I wish you would speak with the cook about the amount of basil she uses."

"And the garlic," added Miss Woods. "It is supposed to enhance instead of hide the flavors. These English!"

Seeing both their host and Evan frowning, Brienne wanted to ask what was amiss. She had no chance. Miss Woods monopolized the conversation with her light-hearted comments about everything and everyone connected with the Polite World. She claimed not to know the English language well, but she clearly had learned enough to heed all the gossip. Louisa Woods had, Brienne discovered quickly, very definite opinions on whom one must defer to and who put on silly airs. London, in Miss Woods's estimation, was a barely tolerable place to live, but it was necessary if she wanted to enjoy the entertainments of the Season.

Mr. Porter said, with a gentle chuckle, "Louisa, you shall wear our ears out with your prattle. Please allow one of the rest of us to make a comment."

She pouted, then gave him a glorious smile. "Of course, Armistead. I want to know all about your guests, so that we can become friends. Tell me, Armistead, how you met Mr. Somerset."

"Evan and I met when I arranged for him to purchase some pieces of art for me." He turned to Evan. "You and St. Clair did great work then, persuading folks to sell work that they had not planned to part with. Is St. Clair still smuggling art from the Continent?"

Brienne expected her grandmother to be shocked at the question, but Grand-mère smiled, her eyes twinkling as brightly as Evan's when he teased her. Grand-mère must have known about this. She wondered how much Evan had told her grandmother on the night he chased after her. Not the complete truth, she guessed, for he now wore that grin that suggested he was keeping the most important secrets to himself.

Evan chuckled and poured more brandy into his glass. "Last I heard, he was reputed to be working for Napoleon in the blockade off the English coast. I am afraid both of us have become quite legitimate."

"That must have been a surprise for quite a few people," his friend returned dryly.

"No one could be more amazed than Dominic and me." He started to add more, then paused when Grand-mère yawned. "Madame LeClerc, I fear we are keeping you from your rest. I know you probably spent last night pacing your room, wondering if today would be the day that your granddaughter arrived.''

''That is true,'' Grand-mère said. ''I know you told me it would take more than a week for your journey, but I admit to being anxious every minute until my dear Brienne was returned to me.'' She gave him a grateful smile.

Brienne did the same. Mr. Porter's household would be quick to reveal to their host how Brienne had taken off and Evan had followed her. Evan's skillful bending of the truth would cover any mistakes she or Grand-mère might make while they were here.

''Forgive us,'' Porter said, setting himself on his feet, ''for delaying you from your rest. My surprise at discovering Evan here has persuaded me to set aside my manners, I fear.''

''Nonsense,'' Grand-mère replied with a smile. ''I am sorry to disrupt your conversation.''

When Evan drew Grand-mère to her feet, then held out his hand to Brienne, she wondered how long they would remain in this grand house on Grosvenor Square. It might be better if she and her grandmother disappeared into the *émigré* community closer to Soho. She must speak with both of them about this right away.

Her plans were dashed when Grand-mère said, as they climbed the stairs to the upper floor, ''Good night and thank you, Evan.''

''For rescuing you from that gabble-grinder?'' He laughed. ''I never thought Porter would attach himself to a prattler. You are most welcome, Madame LeClerc, for, to admit the truth, I was hoping to spare my ears as well as yours.''

''Grand-mère—''

Patting Brienne's hand, she interrupted with, ''Tomorrow, child. I know you have many questions, but Evan is right. I am exhausted from pacing the nights away in anticipation of your homecoming.''

"I am so sorry, Grand-mère," Brienne said. "When you hear what kept us from returning posthaste, you will understand.''

"I hope so." She wore the stern expression that Brienne had seen so seldom. "However, that must wait for the morrow. My mind is paralyzed with fatigue. After a good night's sleep, I will be looking forward to hearing why you were so addlepated, child." She put her hand on Evan's arm as they paused by her door. "Thank you again for bringing my strong-willed granddaughter to me.''

"My pleasure, madame." His smile lasted while Grand-mère kissed Brienne good night and went into her room. It disappeared as soon as her door closed. In a taut whisper, he said, "Brienne, I have a few things I need to say to you that cannot wait for the morrow.''

"I guessed that.''

Leading her to the room she had used when she last was in this grand house, he said, "I had no idea that Porter would be here now.''

"I guessed that, too." She glanced behind them and, seeing no one, asked, "Do you want me and Grand-mère to leave?''

"No!" He chuckled at his own vehemence that narrowed her eyes. "For many reasons, honey, but the most important one other than I want you here with me is that I want to keep my eye on you. Lagrille's men may have followed us back to London. We cannot be certain of anything until they reveal themselves.''

Brienne shivered as she opened her door. She drew him into her sitting room. Closing the door, she leaned back against it.

"You shall ruin your reputation with these antics," Evan said as he faced her. He picked up a book from a table and thumbed through it, but she did not believe his nonchalance. Through his sleeve, she had felt the muscles that were tightly coiled, waiting to spring out in any direction at the first sign of trouble.

"My reputation is pretty much in tatters now," she replied.

"No one knows that but you and me." He gave her a smile. "I do like to keep some things secret."

"You keep too much secret." She sat in a chair by the window. "I am not as worried about my reputation as I am about my grandmother. Can we trust Mr. Porter?"

"He has been my friend for several years."

"Mayhap I should ask that differently." She dampened her arid lips. "Can *I* trust him?"

He closed the book and set it on the table. "One of these days, Brienne, you are going to learn that your allies and mine are the same."

"You were the one who told me I was too trusting."

"Why do you only heed me when you can toss my words back into my face at the worst possible time?"

She knew she had hurt him with her comment, but she could not be too careful. She wanted to trust him. With every bit of her being, she wanted to trust him, but the wariness she had seen in his eyes downstairs warned her more than his words of the danger surrounding them. "I would do anything to protect Grand-mère."

"As I would."

"Would you? Really?"

Sadness dimmed his eyes. "I cannot convince you to take me at my word, and I hope I never have to prove that to you."

"I hope not either." She hesitated, then asked, "What of Miss Woods? I fear we intruded upon what was to be a tryst here this evening."

"You are learning, honey."

"Don't forget that I often saw gentlemen and their latest conquests at L'Enfant de la Patrie."

"I am sure you did. You were far enough from Mayfair to keep a chap from fearing his wife would discover him with his incognita, but still close enough to be an easy drive." His smile returned. "I suspect Miss Woods was not happy about our interruption of her plans with Porter or to discover you are sleeping here in what was her room."

"I thought she was Mr. Porter's mistress."

"In spite of what you have seen, you still have a lot to learn about the Polite World, honey. A young woman who does not negotiate for her own private rooms as part of her agreement to become a man's mistress has little hope of obtaining a grand settlement when the time comes for him to replace her."

"You know so much about the *ton* that one would suspect you are a part of it."

He laughed. "On occasion as the need arose." Drawing her into his arms, he murmured as he caressed her neck with swift kisses, "But there are many of their ways that I never took as my own."

"Such as going from one mistress to the next?"

"Why are you asking such questions when I could be holding you in that bed?"

"After you bathe." She drew back and tapped the front of his filthy waistcoat. "You are abominable, Mr. Somerset."

"And you are stubborn, Miss LeClerc." His fingers sifted through her hair, letting it fall around them. "And so enticing that I will obey your command . . . if you will scrub my back for me."

"You might be able to persuade me." Her nose wrinkled. "Although the water should be chilly by now."

"Then, I shall let your touch warm it up as you warm me."

As she took his hand and crossed the hall to his room, she thought only of the joy of being in his arms, delighting in the touch that drove her to the apex of ecstasy. It was hours later, as he slept, his cheek against her breast, and she stared up at the design on the wooden canopy over them, that she realized how he had changed the subject when she probed too closely to his past.

He was hiding something that was buried so deeply she could not guess what it might be. She shuddered as she imagined what might cause it to emerge and hoped that moment would not doom them all.

Chapter Fifteen

The tap of rain against the window was the only other sound as Brienne entered her grandmother's room. It was as ornate as her room, only decorated in subdued red and blues, giving it a more masculine aura. The furniture was heavy, like the chairs in the book-room downstairs. She wondered why her grandmother had chosen it, then decided mayhap Grand-mère liked the solid sensation of this furniture after their lives had been twisted inside out.

Lamps kept the dreary day at bay, creating pools of light on the dark rug. It was cozy, in spite of its elegance and the high ceiling. Going to where her grandmother was reading the morning newspaper by a brass lamp, Brienne bent and kissed her on the cheek, keeping her hands behind her back.

Grand-mère patted her cheek. "Child, it is so good to see you here and safe."

"I am sorry I frightened you by leaving as I did. Maman wished for me to go without delay, and I promised I would." She hesitated, then sat on the floor beside her grandmother, resting her head against Grand-mère's knee as she had done when she was a little girl. "Forgive me, Grand-mère."

"I only want you to promise me not to be so foolish again."

"I promise." She hoped it was a vow she could keep. Setting the dirty bag on her lap, she opened it carefully and took out the wooden box. She had checked inside the box before coming to her grandmother's rooms. The vase was chipped near the base, but it was still in one piece. "Grand-mère, would you keep this box in a safe place for me?"

"A safe place?"

"A place where no one will find it."

"What is in the box, child?"

"The miniature of my father." She looked down at her hands, not wanting to let her grandmother know that she was not being totally honest. The miniature *was* inside, but that was not why she wanted to conceal this box. She wished she did not have to ask Grand-mère, but she could not involve Evan. He seemed to have accepted that the vase had been destroyed, and she did not want to resurrect any questions in his mind. "I took the miniature with me when we fled the apartment over L'Enfant de la Patrie. The frame is broken, but the picture has not been harmed. I do not want to lose it. It is all I have of him."

Folding the newspaper, her grandmother put it beside her on the chair. She took the box and set it on the table beside her before cupping Brienne's chin. "You know that is not exactly true, child. You have a legacy from him that is far more than a single portrait."

"So, Grand-mère, what Evan told me is true?"

She lowered her voice, even though they were speaking in French, which none of the servants should understand, but Brienne knew her grandmother wanted to be cautious when she said, "If he told you that you are the daughter of a *duc*, it is true."

"And the estate?"

"Is yours if your older brother is, indeed, dead as your mother—as Lucile and I believed."

Putting her hand on her grandmother's knee, she said, "You are my *grand-mère*, and Maman was my *maman*. Nothing can change that."

"You are a dear child, but you know, as I do, that when you claim your heritage, nothing will be the same."

"If I do not—"

"You will negate all that Lucile and I have done for you." She brushed Brienne's cheek with quivering fingers. "Child, we would have returned to France years ago if we had not known that you were in danger from those who would like to claim what was your father's." She sighed. "How I have longed for the sound of the Loire passing beneath my window! The Thames is loud and dirty. The Loire is as pretty as a poem."

"I never guessed what you sacrificed for me."

"It was worth it to see you grow up so I can see both the *duc* and the *duchesse* in you." She sighed again. "I should have told you years ago, but first you were too young, then that dirty Corsican claimed France for his own and began to make war on his neighbors." A smile played with her lips. "Brienne. That is something else I kept from you."

"My name is not really Brienne?"

"Yes, it is Brienne, but I never told you that you were named for the military school both your father and Napoleon attended. Your grandfather, the old *duc*, insisted on your father receiving a stringent education, despite the rank that was his from his birth." She laughed. "No one gainsaid the old *duc*. He was as stubborn as you are."

Looking past her grandmother to the box, she whis-

pered, "Still I ask that you hide this box. I do not want
to chance losing Papa's picture."

"You may be right." Grand-mère stood and carried
the box into the other room with Brienne following. Opening the armoire that faced her bed, she lifted out all the
blankets stored in a lower drawer. She set the box inside
and replaced the blankets. "It should be safe here, child.
The weather is growing warmer each day, so there will
be no need of extra blankets."

"Thank you."

"You can thank me by telling me the truth."

"About what?"

"You and Evan Somerset."

She did not hesitate. Grand-mère would know if she
was lying about this. "I believe I am in love with him,
Grand-mère."

"I was afraid of that." She sat on a petit-point stool
at the foot of the bed. "He has more than his share of
charm, and I feared that he would use it upon you."

"But you sent him to find me."

"Yes, but I might have chosen another if I had had
any other choice." She took Brienne's hands. "Child, do
not mistake my words. I like Evan very much. He honored
his promise to return you to me when he had no reason
to take upon the obligation of finding you. He gave us a
roof when we had none."

"But?"

"You are the daughter of a *duc*. It would not be right
for you to marry a man who has made his living smuggling
art from the châteaux of your neighbors so it could deco-
rate some English country house." Coming to her feet,
she wrung her hands in her gown as if she were wearing
the apron she always had used in the kitchen of L'Enfant
de la Patrie. "You never showed any interest in the lads
who were intrigued with you, so I held my tongue. But
now I can no longer do that."

"Grand-mère—"

"I will accept no arguments about this, child. When you were given into our care, I vowed that I would see you regain what was rightfully yours and make your father proud." Her gaze grew distant. "Lucile readily agreed, for, witless fool that she was, she was madly in love with your father."

"He and she were lovers?"

"Of course not!" Grand-mère scowled. "She was my daughter, but I knew for many years that she was weak-minded and lost in her own fantasies. When your father spoke a kind greeting to her, as he did to all the servants, she mistook that for a flirtation. She believed until her final breath that he loved her."

"She told me that often."

" 'Twas her love for him that enabled her to love you, even though you were the *duchesse's* child." She straightened her shoulders. "Now you can understand why you must put an end to this *affaire de coeur* between you and Evan. When we can return to France to claim Château Tonnere du Grêlon, you must be prepared to marry a man who will be the proper father of your father's heir, for now, in the wake of the guillotine's vengeance, there is no one left alive to claim it."

"But I believe I love Evan."

"I know, child, but that is the tragedy of your birth. To those who are given so much, so many sacrifices must be asked for in return." She patted Brienne's cheek. "Child, think well about this, for you cannot deny what you are much longer. Soon you shall be telling everyone that you are, in truth, Brienne Levesque, daughter of the *Duc* of the Château Tonnere du Grêlon. So long I have waited for the day. I hope it is everything I have prayed it will be."

"I hope so, too," Brienne said, because she did not want to distress her grandmother. She had not considered that making her grandmother's dreams come true might put an end to hers.

In the rain, a lone person hurried across the grass in the middle of the square to run inside a house on its south side. Even when the door had closed behind the man, Brienne did not turn from the window. She was not accustomed to having her hands idle. At L'Enfant de la Patrie, she always was busy preparing the evening's meal and cleaning and chatting with Grand-mère and Maman. She had shopped and cooked while with the Teatro Caparelli as well as helping with the performance twice a day.

Now she had nothing to do.

This was the life Grand-mère wished for her. A life where servants waited upon her every wish, and she had to do no more than give them orders and entertain her callers.

"I shall go crazy," she muttered as she watched a raindrop slip along the window before vanishing amid dozens more as the wind struck the glass.

"Is something amiss?"

Whirling, Brienne saw Mr. Porter in the doorway. She gave a strained laugh as he entered the dusky room. "I did not realize anyone was nearby."

"Talking to one's self is not a crime." He lit several more lamps and gave her a sympathetic smile. "That you are alone when you are so obviously distressed is a crime, however."

"I did not realize it was that obvious." She stepped away from the window when he motioned for her to sit on one of the chairs nearer the hearth. His manners suggested she was, without question, the fine lady that Grand-mère claimed her to be.

Sitting, she folded her hands in her lap. He took a chair

facing her, his dark coat falling back to reveal the merry color of his red-striped vest.

"Mayhap I spoke out of hand," he said, "but I believed I heard a large sigh from you as I passed the door."

"To admit the truth, I find it odd to have so much time and so little to do, Mr. Porter."

"Please call me Armistead, Miss LeClerc."

"If you will address me as Brienne."

He dipped his head toward her. "I would be honored to do so." His brows lowered as he pyramided his fingers before him. "I do not like to have my guests suffering from ennui. How may I relieve this for you?"

"I am afraid short of allowing me to take over your kitchen, which I can assure you that your cook would not welcome, I fear there is nothing."

"You cook, Brienne?"

"I prepared all the meals at L'Enfant de la Patrie."

He leaned forward and smiled. "You are *that* Miss LeClerc? I have heard wondrous things about the fare available at your salon."

"It is available no longer, I am afraid." Brienne quickly explained how the building had burned, but took care to give no hint that the fire had been set. "If it had not been for Evan, I am afraid we might not have escaped as we did."

"Such a tragedy that you lost everything."

"I have my grandmother with me still."

He shook his head with a sad smile. "I would be lamenting very hard if such a thing had happened to me. I enjoy my house and all it contains."

"Our house did not contain treasures as this one does." She rose and went to look at one of the paintings on the wall. "I know very little about art, but this is a lovely picture. It looks as if the river could flow right past the frame and into my hands. The flowers are so realistic that I believe if I tried hard enough, I could smell their fragrance.''

"That is one of my favorites, too. It is of the Loire region of France.''

"The Loire?'' Her voice squeaked on the two words.

"Does that disturb you, Brienne?''

Turning, she forced a smile. Grand-mère had impressed on her that the secret of Brienne's past must be guarded with as much care now as it had been since they had come to London. Now, barely an hour later, Brienne risked revealing the truth by a silly reaction to nothing.

"Just surprised that you would have a picture of something French in your parlor.''

Armistead chuckled. "I do not tell everyone who admires the painting the truth, because I know that the hatred for Napoleon runs deeply here in London. However, as you are an *émigré*—''

"Did my grandmother tell you that?''

"You usually call her Grand-mère, which is what made me assume you were born in France. Certainly you speak English without a hint of an accent, so have I made an error in my assumption?''

"No.'' She was being foolish to jump on every word he spoke. How had Grand-mère and Maman succeeded in keeping even Brienne from suspecting the truth all these years? "I was simply curious.''

"As you are about why the painting is here. It is here because I think it well done. Do you recognize the spot where it was painted?''

"I recall nothing of France. I was not much more than a baby when I came to London.'' Brienne knew she had to change the subject which was veering too close to the secret of her past.

She was saved from making some inane comment when Miss Woods rushed into the room. The young woman's smile broadened when she glanced at Brienne, but she hurried to Armistead's side.

"Look what was just delivered for you," she said, excitement in every word. "An invitation to Lady Jacington's assembly." Looking at Brienne, she added, "Lady Jacington is one of the premier hostesses of the London Season. An invitation to her soirée is as hoped for as one to Almack's." She gripped Armistead's arm. "And you have been invited."

He unfolded the paper and smiled. "It appears you are quite correct, Louisa."

"Shall we go?"

"It is the same evening that you promised to join Mrs. Townsend for cards and conversation. You know how excited she is to have you join her. She has been so pleased with your progress with your English lessons." He looked past Miss Woods to Brienne. "Do you have plans for Monday next, Brienne?"

"No, but I cannot go to such an assembly."

"Why not?" he asked.

"I have nothing to wear, and I am in mourning for my mother."

Miss Woods grasped Brienne's hands. "I am sure I can find you something to wear that will be in keeping with your mourning, but will allow you to attend."

"Otherwise I must send our regrets to Lady Jacington," Armistead added.

"Our regrets?" Brienne asked.

"I would be a most unworthy host to leave my guests to attend an assembly without them."

"Oh," moaned Miss Woods, "that would be unspeakable. You have waited for this invitation for more than two years, Armistead."

Brienne sighed. "Let me discuss this with my grandmother. If she is willing to let me set aside my mourning for that one night, I shall join you, Armistead." She smiled weakly. "I want you to know I appreciate you asking me to go to this assembly."

"I hope you will be able to attend." He gave her an answering smile. "I can assure you that it will be a night unlike any other you have ever experienced."

As Miss Woods began to prattle about all the guests and who would be there and who would be snubbed by not being invited, Brienne could not ignore the pulse of excitement racing through her at the idea of attending one of the soirées she had heard discussed at L'Enfant de la Patrie. She hoped Grand-mère would agree for her to go.

Evan shook water out of his hair as he entered the house. In spite of the rain, today had been a good one. He had woken at dawn to savor Brienne's beguiling kisses before he had left the house on errands that had already been postponed for too long.

His pocket was now lighter a few guineas, but he had the information he needed. The men who had attacked Brienne at L'Enfant de la Patrie were no longer in London. Whether they had sailed or simply left London for another part of England or had been murdered down by the docks did not matter to him. They were not here to cause more trouble for her.

Finding out about Lagrille and his men had been less productive. Several men in the taverns where he had bought enough ale to loosen everyone's tongues had been approached as Evan had to do some work for this Frenchman, but no one knew who he was.

Evan handed Hitchcock his drenched overcoat and hat, ignoring the butler's disgusted frown. It was the same whether Evan arrived at the door in sunshine or amidst a storm. The butler was not as annoyed at the wet clothes as he was by the fact that Evan was still welcomed here.

"Where is Miss LeClerc?" Evan asked as he glanced toward the stairs.

"She is with Mr. Porter and her grandmother in the small parlor, sir." The first and last words were spoken reluctantly.

Chuckling to himself as he went up the stairs, he wondered how Hitchcock would change his ways if he knew that Brienne could claim the title of *duchesse*. The butler would endeavor to endear himself to her by groveling to make up for this cool arrogance.

A slender form burst out of a doorway, bumping into him. For a moment, a pulse of anticipation rushed through him, but then he realized he was steadying Miss Woods, not Brienne.

"Pardon me," he said as he drew his hands back. "I was lost in my thoughts, and I did not watch where I was going."

Patting her brown curls back into place, she smiled. "I must plead guilty to the same, Mr. Somerset. Pardon me." She looked down with dismay at the wet spots on her gown. "Oh, dear."

"I fear I brought some of the day's dampness into the house with me. I regret ruining your dress."

" 'Tis not ruined." She laughed again. "Water will quickly dry." She brushed at the spots, her fingers lingering along her bodice. Slowly she looked up at him with a seductive tilt to her lips.

Evan told himself he must be mistaken. Miss Woods was Porter's mistress. She would be a fool to entice another man while Porter was keeping her so well. Or did she know of her lover's plans to garner the favor of another lady? If that were so, then she might be looking for another man to become her protector.

"I am glad," he said. "If you will excuse me . . ."

"Must you go?" She edged closer to him, her hand sliding along the banister as her lips parted in an invitation to taste them. "Porter has told me so much about you, but I would like to get to know you better myself."

She was not subtle, that was for certain. Resisting the urge to laugh at her overt offer, he folded his arms in front of him and smiled. "I am afraid, Miss Woods, that you would find the telling of my life story boring."

"Not from what Armistead tells me." She slipped her hand onto his sleeve and stepped closer. Regarding him with wide, brown eyes, she whispered, "Did you really smuggle art right beneath the noses of the French and British officials?"

"That is all in the past."

"And what is in your future?" She glided her fingers along his arm toward his shoulder. "Do you intend to enjoy the prizes from your hard-won labors?"

Laughter came from the parlor. He stepped away from Miss Woods as the lilt of Brienne's laugh caressed his ears. Except when she was in his arms, he had heard that laugh too seldom. He wanted to hear it more, and he wanted her in his arms again so he could delight in her sweet touch.

Evan strode into the parlor with a cheery, "Good afternoon."

As Porter urged Miss Woods, who had followed Evan into the parlor, to pour their guest a cup of tea, Evan looked at Brienne with a smile. She lowered her eyes, not meeting his. Every instinct shouted that something was amiss with her, but why had she been laughing just moments ago?

The answer was simple. Whatever was amiss had to do with him. Something had happened since he had left her this morning. He could not ask what it was when Porter and his mistress as well as her grandmother would be privy to the conversation.

"Good afternoon, Madame LeClerc," he said as he accepted the cup of steaming tea from Miss Woods.

"You arrived just in time," Madame LeClerc said, delicately balancing her own tea. "Armistead was telling Brienne about all the people she would have a chance to meet at Lady Jacington's party."

"Party?" he asked, glancing at Brienne.

This time, she did not lower her eyes. "Armistead has been invited to this assembly, and he did not want to attend alone. Grand-mère thought it might be a good idea for me to accept his offer to go with him."

"Is that so?" He clenched his teeth to keep from spitting out the words he really wanted to say. Was Madame LeClerc out of her mind? Brienne should be avoiding any place where she would stand out as a target for Lagrille's men. Forcing his jaw to unclench, he smiled as he said, "I think we shall have a wondrous time."

He noticed a tic over Porter's left brow as their host said, "I believe you are right, Somerset. Louisa has offered Brienne one of her gowns. As the two of them are of a size, it should fit with few alterations." He lifted his hands and laughed. "That is something that concerns the ladies more than it does us. Madame LeClerc has offered to help with any work needed to have Brienne ready on Monday next."

"It seems you have it all planned," Evan replied, "so there is nothing for me to do but say thank you, Porter, for offering to act as a duenna for Brienne and me."

His smile stiffened. "Madame LeClerc has offered to play that rôle."

Evan laughed. "Then, I guess we shall all have an entertaining evening together."

Porter continued to smile, but his eyes fired daggers at Evan. Resisting the urge to laugh again, Evan wondered if his friend had honestly thought Evan would step aside to allow Porter to escort Brienne to this assembly.

He glanced at Miss Woods, who was oddly silent. No one had mentioned her attending. Did the young woman suspect that Porter had set his cap on another woman? That would certainly explain her actions in the hall, although he wondered if she knew the state of his empty pockets. His fingers tightened on the china saucer. Miss Woods had prattled about Porter telling her all about Evan's past.

All? He forced himself to relax. Porter did not know *all* about his past.

For as long as he was able, Evan endured the conversation about the soirée and who might be there. Then he set himself on his feet. Holding his hand out to Brienne, he asked, "Will you excuse us? I need to speak with Brienne alone."

Madame LeClerc cleared her throat and said, "Brienne needs to select her gown for the assembly, so that I may begin any alterations that are necessary."

"I shall have her back to you straightaway." He struggled to keep his smile in place. Madame LeClerc's voice had been as cold as an executioner's, and he had not missed how Brienne had flinched at her grandmother's tone. "Brienne?"

For a long moment, she did not move. She stared straight ahead; then slowly her fingers rose to settle on his palm. He closed his over them before she could change her mind. Bringing her to her feet, he mumbled something he hoped the others would take as a polite good afternoon. He did not want to be delayed from finding out what was wrong by some insipid prattle.

Evan led Brienne into Porter's book-room, which was even darker as rain ran in streams along the windows, and closed the door. When he saw her walking beside the shelves, running her fingers along the books he wondered if Porter had ever read, he knew he had not been wrong about something being amiss. If it had not been, she would not be putting space between them. Rather, she would be in his arms.

"They are gone," Evan said without preamble.

"They?" She faced him, but kept most of the length of the room between them. Even so, he could see how stiff her shoulders were. He wondered what burden had been placed on them now.

"The men who came to your salon to get that vase." His jaw tightened. "The ones I suspect set fire to L'Enfant de la Patrie."

"Oh." She gave him a small smile. "I guess that should be a relief."

"It might be a relief, if you were not acting as witless as a chucklehead."

"I am as surprised as you that Grand-mère wishes for me to go to Lady Jacington's party."

He was glad she had not dissembled. Crossing the room, he folded her hands in his before lifting them to his lips. The fire glowed within her eyes, sweeping away the dullness. They widened when he whispered, "So your grandmother is ready to fire you off into the *ton* and find you a proper husband for a *duchesse*."

"She is adamant that I must think only of my obligations." She drew her hands out of his. When he reached for them, she put her fingers up to his cheeks, startling him, for he had not expected her to gainsay her grandmother's wishes. He understood when she asked, "But how can I think only of my obligations when I wish only to think of you?"

With a moan, he pulled her into his arms. He tasted despair on her lips, a despair that had not been there even at the bleakest moments when they had escaped the fire or when they had fled from Marksen's smugglers. He did not want to believe that even more dismal times awaited them, but he knew she did. He should ask her if she would heed her grandmother's wishes to find a proper match, but he did not want to know the answer. He knew he would learn it all too soon.

Chapter Sixteen

Brienne was sure she had been swept into the tale of *The Golden Lion*. The painted backdrop on the Caparellis' stage was a poor imitation of the glorious gilt and paint decorating the ballroom. As she stood beneath the center arch of the trio opening onto the large room, she could not keep from staring at the crystal chandeliers.

"Can you imagine what the ballroom at Château Tonnere du Grêlon must be like?" Evan whispered as he lifted off her black silk cloak and handed it to a footman.

She straightened the ribbons on her sedate gown. It was a pearl gray, the most subdued frock among Louisa's vast wardrobe. She knew she appeared very somber compared to Evan's perfect evening wear with a black coat and white waistcoat over silver-colored breeches. "The château may have been abandoned for years. By now, it may be the home to nothing but birds and rodents."

He laughed. "Mayhap, but I prefer to think of it as glorious as your sweetest fantasy, just waiting there for you whenever you want to claim it."

Closing her eyes, she savored the gentle caress of his finger along her bared shoulder. "No wonder you enjoyed being on the stage. You live in a world where make-believe is real."

"*Au contraire*." He laughed when she regarded him with amazement. He continued in barely accented French, "You should know by now, Brienne, that a man who has made his living shifting artworks from France to England must be able to speak both languages with ease."

"Your accent betrays you as an Englishman."

"Ah, but when the situation required not making that fact known, I could depend on my partner to handle all the negotiations."

"Your partner Dominic St. Clair?"

"One and the same." He put his arm around her waist. "However, you should not speak his name too loudly here. Although many of these members of the Polite World have arranged for our services, they do not want to admit to that among their comrades."

"How marvelous!" Grand-mère smiled as she came to stand beside them, her expression telling Brienne that Grand-mère was recalling similar gatherings at Château Tonnere du Grêlon. "I have so often imagined you at such an assembly, Brienne." She adjusted the feather laced through Brienne's hair that had been curled to drop along her nape.

Evan laughed. "You are a doting watch-dog, Madame LeClerc."

Grand-mère gave him the same tense smile she had offered Evan since their return to London. "It is my duty, which I take very seriously."

"And she does it well." Armistead joined them. He scanned the room in front of them. "May I?" He held out his arm to Grand-mère.

Brienne watched in silence as Armistead led Grand-mère into the ballroom. His kindness was a contrast to

Grand-mère's growing coolness to Evan. Evan had not said anything more about it, although she guessed he must find it vexing. Not certain what to say to him, she smiled as a woman with hair as gray as Grand-mère's hurried over to them.

Jewels glittered on each of her fingers, around her neck, and at her ears. Her gown had as many flounces as a young miss's. Although she waved a fan that was twice as large as the one hooked to Brienne's wrist with lace, her round face glowed with perspiration.

"Good evening," she said. "I am Lady Jacington, your hostess."

Evan bowed and introduced himself and then Brienne before adding, "We were asked to join this assembly this evening by Armistead Porter, who is our host during our visit to London."

"Oh, Mr. Porter! He is such a witty man!" She gushed like a girl. "Is he here?"

"He is with my grandmother," Brienne said, glancing toward where Grand-mère was chattering with Armistead as steadily as Miss Woods had.

"I must go and greet them." Lady Jacington scurried away, clearly reveling in her position as hostess this evening.

"Shall we jump into the jumble of guests and see how we can amuse ourselves?" Evan asked.

As she put her hand on his arm, she said, "Of course."

"I thought you might rather find a corner where we can be alone and discover very special ways to amuse each other."

She could not mistake his words' meaning when he smiled with the yearning that surged within her. Hoping her voice remained steady as she walked with him into the crowded ballroom, she said, "I doubt if Lady Jacington would appreciate us ignoring her efforts as a hostess."

"A hostess's duty is to make sure each guest has what

he or she wishes.'' He whispered against her ear, ''And you know well what I wish, honey.''

''By Jove, Somerset!'' called a man before she could answer. ''I did not expect to see you here.''

Brienne backed away as a man grasped Evan's hand and shook it with enthusiasm. The man's hair was as dark as hers, and she noted the undeniable hint of a French accent on his English. She had not guessed that another *émigré* had found a welcome among the English *élite*. His clothes were of the most elegant cut, and she saw a flash of gold on the hand that gripped Evan's. This man's experiences since he fled France had clearly been different from her own.

''Devereux, you old rooster!'' Evan chuckled. ''I thought you were in America.''

''Not a comfortable place to be when everyone is clamoring for war. I decided to hie it back to England where I, at least, know my enemies.''

Evan laughed again, then turned to Brienne. ''Brienne, this is an old friend. Louis Devereux. Devereux, a new friend of mine, Brienne LeClerc.''

Mr. Devereux took her hand and bowed over it with a grace that suggested he had learned his courtly manners in the corridors of Versailles. ''Somerset, I would be remiss not to note that your taste in friends has improved decidedly. Miss LeClerc, it is indeed a pleasure.'' Without a pause, he added, ''So what are you doing here, Somerset? I had heard from someone that you had accepted some commission that had taken you away from Town.''

''I chose instead to let Porter play host to me while I was here.'' Evan's tone suggested that there had been no reason for his choice more important than which cravat he would wear tonight.

''Porter is here?'' His nose wrinkled. ''I have avoided him since he served as a second in that tragic duel between Lord—''

"I recall you telling me that you never wanted to talk about that." Evan chuckled.

"You are quite right, for why would I speak of that when I could be eloquent in my admiration of Miss LeClerc?"

Brienne smiled and replied in French, "I suspect, Monsieur Devereux, that you would prove to be eloquent on almost any subject."

"She has seen through your façade with ease," Evan said in English as he took a glass of wine from a passing tray and handed it to Brienne. "I should have warned you. Brienne has no use for flummery."

"Then, how can she tolerate you?" Mr. Devereux laughed. "Ah, even where the mind is serious, the heart can be won by frivolity."

Evan grimaced. "You may be living here now, but you still have a Gallic delight in chivalry."

"Miss LeClerc understands, don't you?"

"I am afraid I have become quite the prosaic English-woman," Brienne replied with a smile. "My grandmother laments about that quite regularly."

Mr. Devereux chuckled. "It is difficult not to assume the ways of our adopted homeland. I have come to appreciate the fine entertainments always awaiting one in London." He bowed again toward Brienne. "I trust I will see you again before the evening is over. Somerset, you have done yourself proud this time."

Evan grinned wryly as his friend vanished into the crowd. "So you have met another of my friends."

"You seem to have all types."

"I meet many different people in my work." Around his finger, he looped one of the curls hanging along her neck. "Some of them are much more special than any of the others."

"Some?" She gave him a sly smile. "I did hear Mr. Devereux say you have done yourself proud *this* time."

"Egad, Brienne, are you going to demand that I humiliate myself among this gathering by wooing you with nothing-sayings?" He drew the curl toward him, and she leaned closer. "When you know so well that there has never been anyone quite like you in my life?"

"And no one like you in mine," she whispered.

"I am glad." He ran his finger along her lips. "I am quite sure that you have not stopped smiling since we arrived."

"This is fun!"

"This?" He looked around the ballroom where more and more people were trying to squeeze into the room. Even a room as large as this one could not hold all the guests Lady Jacington had invited. "So you enjoy prattling about nothing?"

She slapped his arm lightly. "You shall not change my mind about this evening with your dreary attitude. I have long been curious about the lives of those who patronized L'Enfant de la Patrie."

His hands framed her face. "And I have long been curious about the flavor of your lips."

"Long curious?" Her laugh was soft. "I believe I recall a very delicious kiss before we left Grosvenor Square."

"That seems an eternity ago when I hunger for another."

As his mouth found hers, she delighted in the pleasures that refused to be forgotten. So easily she could recreate the sight of his head pressed close to her as his mouth explored her body. Her memory's ear could detect the rasp of his laugh as she found paradise in his arms. She yearned for his body against hers, propelling her into the ecstasy which had been agonizingly exquisite.

"Brienne!"

Pulling herself out of Evan's arms took every bit of her willpower when there was no place she would rather be. She faced her grandmother, who wore a disapproving frown.

Grand-mère said nothing, but she did not need to as she continued across the ballroom. She took her place among the other dowagers, nodding to them as if she were the hostess of this gathering. Grand-mère could not hide how much she missed the elegance of the life she had known in France. Even as a servant, she had been the witness to countless balls and gatherings.

Brienne sighed. "This change of heart she has had about you is going to be troublesome."

"An understatement if I ever heard one." Evan brushed the back of his fingers against her face; then his face hardened as he looked past her. "Will you excuse me? I see someone I must speak with."

"Is something else wrong, Evan?"

"No, just some business that remains uncompleted."

"Lagrille—"

"Do not speak his name here." Again he touched her face lightly. "This is other business, honey, from before you got your life entangled with mine."

"I like being entangled with you."

His eyes sparkled as he kissed her finger, then pressed it to her lips. "Keep that thought, honey. We need not stay late at this assembly tonight." Again he looked past her. "I have to go."

She nodded. "Go and hurry back."

"While I am speaking with—while I am gone, sit with your grandmother. You should not be alone." He gave her a wry grin when she gasped. "Don't look dismayed. I meant only that you should not be unescorted here. A young woman who wanders about alone gives the suggestion to men with indecent thoughts upon their minds that she would be willing to partake of their favors."

"Go!" She gave him a gentle shove. "I have been

watching over myself since Grand-mère trusted me out of the salon on my own. I believe I can walk across a ballroom without getting into trouble.''

"We shall see. I suspect there are more than a few so-called gentlemen here who would like to prove you wrong."

"You worry like an old tough."

With a laugh, he winked and walked away in pursuit of whomever he sought to find.

Brienne laughed quietly as she went in the opposite direction. No matter where they were or what they were doing, Evan found a way to make the situation amusing. She wondered what sort of disaster would make him lose his sense of humor that had saved them so many times from despair.

The ballroom surely was even more chock-full than before. Amid what seemed to be every soul in the Polite World, she found the crowd smothering. She bumped into one person, then another as she tried to make her way toward her grandmother. Bits of conversation chased her. As they had at L'Enfant de la Patrie, the guests here shared gossip about others in the *ton*. She heard a few comments about the progress of the English forces against Napoleon, but clearly this gathering was more concerned with discussing the latest in fashion than the situation on the Spanish Peninsula.

Brienne tried to squeeze past two women who were enthusiastically discussing someone who seemed to have made a horrible *faux pas*. So intent were they on heaping blame on that poor soul whom they did not name that they ignored her requests to excuse her and allow her to pass. After saying, "Pardon me" for a third time, she gave up and edged to her right.

"Pardon me," she said yet again when she bumped into a man.

"Pardon *me*," he replied. He brushed at his sleeve

where something had splattered. "I trust I did not spill any wine on you."

"No, I am fine." She flashed a quick smile at him as she looked to where her grandmother seemed to be separated from her by a vast moat of humanity.

"Ah, here you are." Lady Jacington somehow maneuvered through the press of her guests with a skill Brienne doubted she could ever emulate. "I was wondering where you were, Miss LeClerc." She put her hand on the arm of the man Brienne had bumped into. "Have you been introduced to Miss LeClerc, my lord?"

"I do not believe I have met Miss LeClerc before." He bowed over her hand.

"It is a pleasure to meet you, my lord." Not wanting to stare, she could not halt herself as he straightened to smile down at her. She was certain she had met him before. Mayhap at L'Enfant de la Patrie, although she could not ask him. There was something unquestioningly familiar about his sparkling eyes and the warm smile beneath his silver hair.

Lady Jacington twittered like a young girl. "My lord, Miss LeClerc knows barely a soul here tonight."

"Just fired-off, are you?"

Brienne hesitated, not sure how to answer that. She was not a miss looking for a husband among the eligible bachelors who had money and a title to keep her in style. None of the bachelors with a title and no funds would be interested in her because she was penniless.

"I am staying with friends in Town, having only recently arrived from the country," she answered, deciding on a facet of the truth. "Lady Jacington was kind enough to invite them to this soirée, and they were kind enough to ask me to join them."

"And are you enjoying yourself, Miss LeClerc?"

"Yes. Lady Jacington is a wonderful hostess."

She was awarded with a smile from the plump woman

as Lady Jacington said, "You can find no one better to speak with, Miss LeClerc, than the earl. He knows everyone in the Polite World."

"Mayhap I once did when I was as young as Miss LeClerc." He chuckled, and again she was struck by the sensation that she had heard this sound before. But where? "My erstwhile tie-mates now worry more about rents and harvests than which rout to attend or which club to join."

Music wove through the conversation, dimming it only a bit. Lady Jacington's smile broadened. "I thought the orchestra would wait until it was time to go into dinner before they began to play."

"I am certain," said the earl, "that you have the situation firmly in control, Lady Jacington. Only you could oversee such a gathering so early in the Season."

"You are too kind, my lord." She glanced at Brienne. "Where are your companions, Miss LeClerc?"

"Busy with other conversations. I thought to see how my grandmother was enjoying herself." She wished she knew of a way to excuse herself without appearing impolite, but she had no idea how.

"Bah!" the lady said. "You should not be sitting with the dowagers. She should not, should she, my lord?"

"I consider her anxiety about her grandmother's welfare most touching and admirable." He smiled, and she fought to remember where she had seen him smiling before.

"A young woman should be dancing." Lady Jacington's tone suggested that getting into a brangle with her on this topic would be a waste of breath. "Don't you believe that, too, my lord?"

The earl gave Brienne a sympathetic grin, and she guessed he found Lady Jacington as amusing and as vexing as she did. "I would be a leather-head to say otherwise."

"I have just the dandy!" Lady Jacington smiled as if

this idea had just occurred to her, although Brienne guessed she had pounced on Brienne and the earl with this very intention in mind. "My lord, your wife has not yet arrived in Town, and Miss LeClerc has so very recently come among us. What would be better than to have her first dance with a respected gentleman instead of one of the rakes that seem to prey on unsuspecting misses?"

Brienne had a suspicion that no one could be as calculating as Lady Jacington was right now. Again she yearned for a way to put an end to this, so she could hurry to Grand-mère's side. Her grandmother would enjoy a laugh about their hostess's very obvious intentions.

"May I?" the earl asked with a bow toward Brienne.

She glanced around the room. If Evan had returned, she did not know where he was. Putting her hand on the earl's arm, she said, "I would be honored."

"No, Miss LeClerc, the honor is mine." He led her to the dance floor, keeping her smiling with lively conversation that seemed intent on putting her at ease.

She smiled as they joined the lines of dancers for the quadrille. How she had loved to dance when Grand-mère taught her in the tiny rooms over the salon! Then she could not have imagined that she would dancing in this splendid house with an earl.

Brienne was certain she had fallen asleep and was dreaming of a fairy tale where she could be a part of the impossible. Yes, her father had been a *duc*, but her life had been L'Enfant de la Patrie. To be on an earl's arm must be a fantasy.

She delighted in every moment. While the earl introduced her to the dancers on either side of them in the line, the orchestra played the first notes of the quadrille. She feared her smile was growing too wide for her face as she curtsied to the earl and let herself get caught up in the intricate pattern of steps. It was far more complicated than the dances Grand-mère had taught her.

When the earl faltered partway through the second pattern, Brienne was startled. His steps had been as elegant as a dancing master's until now. "My lord, you should walk to the left and . . ." She saw him scowling at someone past her and looked over her shoulder to meet Evan's furious gaze.

She had been so caught up in the dance that she had not noticed Evan coming toward them. Why was he angry with her? She had not done anything to call attention to herself. The dance floor was crowded, and she and the earl were in the middle of the line.

Then she realized his gaze was riveted on the man beside her. Around them, the other dancers paused. The music continued on, but no one moved. Even the conversation from around the dance floor vanished as every eye watched her and the two men.

Evan bowed his head the merest bit. "Good evening, my lord."

"It was until now." The earl's voice was as frigid as Evan's gaze. "If you will step aside, the dance you have interrupted may continue."

"I shall." Holding out his hand to Brienne, he said, "We both shall step aside."

"Do you wish me to believe that Miss LeClerc is acquainted with you?"

"Quite well." His lips curled into a stiff smile. "Brienne?"

Not sure what was happening, but knowing that the polite words covered emotions that could easily explode, she placed her hand on Evan's. She must put an end to this without delay. Her attempt to smile was futile as she said, "Thank you, my lord, for asking me to stand up with you. I enjoyed the chance to dance."

"*Your* company was a pleasure, Miss LeClerc." The earl strode away.

"Evan?" she asked, not sure which question to pose first when so many pummeled her lips.

"Not here." He drew her hand within his arm and led her in the opposite direction.

Knowing that no one in the ballroom was looking anywhere save at her and Evan, Brienne stared straight ahead, pretending to be indifferent to the heads that bowed and the hiss of whispers as they passed. She thought Grandmère would rush after them, but when Evan led her into a small chamber near the stairs, they were alone.

He shut the door. "Brienne, how could you be so unthinking? You drew everyone's attention to you."

"Me? No one paid me any mind while I was dancing. 'Twas your interruption that created the hullabaloo."

With a curse, he slammed his fist against the door frame. She gasped. Never during all the crises she had weathered with him had she seen him in such a huff. He had controlled his emotions, releasing them only when he held her in his arms. What had unsettled him so now?

"You are right," he growled.

"I am?" She had not expected him to admit to that.

He snarled another oath. "I made an ass of myself and a spectacle of you."

Hearing a smidgen of amusement return to his voice, she frowned. There was nothing humorous about this. "That cannot be changed, but, mayhap you will explain why you spoke so rudely to the earl."

"The earl? Don't you know his name?"

"Lady Jacington never said."

He laughed icily. " 'Tis no surprise. The dowager viscountess has garnered a reputation for creating controversial situations and then watching everyone's reactions. That is why so many come to her assemblies. They know that something is bound to happen to entertain them. This chance meeting was something she simply could not resist exploiting for her guests' merriment."

"But you were contemptible to him."

"Because familiarity, they say, breeds contempt."

"You know him?" she asked, again startled. This was getting more and more confusing.

"Yes."

"For how long?"

"All my life." His lips straightened. "He is my father."

Chapter Seventeen

"Your father?" Brienne stared at Evan, sure she had misunderstood him. Then she knew she had not. No wonder the earl's smile and laugh had been familiar. They were his most obvious legacy to his son. She recalled the few comments Evan had made about his family. None of them had been complimentary, but the earl had been the epitome of graciousness to her.

"The Earl of Sommerton to be exact," Evan replied, each word bitten off as if it tasted horrible in his mouth.

"Evan," she whispered, putting her hand on his sleeve, "if your father is here, this is your chance to heal the wounds that fester between you."

"You want me to apologize to *him?*" His laugh was raw. "I have warned you before that you should not think that your family is like all others."

"But he is your father!"

"I am aware of that to my eternal regret." He drew her hand off his sleeve and folded it between his. "Do not interfere in what you so obviously cannot understand.

I have no need for a family." He gave another terse laugh. "Nor do I have a use for one. I have made my own life, and it has no place for them in it."

"That is absurd. You may need your family someday. What will you do then?"

"I don't know, but is it worth the cost of denying everything I hold within my soul?" With a scowl, he tapped the top of her fan. "Haven't you learned the truth, Brienne? Your grandmother has made it clear to me since our return to Grosvenor Square that I am not, in her opinion, the proper suitor for her granddaughter, the *duchesse* of Château Tonnere du Grêlon." His laugh was still strained. "Do you think she will change her mind when she learns that I am an earl's heir, or is an English heir still an improper suitor for her granddaughter?"

"You are his heir?" She had been certain she could not be more shocked, but she was. How many more secrets had he kept from her?

"Why so startled, Brienne? You have chided me often for being overly familiar with the ways of the *ton*. That is because I was once a part of the Polite World before I decided I would rather live my life as I saw fit instead of letting someone else dictate it for me. As you are allowing your grandmother and all your dead ancestors to dictate yours."

"Please do not be hateful. I want to help you and your father." She hesitated before asking, "What of your mother, Evan?"

"She offered the ultimatum that persuaded me to leave Sommerton Hall."

Brienne sank to the settee behind her. "I do not understand. To have both a mother and a father is something I used to wish for every night."

"This is not about fairy tales. We are not in a play where everything works out in the end."

Taking his hand, she said, "It could. If you wish, I would speak to your father and—"

"And I am telling you that there is nothing you can do. This is not one of your sauces, Brienne, where a pinch of some spice can save it." He opened the door and turned on his heel, firing over his shoulder, "I pity you that you are so caught up in your desire to fulfill your grandmother's dream of you claiming that dashed château that you fail to see that you are trading everything that is Brienne LeClerc for it."

Brienne stared after him as he stormed back to the ballroom. How could she argue with him when she had asked herself the same question?

Slowly she rose. She could not go to Lord Sommerton, for Evan would view that as a betrayal. That would only exacerbate the anger between father and son. Mayhap Grand-mère could help. Or mayhap she would not, for Grand-mère wanted Evan out of her granddaughter's life.

Waiting here would gain no one anything. Going to the door, Brienne blinked back tears as she heard a lighthearted melody from the orchestra. It was similar to the quadrille she had begun with Lord Sommerton.

She wiped a vagrant tear away and went to the closest arch opening into the ballroom. Many more people were now dancing, but the crowd had lessened. Few men remained, save for those who were dancing. She suspected the men had sought privacy in another room to enjoy brandy, cigars, and cards.

"Brienne, are you all right?" Armistead stepped around the arch. "You look distressed."

"Yes, thank you, I am fine." She told the lie easily as she looked toward the chairs the dowagers had made their own. "Where is Grand-mère?"

"I believe she was seeking Lady Jacington to discuss something with her. She looked in quite a pelter, so I did not get in her way."

Brienne suspected Grand-mère intended to ring their hostess a regular peal for putting Brienne into such a scandalous situation on her first night among the *ton*. How she wished Evan stood here now to point out what was amusing about the whole of this! How she wished she was in his arms!

"Did you see Evan in the ballroom?" she asked, although she guessed he had left the house to avoid encountering his father again.

"I have not seen him." He lowered his voice. "Brienne, I heard talk of an incident—"

She held up her hands. "Please say no more."

"You *are* distressed, Brienne. Would you like me to take you out on the terrace until you can compose yourself?"

"That might not be a bad idea." She glanced again into the ballroom. "But what of the lady you want to impress? Evan told me that you had a *tendre* for a young woman among the Polite World."

"She will wait." He offered his arm and drew her fingers within it. "No doubt, someone else will gladly keep her company when I cannot be by her side."

"Her heart is that fickle?"

"No, her heart is constant."

Brienne was baffled by his easy smile. He was not speaking of Louisa. These ways of the *ton* were something she never would understand. *Bourgeoisie*, her grandmother had called her in a scolding tone. Mayhap, but it had less to do with the ways of her class than the longings of her heart.

She wanted Evan to remain in her heart, but she feared his had no room for anything but hatred. In addition, she knew he had that unfinished business with Lagrille. Although he had not said anything since their arrival back in London about going into hiding, she knew it was only because he was not sure that she was safe from Lagrille's men.

Or did he linger because he shared her craving for what they experienced when they were alone and eager kisses swept away all thoughts of anything but pleasure? She wanted to believe that, but she could never be certain with Evan.

"Talking often lessens one's burdens," Armistead said, as he put his hand over hers on his arm.

"I have nothing to say." She glanced at him when she heard the strain in his voice. No sign of it was visible on his face.

"Then, you are a rare woman. Louisa is never without something to say. My ears suffer from her prattling."

"Then, why— It is none of my business."

"To speak of why I have not put Louisa out of my life?" He smiled. "You are right, but not because I mind you inquiring into such a private matter. Speaking of such things is not appropriate for me to do with a lady like you." He opened a door and ushered her out onto the small terrace that was edged by potted shrubs.

She was sure she saw someone moving over by the bushes. She wished Armistead would walk in the other direction. Being set upon by some vagrant would make this whole evening a complete disaster.

Before she could suggest returning to the ballroom, she heard, "Ah, here you are, child."

Grand-mère bustled out of the door and over to them. "Come back into the ballroom before you catch your death of cold. Spring has been battered back by this wintry chill tonight."

Brienne had not noticed if the night was warm or cold, but she nodded. "Mayhap we should bid our hostess a good evening."

"An excellent idea." She turned to Armistead. "Lady

Jacington has offered us a carriage to return to Grosvenor Square, so you need not curtail your evening.''

"I would gladly escort you home," he replied, the underlying tension still laced through his voice.

"That is not necessary." Grand-mère's tone suggested that she would have preferred to have used the word "desirable" instead of "necessary." "Let us go, Brienne."

Evan's voice whispered through Brienne's mind, chiding her for heeding her grandmother's orders instead of thinking on her own. Just now, she was grateful for Grand-mère's intrusion. Armistead's nervousness was disquieting, or mayhap 'twas no more than her own despair at Evan's cold words about his father.

"You are right, Grand-mère," she said quietly. "Thank you, Armistead, for being so kind."

"Brienne, I wished to show you—"

"It will have to wait." Grand-mère took Brienne's arm. "I do not want her sickening."

Going with her grandmother into the house to collect their cloaks, Brienne did not glance toward the ballroom. The fairy tale had died here tonight.

Hitchcock paused in the doorway of the small parlor where Brienne had tried to lose herself in a novel. She would rather think of the silly troubles of the hero in the story than recall that Evan had not come back to the house on Grosvenor Square last night. She had chosen this room, with its view of the front of the house, in hopes of seeing him. The afternoon was nearly gone, and still there was no sign of him.

"Miss LeClerc, a gentleman is here to see you." The butler did not hide his incredulity that someone might call on her.

Although she knew he must know the name of the

caller, she would not ask. She set herself on her feet. "Please show him in."

He mumbled something that she suspected she should not ask him to repeat.

Brienne checked her appearance quickly in the glass by the hearth. It was impossible to hide the signs of her sleepless night, for shadows clung beneath her eyes.

At the sound of footfalls, she turned, preparing to smile. It never reached her lips as she gasped, "Lord Sommerton! I did not expect—" She knew she was blushing when her face grew hot.

The earl gave her a sympathetic smile. "Do not apologize, Miss LeClerc. I am sure that I am the last one you expected to call on you while you are living under the same roof as my son."

"Evan is not here."

"I did not call to speak with him, but with you." He gestured toward a chair. "May I?"

"Of course. I shall ring for tea."

Brienne went to the bellpull. As she waited for a maid to answer it, she knew she should offer the earl some light conversation, but nothing came to mind.

Every moment became more strained with silence. When she gave the maid the request for tea, she wished she could ask as well for someone to help her. Grand-mère would know what to say and do. Armistead had gracious manners. Evan . . . *Mon Dieu*, she did not want Evan here now when she would be between the icy daggers in the men's eyes.

As she sat again, the earl said, "I am sorry that you were a witness to what happened last evening. I should have held my tongue, but I was amazed to see my son at Lady Jacington's party."

"Evan said he has not been among the *ton* as one of them in a while."

"You are very discreet to choose such words, Miss

LeClerc. I know well how my son has spent the past decade." He sighed. "You find the whole of this chasm between my son and his family incomprehensible, don't you?"

She nodded, but waited until the maid had set a tray on a table beside her before she said, "My family has always been very close, my lord. I thought that is how all families are." She poured a cup of tea and handed it to him.

"How they are *supposed* to be." Lord Sommerton set the cup on another table and rubbed his hands together. "I fear it is too late for anything to change."

"Do you?" She knew she was being bold, but she might never have this chance again. As she prepared another cup for herself, she asked, "Would you have called here, my lord, if you were not willing to reach a compromise?"

"Do not think your kind and generous heart beats in the chests of the Somerset family." He smiled sadly when she looked up at him. "I came here solely to apologize for my unspeakable behavior last night with abandoning you in the middle of a dance. I trust you will forgive me."

Although she wanted to tell him that she would gladly forgive him if he offered the same apology to his son, she knew it would be just a waste of her breath. Both father and son had elected to hate each other.

"Yes, my lord. I accept your apology." She hesitated. "May I ask what caused this rift?"

"Evan never told you?"

She shook her head. "He speaks so seldom of his past."

"Then, I shall respect his wishes and remain as reticent."

"You will?" She put her fingers to her lips. "Forgive me, my lord. I should not have said such a thing."

"Nonsense. You have every right to assume that I care

nothing about my son.'' He stood. ''It appears Evan has learned something if he has been wise enough to welcome a warm-hearted woman like you into his life.'' Taking her hand, he bowed over it. ''I appreciate you receiving me, Miss LeClerc.''

''My lord?''

''Yes?'' he asked, pausing as he was walking to the door.

Rising, Brienne clasped her hands in front of her. ''Please know that you are welcome to call whenever you wish, my lord.''

''As you are at the family's townhouse on Berkeley Square.''

''Thank you.''

She sat when he took his leave. The question she had not asked as well as the answer he had not given still hung in the air to taunt her. Did the earl know where his son was? She had not known how to ask or how he might answer. Or if she truly wanted to know the answer.

Evan climbed the stairs, pushing his hair back out of his eyes. He had avoided meeting anyone since he had entered the house through the laundry, an easy task when the hour must be the second past midnight. A single light burned in the upper hallway, but his eyes had become accustomed to the darkness hours ago.

Opening the door to his room, he was amazed to see a single candle burning. He closed the door and drew off his coat. As he turned to toss it onto a chair, he froze, noticing the shadows move.

He said nothing when Brienne stepped into the small pool of light. He was uncertain if he could even think of something to say when she looked so luscious in her silken nightdress that accented her enchanting curves.

She took his coat. Folding it over the arm of the chair, she loosened his cravat.

His arm was around her waist and his mouth on hers before she could draw away his cravat. Her sweet breath pulsed into his mouth, seeking to warm every inch of him. "Were you acting, princess, when you told me on the stage that you would be mine?" he whispered against her soft cheek.

With a laugh, she gave him a coquettish smile. "You dare much, sir, to believe you may hold a princess so intimately."

"This is not as intimately as I wish to hold you, honey."

" 'Tis not as intimately as I wish to be held." She put her hand on his head and brought his mouth back to hers.

A craving gnawed at him. Had she guessed how completely his thoughts had been of her for the past day? At the realization, Evan drew out of her arms. When she regarded him with hurt and astonishment, he brushed her cheek with eager fingers.

"Honey, I did not expect to find you here." He laughed. "Or for you to be so forgiving of the fact that I walked out on you at Lady Jacington's assembly."

"It has given me some time to think." She ran her finger along his nose, a playful motion that sent a splinter of need cutting through him. "I have had so little time to think since you burst into my life, Evan." Her lips curved up in a seductive smile. "What I thought of when I had a chance to think was of this." Those enchanting lips brushed his.

With a moan, he deepened the kiss until she softened in his arms. Every fiber urged him to lean her back on his bed and savor her. His groan was heartfelt as he took her arms and lowered them from his shoulders. First. . . .

"Honey, I am glad you are here. That way, what I have to tell you does not have to wait until the morning."

"Evan, we can talk later."

"We must talk now." His laugh was self-deprecatory. "I cannot believe I said that when I want you so, honey, but you need to understand where I have been." He drew her down to sit on the chaise longue by where the candle offered such a small pool of light. "Do you know why I left the assembly last night?"

"Because your father—"

"No, honey. That was a serendipitous excuse. I had an appointment to meet someone at the assembly."

"Mr. Devereux?"

He smiled. "It is not easy to hoax you. I wanted to speak with him and another friend whom you have not met. Then I had arranged to speak with another person who was not in attendance."

"Which is why you had to leave?"

"Yes." He gazed into her dark eyes, yearning to put aside what he had to tell her so he could watch them close as he tilted her lips under his. Curving his hand along her cheek, he whispered, "I learned that Lagrille is in London."

Brienne pulled back, horror strangling her. "Where?"

"That is the question I have not yet gotten an answer to." His mouth twisted into a frown. "But I learned enough to know you need to get out of London."

"To the Teatro Caparelli?"

"No, he followed you there." He hesitated, then said, "It may be time to cross the Channel."

"Go to France?" She shook her head. "No."

"If you want to claim your father's château—"

"Forget the château."

"Forget it? What about your promise to your mother?"

She leaned her head against his shoulder. "Maman may have lost rational thought by the time she asked me to go. At the time, I was so distressed I did not think clearly either. You and Grand-mère have persuaded me of that. *Mon Dieu*, Maman warned me to watch out for a door.

That makes no sense at all.'' She ran her hand across his chest, her fingers pausing over the rapid beat of his heart. ''Also I will not risk your life for Château Tonnere du Grêlon.''

''I do not think I am worth giving up a château and a title for.''

''Mayhap not.'' She smiled when he chuckled. ''But I refuse to risk the life of the man I love.''

Evan pulled her back and stared at her. ''Love? Have *you* lost your mind?''

''Mayhap, but I know I have lost my heart to you.''

Standing, he pulled off his collar and tossed it onto another chair. He frowned when he heard footsteps beyond the door, but ignored them when a door opened on the other side of the hall. He looked back at Brienne, a most pleasing prospect, but one he must ignore as he said, ''Honey, I have warned you about believing in fairy tales.''

''This is not a fairy tale. My love for you is real.''

He clasped her face between his hands. ''I know, as mine is for you.''

''If that is so—''

''Hush, honey. Let me say what I must. You have seen the danger surrounding my work. I do not want you to be its victim again.''

Shaking off his hands, she rose. ''I would not want to be accused of standing in the way of your larceny and skulduggery. Foolish me! I thought you might consider my love more important.''

''It is more important.''

''Then—''

''No, honey. Let me finish.''

As her chin rose in defiance, Brienne said, ''You are finished. If you will excuse me, I will return to my room. Good night.''

He pulled her back to him. "If you think I am going to let you leave, you are crazier than I thought."

"Then, I am crazier than you thought. I love you, don't I? What could be more insane than that?"

"Nothing," he said sadly, "except me loving you."

"But one day you will go and I shall never see you again, won't you?"

"Can it be any other way? For me, it would be wonderful to have a place to go where I always would find a warm welcome and loving arms. For you, that is wrong. You need someone you can depend on to be with you every night of your life."

"Maman waited foolishly for love."

"You have too much joy within you to waste your life pining for a man who has ruined his life and now could ruin yours."

When Brienne stepped away, she wished she could be angry. How could she when Evan was being brutally honest as she had longed him to be?

She held out her hand to him. "If our time together must be short, Evan, I do not want to use it arguing with you. I want your love for as long as I can have it."

"My love is yours forever, honey." He put his hand in hers. His eyes sparked with a mixture of grief and fury. "I cannot make you many vows, but this one I mean sincerely. When I must leave you, my heart shall stay behind."

Evan led her to the bed. When he sat her on it, he gazed down at her. His arms encircled her waist and tugged her against him.

As her fingers messed his hair, she whispered, "You are going to be my undoing, Evan Somerset."

He reached for the ribbons closing her nightdress. "That is exactly what I had in mind, and I shall be undoing you right now." When she laughed, he captured her lips with his fevered yearning. "Help me," he breathed against her lips.

"Help you?"

"Help me turn my bed once more into paradise with your love." Leaning her back on the pillows, he placed a flurry of kisses across her face.

She held her arms out to him. "Love me tonight." *And every day for as long as I live.*

"You need not ask," he whispered as he ran his fingers along her. The silk caught fire between his skin and hers. "I cannot think of anything I would rather do."

He sat beside her and pulled off his boots. As he began to loosen his shirt, her fingers brushed his aside. He smiled as she slid his sleeves down his arms. A powerful shock rushed through her as his chest pressed against her bare skin above the nightdress.

With a moan, he pushed her back into the mattress. She lovingly massaged the muscles along his back and smiled when his mouth swept along her neck, leaving blazing embers.

She gasped as his hands moved along her breast. As his mouth returned to hers, she tangled her fingers in his hair. An eager sigh escaped her lips when his fingers twisted through the ribbons on her bodice, drawing them apart.

Slowly, excruciatingly slowly, he slid the material aside. Lowering his head, he tasted the tip of one breast. The explosion of sensation stripped her of all but the naked power of his mouth on her skin. He drew her up onto her knees, the bed rustling like a whispered song. When he lifted the opened gown over her head, he smiled and let his hands slip along her.

"You must have been sure I would come back to you," he murmured. "Or do you sleep every night with nothing beneath your nightdress?"

"I had hoped you would come back." She pressed his

hand between her breasts. "It was empty here, but I knew my heart was with you."

He leaned her back into the nest of pillows and pulled her into his arms. Tilting her face up, he kissed her until her body slanted into his. She slid her arms along his bare back as his mouth moved along her neck and then lower when he placed enticing nibbles along her breasts. She cried out in ecstasy. His tongue etched a path along her, and she quivered with the need that ached through her.

The flame inside her burst into an inferno as she unbuttoned his breeches and pushed them aside. Urging him onto his back, she leaned over him and began to explore him as he had her. The flavors of his skin were more delicious than her best sauce. Gazing into his face which revealed his rapture, she reveled that she could bring such joy to him.

His mouth took hers as he pushed her back into the pillows. She clutched him like a castaway clinging to a raft on a frenzied sea. Her fingers brought his mouth to hers, blistering her with the fire of his passion. Slowly her eyes opened. She met the intensity of his blue eyes. She could not escape his gaze as he moved over her.

Her arms enfolded him to her as he brought them together. His mouth covered hers to sample her heated breath. His slow, gentle movements matched the caress of his tongue on hers. When she trembled, all gentleness vanished. A frenzy roiled through her. Even his breath, husky in her ear, and her hands pressed against his back urging him closer disappeared. She was only the motion, with him, part of him. The tremors intensified until an internal explosion erupted outward in exultation. This was perfection. A perfection she never wanted to lose.

* * *

Opening his eyes, Evan sighed when he saw the first light of dawn edging past the sides of the drapes. The night was gone, and now the troubles of the day could no longer be ignored.

Did Brienne guess how much he had not told her last night? Several contacts had informed him that Lagrille was in London. Nobody could tell him where, but he guessed from their comments that Lagrille had garnered a place for himself among the Polite World. Lagrille could not be living with the *émigrés*, for Evan had already checked with that close-knit community.

Lagrille! Who was this man? Why he wanted Brienne was obvious. That blasted château!

He smiled as he gazed down at her face resting on his chest. This was why he wanted Brienne, to share these moments when she relinquished her stern self-control to delight in passion. All he wanted was to lie next to her and touch her. If he could spend the rest of his life concentrating on loving her, he would be in heaven.

With a sigh, he knew it was impossible. Even as he held her while she slept, other thoughts invaded his mind, dimming his contentment.

"What is it?" she asked as she opened her eyes. "Evan, you sound so sad."

"Sad? When I hold you?" He smiled and kissed her lightly. "Never, honey."

"But something is bothering you. What else did you discover?"

Evan almost laughed. Somehow, Brienne was learning to discern his thoughts as no one else ever had. When she brushed the worried creases from his forehead with loving fingers, he kissed her wrist and heard the intake of her eager breath.

"Only enough," he said, "to know I have much more to discover before I can keep you safe in London." He stood and pulled on his breeches. "I know of only one place you might be safe."

"Where?"

"Where I should have taken you as soon as we came ashore from Marksen's ship. To Sommerton Hall."

Brienne sat up and stared at him. "Your family's manor house?"

He could not keep his finger from caressing the downy warmth between her breasts. When she pulled the blanket up to her chin and glowered at him, he reached for her nightdress and dropped it on her lap. "It is north and west of York. Lagrille will not be able to reach it without being seen."

"And where will you go?"

"To do what I must to make sure Lagrille does not try to reach Sommerton Hall."

"No, I will not go there and leave you here to deal with him alone."

As if she had not spoken, Evan continued, "I shall send your grandmother to you as soon as I know she will not be followed." He frowned and shook his head as he pulled on his shirt. "By Jove, this would be so much easier if you had not attended Lady Jacington's soirée where so many people saw you and Madame LeClerc together."

Brienne leaped from the bed and grasped his arm. "Let Lagrille have the château if that is what he wants. I refuse to let you die for it."

With a sad smile, he shook his head. "That will not work. He cannot claim it without you."

"Evan, listen to me. I—"

A knock was set on the door. When she gasped, Evan patted her hand before going to open it.

He frowned. What was Hitchcock doing at his door? The butler usually avoided him. When Hitchcock looked past him as if he were invisible, his frown deepened.

"Miss LeClerc, this was found in your grandmother's room."

"Grand-mère's room?" She pulled on a rose-pink wrapper that Evan had not noticed last night. Coming to the door, she asked in a puzzled tone, "What did you find there?"

"This." He placed a small, folded sheet of paper in her hand.

Brienne opened it and cried, "Oh, no!"

"What is it?" Evan asked.

She raised her eyes, and he nearly recoiled from her horror. He understood it when she whispered, "Lagrille has abducted Grand-mère."

Chapter Eighteen

"Grand-mère has been abducted." Brienne could not halt herself from repeating the words. Mayhap if she said them enough, the whole of this would go away and never have happened.

Evan took the note from her numb fingers. As he scanned the short missive, she knew what he was reading. The few words, written in French, were imprinted upon her eyes, so that each time she blinked they burned brightly against the darkness.

> *I have had Madame LeClerc taken from your house. She will be returned to you when you have followed my orders.*

It was signed simply "Lagrille."

Turning the note over, Evan frowned. "What orders is he referring to?"

"I don't know," she whispered. "That is all it says."

Pushing past Hitchcock, he rushed down the hallway.

Brienne followed, knowing where he must be headed. When he threw open the door to her grandmother's room and shouted out Grand-mère's name, she held her breath in hopes of hearing her grandmother answer.

"No," Evan said as she reached the doorway. "I think it would be better if you did not go in."

"Stop coddling me, Evan. She is my grandmother!"

"Exactly."

She pushed past him as he had done to Hitchcock. He seized her arms, spinning her away from the door, but not before she saw the disaster that had been her grandmother's sitting room. It looked like the salon after the sailors had attacked her.

"*Mon Dieu*," she groaned.

Evan released her with a more vicious curse. "I did not want you to see this, but now that you have . . ."

Brienne put her hand on the door frame, not sure she could trust her knees as she stared at the upset chairs and broken table. Pictures were pulled from the walls, their broken frames lying atop where they were scattered across the floor. A newspaper had been pulled apart and thrown everywhere.

"How was it that no one heard this?" Brienne gasped. "We could not hear from the front of the house, but someone must have heard this."

"That is my question as well. Were all your servants senseless last night?"

At Evan's question, she looked over her shoulder to see Armistead behind them. Louisa stood beside him, her hands over her mouth and her eyes wide. Armistead's jaw worked as his gaze swept over the room.

"What is the meaning of this?" Armistead frowned. "I welcomed you and your companions into my house, Somerset, and *this* is how you repay me?"

"*This* is not my handiwork," Evan said. "Brienne's

grandmother has been kidnapped.'' He thrust the note into his friend's hand. ''See for yourself.''

''Kidnapped?'' Louisa collapsed in a swoon.

Rolling his eyes, Evan knelt beside her as he called, ''Hitchcock, bring the *sal volatile* to wake her.''

''Forgive me,'' Armistead said as he handed the note to Brienne. ''I should not have assumed you were involved in this.''

Her forehead furrowed when she saw a glint in his eyes which avoided hers. Did he find something about this amusing? She started to ask that, then halted herself. He might be simply grateful that his mistress had not been the one stolen from the house.

''Why,'' Armistead went on when she remained silent, ''would anyone want to abduct Madame LeClerc? She seemed like such a harmless old woman.''

''Seems!'' cried Brienne, unable to restrain herself at his comment. ''She is not dead.'' She went into the room and lifted a small table upright.

Sobs burst from her. This reminded her too much of the day when she had been assaulted and the salon almost destroyed, the day Evan had burst into her life at the very moment everything she had always believed was shattering like the figurines that had been smashed on the hearth. Sitting on the settee, she covered her face with her hands.

''I am so sorry, honey,'' Evan said as he sat beside her. Drawing her into his arms, he turned her against his chest. She clutched his shirt as she had the night Maman had died and wondered if all the pain of the past few weeks had gathered together to be inflicted upon her anew.

A commotion in the hallway brought Brienne's head up. She saw Louisa being carried away from the door. With a sigh, she leaned back against the settee and stared up at the ceiling which was the only unchanged part of this room.

"She will be fine," Armistead said as he came into the room. "She has a habit of doing that whenever things become too disagreeable."

Although she wanted to fire back that this was far worse than disagreeable, Brienne held her tongue. She could not let him put her nose out of joint with every word he spoke. He was upset as well.

"They were quite thorough, I see." Armistead picked up a shard of a broken shepherd. "I was rather fond of this piece."

"We must find Grand-mère," Brienne said, turning to Evan.

He was staring across the room, and she guessed he was not looking at the damage. His gaze was turned inward. What was he planning? She wanted to ask, but she could not when Armistead was prowling the room, frowning more fiercely as he viewed the destruction from every angle.

"But where to begin?" Their host grimaced when glass crunched beneath his feet.

Evan nodded, his eyes focusing as he turned toward her. "Until we know what this Lagrille wants, we can do nothing. Do you have any idea why someone with that name would want your grandmother?"

"What do you mean?" She wanted to shake him. This was not the time for one of his jests.

"Just what I asked you, Brienne. Armistead is right. Your grandmother is a harmless old woman. I cannot imagine a single reason why someone would want to kidnap her." His gaze drilled her. "Can you?"

Her hands clenched in her lap as she realized that the hoax was not meant for her, but for Armistead. Evan wanted to assure that their host could not guess even a hint of the truth.

Lowering her gaze to her hands, she said, her voice trembling, "I am at a loss, too."

He put his hands over hers, but his words were for Armistead. "As soon as Brienne is dressed, I think we should meet to discuss this ... somewhere else." He glanced around the room. "This is too distressing for all of us."

" 'Tis the hour for breakfast." Armistead went to the door. "I shall have it readied to be served when Brienne joins us."

"In the meantime, we shall talk."

Brienne wanted to plead with Evan to come with her. She had so many questions to ask him, so much she needed to tell him, but he drew her to her feet. "Evan," she whispered, "in Grand-mère's bedchamber—"

"Later, honey," he murmured. Raising his voice, he said, "Do not be long, Brienne. I doubt if this Lagrille will wait long to make his wishes known to us. We need to be prepared."

Going to the door, she looked back at the two men. Evan stood in the middle of the room, his gaze again distant. Beyond him, Armistead was gathering up the broken fragments of another figurine. His scowl was as fearsome as a thunderstorm, and she recalled how he had spoken of his affection for his possessions.

A shudder ran along her, for she knew it was what she still possessed that had led to this horror.

Brienne was amazed to see Louisa looking serene and sitting at the large table in the breakfast-parlor. No one greeted Brienne as she entered. From Evan's stiff expression, she guessed this uncomfortable silence had been going on for a while.

He gave her a bolstering smile as he came over to the door. "How are you doing, Brienne?"

"As well as can be expected." She glanced at the table. "We are wasting time just sitting here."

"I expect we will hear from Lagrille before midday."

"You do?"

His smile became feral. "Why should he delay?"

To that, Brienne had no answer. Going with Evan to the table, she thanked him as he seated her. Silence descended again around the table as heaping plates were set in front of them. She picked up her fork and looked at hers. Her stomach threatened to embarrass her on her first bite.

"To answer your question, Somerset," Armistead said in a vexed voice, "I have had Hitchcock speak to the staff as well as the neighbors. Nobody saw anyone strange come into the house last night."

"Or this morning?" Evan asked.

"I told you. No."

Brienne put down her fork. It was senseless to try to eat when she could not swallow past the fear clamping around her throat.

"Someone must have seen something!" Evan argued.

"Yes, I was able to slip into the house last night without being noted, but I was not taking a woman with me who did not want to go."

Louisa toyed with her muffin. "If they had knocked her senseless—"

"Don't even say such a thing!" Brienne cried.

Evan put his hand over hers. "Honey, we have to consider every possibility, no matter how heinous."

Pushing away from the table, she stood. She went to the window overlooking the garden at the back of the house. No doubt, the blackguards who had taken her grandmother had come this way. That would explain why none of the neighbors had seen anyone suspicious, but how could no one have seen them when they came through the kitchens?

"Brienne," Evan said as he put his hands on her shoulders, "mayhap you should retire so you can compose yourself."

"I am quite—" She bit back the rest of her retort when she saw the tension tightening his face. Letting her shoulders droop, she said, "Mayhap you are right, Evan. Will you assist me to my room?"

"Of course." His expression remained grim as he turned toward the table. "If you will excuse us, Porter."

"I will have the servants continue to question anyone who might have been on the square last night," Armistead said. Coming around the table, he squeezed Brienne's hand. "You know I will do all I can to make this come to rights."

"Thank you." She added nothing else as she went out of the breakfast-parlor with Evan.

He held out his hand, and she slipped hers into it, lacing her fingers through his. As they went along the passage, he gave her a reassuring smile. She appreciated his effort, for his tension tightened his grip around her fingers, and she knew he was as anxious about Grand-mère as she was.

When they entered the small parlor, he closed the door. He pulled her to the far side of the room and into his arms. She started to speak, but he put his fingers to her lips.

"Whisper," he said so quietly she could hardly hear him. "I do not know who in this house has betrayed us, but someone has."

"Hitchcock?"

He chuckled. "He is an obvious choice. It has to be someone who has a position of authority here."

"Evan, we must do something. Poor Grand-mère! I do not want to think about how frightened she must be."

"What do you suggest we do when we have no idea where your grandmother may be?"

"Your father is wealthy. He would be able to hire Bow Street Runners to seek Grand-mère."

"No."

"But, Evan, 'tis Grand-mère." Tears fell along her face, and she did not wipe them away. It was useless, for more would follow.

"No."

"I cannot believe you would let your hate for him keep you from getting the best possible help for my grandmother." She stepped out of his arms.

He grasped her hands and kept her from walking away. "Brienne, when you do business with the devil, the price is your soul."

"The price may be my grandmother's life."

His lips curled in a caricature of a smile. "Do not worry about that, honey. I have a few connections of my own that should help me find your grandmother far more quickly than the Bow Street Runners could."

"More friends?"

"Why are you sneering when my friends have proven to be so helpful since we met?" He released her fingers and sifted his through her hair. "Honey, I would not do anything to risk your grandmother. You know that, don't you?"

"Yes."

"But?"

"I did not say but."

"No, but I heard it in your voice." Evan stepped back, his hands falling to his sides. "You think I would put my anger with my father ahead of finding your grandmother."

She could not deny the truth. "Yes."

"You are wrong. Too bad Dominic is not here. He could assure you that I keep my promises, no matter how high the cost might be." He drew her down to a settee. "None of this makes sense. Why did they take your grandmother instead of you?"

"I was with you last night."

His smile was fleeting. "Yes, you were." He sighed.

"If you recall, that did not halt Lagrille's henchmen from slaying Angiola's lover."

Brienne surged to her feet, unable to sit still when he spoke of such things. "Evan, how will we get Grandmère back safely?"

"By giving them whatever they want." He pounded his fist into the arm of the sofa. "But what could it be?"

"The vase," she whispered.

"Then, they are one case of arson too late to get it."

"No, they are not."

Evan slowly stood as he stared at Brienne's colorless face. He wanted to believe that he had misunderstood her. When she backed away as he walked toward her, he caught her by the elbows and brought her close to him. "What did you say?" He had to squeeze each word out past his rigid lips.

"The vase was not destroyed in the fire."

"You told me—"

She yanked herself away. "Why should I have trusted you when I did not know anything about you except that you brought all this trouble into our lives?"

"That was weeks ago. During all that time, it never crossed your mind to confide in me?"

"It crossed my mind."

"But you did not trust me with the truth." He snarled a curse, then realized it was his father's favorite one. He chose another oath, but it offered no more satisfaction. "Brienne, do you have the vase now?"

"I know where it is."

"Then, let's get it. I will order a carriage and—"

Putting her hand on his, she said, "There is no need for a carriage. Come with me."

"Where?"

"Grand-mère's chamber."

"The vase is here in the house?" Astonishment widened his eyes.

She nodded.

"Damn! This makes it harder."

"Harder? All we need to do is go and retrieve it."

"I told you that we may have an enemy in this house."
He smiled abruptly. "Shriek with hysteria."

"Excuse me?"

"We don't want anyone to intrude. Even Hitchcock
will avoid the room if he hears you howling with despair."
His smile turned grim. "Didn't you see his face when
Miss Woods fell into her swoon?"

She shook her head. "All I could see was the destruction
to Grand-mère's sitting room."

"I would say that you should trust me on this, but I
suspect that is not possible."

Brienne wanted to tell him that he was wrong. She did
trust him now. How would he react if she told him that
she had not revealed the truth about the vase because she
had feared he would take the vase and leave to deliver
it to Lagrille and never come back? She had been afraid—
she *was* afraid—that Lagrille would slay him. She also
feared, once his job was completed, Evan would not return
to her arms. Had he not said as much last night?

Now she had no choice, save to sacrifice her grandmother. That she could not do.

As Evan opened the door, Brienne's cries echoed
through the house. She noticed maids watching in sympathy as he helped her up the stairs.

"Yes, honey, it will be all right," he said, just loud
enough so that no one could mistake what was going
on. "If it makes you feel better, we will wait in your
grandmother's chambers until we know what to do next."

Even though her throat was raw from her keening, she
did not cease until they were inside and the door was
shut.

"Enough!" He grinned. "My ears are going to ring
for a month."

Brienne motioned toward the bedchamber. "If it has not been stolen, the vase is in here."

She stepped around the upended chairs and went to the armoire. She threw the door open and knelt to pull out the drawer where the box had been hidden.

Lifting out the blankets, she almost smiled when she saw the box was undisturbed. How could she smile when Evan now would leave to risk his life to save her grandmother? She handed him the blankets and took the box out of the drawer.

He tossed the blankets onto the bed and squatted beside her. Smoothing a strand of hair back behind her ear, he said nothing as he waited with extraordinary patience for her to open the box.

His gentleness almost undid her, but she swallowed the hot tears and lifted the top. She touched the battered frame of her father's picture, then picked up the vase and placed it in his hand.

"Be careful, Evan," she whispered. "I don't want to lose both you and Grand-mère."

"If it works out as I hope, your grandmother will be back with you in ripping time."

"And you?" She had to ask the question.

Standing, he sighed. "I shall not make you any promises I cannot keep." He looked at the vase. "However, I am sure you will be seeing me soon. If Lagrille wants this vase in order to get to you, I will be back to make sure he does not mistreat you."

"If you can." She let him help her to her feet.

"You have known from the onset, honey, that my work is not without its risks."

"Which is why you love it?"

"Which is why I *loved* it." He sighed as he slipped the vase under his coat. "Of late, it has lost its charms as I have come to know yours."

She savored his kiss, even though it was tainted with

farewell. As she locked her fingers behind his nape, she leaned into his strength, taking care not to bump the vase.

He took her hands, drew them down, and folded them between his. "Stay close to the house. Porter will make sure you are never alone."

"But if he is our enemy—"

"You must assume everyone is now." He raised her hands to his lips, kissing one, then the other before relinquishing them with a sad smile. "Save for me. You believe that, don't you?"

"Yes. I would not have given you the vase otherwise."

"Honey, then trust me that I would not leave you here if I had any other choice that would keep you safe. Trust me that although it may appear so, you are not alone."

"Not alone? What do you mean?"

"Trust me, honey."

"Without an explanation?" Brienne took a deep breath and let it slide past her clamped lips. "You never make it easy for me, Evan."

He caressed her cheek. "You will be safe here. If you must leave, take Porter or one of the stronger footmen with you."

"But, if I went with you—"

He seized her arms and kissed her fiercely. "Honey, you need to stay here where you will be safe."

"Lagrille's men took Grand-mère from the house!"

"Why, do you think?"

Her shoulders sagged as she dropped onto a trunk at the foot of the bed. "To persuade me to give chase. Evan, I know that, but I cannot leave her to them."

"I will make them sorry that they were so stupid." He knelt beside her. "Honey, I know it is hard for you to trust me, but you must."

"Am I intruding?" asked Armistead from near the door.

"No. Come in." Evan stood and took Brienne's hand.

Placing it in his friend's hand, he said, "Guard her well while I see if I can find her grandmother."

"I will guard her well." He gripped her fingers. "You take care of her grandmother, and I shall take care of Brienne."

"Be careful, Evan," she said, drawing her hand out of Armistead's. "I love you." When Evan frowned, she added hastily, "Tell Grand-mère that when you find her." She shivered, knowing he also suspected their host of being involved in all of this. He was right to be suspicious of everyone. She must copy him in this. Anyone could be their enemy.

"I will be careful," he said, then was gone.

She stared at the empty doorway, hoping she would see him walk back through it again soon.

Chapter Nineteen

"*Have a gathering here now?*" Brienne stared at Louisa, certain she had misheard Louisa's question.

"*It will help you get your mind off your anxiety about your grandmother.*"

As Brienne drew on her slippers, she wished she had put an end to the conversation at that point. If she had, she might not have had Armistead add his voice to Louisa's to persuade her that the soirée planned for this evening should not be canceled. She had agreed to that readily. When she had asked for them to excuse her from attending, the persuasion had begun in earnest. She had relented so they would leave her alone. She wanted time alone to consider what she should do next.

Louisa and Armistead were waiting when Brienne came out of her room. That surprised her, for she had guessed they would be with their guests who had been arriving in lovely carriages for the past half hour.

Holding out a glass of wine, Louisa said, "I thought you might want this before you joined us."

"Thank you." She took a sip, noticing how her hands trembled. "This is very good."

Armistead smiled. "Do not ask where I obtained it, Brienne."

"I won't." She did not want to think of Marksen and the other smugglers. If she had not hied out of London so thoughtlessly, Grand-mère might not be in danger now. She took another sip.

Armistead offered his arm to his mistress as they went down the stairs. Louisa prattled about things that Brienne could not care about when she was so worried. When Armistead took her wineglass as they reached the floor where the guests were gathered, Brienne was startled to see the glass was empty.

"There is more in the parlor," he said with a smile.

She shook away the sensation that he was amused with her. No doubt, he was simply anticipating enjoying the company of his tie-mates and putting the horror of Grand-mère's abduction out of his mind. She wished she could do the same.

As she went to a wide archway that had previously been closed, all words were stripped from her by the view of wealth displayed with arrogant pride. Gold columns edged the wall of the upper floor. Plaster cupids were embossed between them and reached for the ceiling which arched up into an inverted bowl. At the top a gigantic chandelier twinkled with scores of candles.

Neither Armistead nor Louisa paused as they entered to admire the benches upholstered in gold brocade or the silk wallcovering in the palest shade of green. Brienne wondered if she could ever become accustomed to such luxury.

Can you imagine what the ballroom at Château Tonnere du Grêlon must be like? Evan's voice rang through her head, teasing and comforting at the same time. She wished he were here so he could tell her that her grandmother was safe. She wished he were here, so she could wrap his arms around her. Although he had been gone only since yesterday, it seemed a lifetime.

In spite of herself, she gasped as she walked through the chamber. It was bigger than the ballroom at Lady Jacington's townhouse, but oddly cozy with dark walls covered with a variety of paintings. She recalled how Armistead had spoken of hiring Evan to arrange for the purchase of art. She wondered if any of these pieces had been smuggled into England from France.

She had no chance to examine them closer. More than a dozen other people were gathered by a hearth on the other side of the room.

Armistead took her arm and led her toward the others. "My friends, you know my dear Louisa, but allow me to introduce you to Brienne LeClerc."

A dowager peered at her through a pince-nez. "Have we met, young lady?"

"No, Lady Heathton, for she has recently entered the Polite World," Armistead said. He smiled at Brienne and gave her a wink.

No wonder he and Evan were friends. They enjoyed hoaxing the rest of the *ton*. A pulse of sorrow rushed through her. She wished Evan and Grand-mère could be here to enjoy this joke.

Brienne greeted each of the others, trying to remember the names spoken so quickly. She listened to their conversation and was amazed how they spoke of names which were familiar from the newspapers. This was still all too strange, especially when she wanted to think only of Grand-mère.

"Oh, he will be arriving a bit later," Armistead said and smiled more broadly.

Knowing that her thoughts had drifted from the conversation, Brienne did not ask whom he was speaking of. She doubted if she had met the person. She wished she was back at L'Enfant de la Patrie where she knew all her neighbors and she had lived in guileless happiness.

Louisa took her arm. "Come and sit, Brienne. You look as if you could use another glass of wine."

"Forgive me for being so unsettled."

"You need not apologize." Her pert nose wrinkled as she said, "I do not want to imagine how frightened you are."

Armistead had been listening, she realized, when he said, "Excuse me, my friends, while I get Miss LeClerc something to ease her thirst."

Brienne thanked him as he brought her another glass of the excellent vintage. Grief pulsed through her. Grand-mère would know where it had been bottled. Although Brienne had learned her grandmother's skills in the kitchen, she never had equaled her grandmother's taste in fine wines.

He sat her on a settee and smiled again when Louisa sat on her other side. When Brienne giggled, she put a tremulous finger over her lips to silence the childish sound.

"No. No more," Brienne said when he offered to refill her glass. "I believe I have had too much wine already."

"A Frenchwoman who would turn away wine?" Armistead laughed and tapped his goblet against hers. "Are you jesting with me? Or is this an act like the one you performed with that Italian *comedia?*"

"Evan told you about Teatro Caparelli?" she gasped. She had not guessed that Evan had been so flippant about what she had thought must be kept secret.

"A *teatro?* Are you an actress, Miss LeClerc?" gushed a woman behind them.

Brienne pushed against the floor to shift so she could look back over her shoulder. Her feet refused to move at first, but then she turned slowly and waited for her eyes to focus. The wine must be more potent than the *vin ordinaire* she had been drinking in the rooms over the salon from her earliest memories.

Armistead answered, "Of course not. Miss LeClerc is not of that low class."

"But you said—"

"Lady Grosbeck, it is true that Miss LeClerc has done some performing, but only as a lark." He smiled at Brienne and squeezed her hand. "She has a true talent in pantomime, I am told."

"My dear, you must do a reading for us!" Lady Grosbeck urged.

"Oh, do!" seconded Louisa, clapping her hands with delight.

"I do not think that would be such a good idea," Brienne answered faintly. Putting her hand up to her head, she was shocked that her fingers refused to follow her wishes just as her feet did. She could not have had too much wine, for this was only her second glass. If she had taken ill, she must excuse herself posthaste.

"Please." Louisa laughed. "It would be so much fun."

Brienne blinked several times, but could not clear her eyes. As when they had pleaded with her to attend this evening, agreeing would be the simplest thing. Then she could excuse herself when the conversation turned to something else.

"I fear I shall disappoint you." At least, her lips still worked.

"I doubt that." Armistead chuckled. "Shall we?"

She rose, and a hand on her back steadied her. Slowly she looked back to Armistead standing behind her. He was smiling in anticipation. "We?" she asked.

"If you would be agreeable," he said as he took her cup from her oddly numb fingers, "I would like to perform the scene with you. I have a love for drama."

"Really?" Her voice seemed to come from the depths

of a bottomless shaft, echoing through her skull. "What scene shall we do?"

"What did Evan tell me that you had performed? Ah, 'twas the tale of the golden lion."

Another man came to stand next to Armistead. "I know that play. May I take the rôle of the king?"

"Yes," Brienne said, "but we cannot do that story with only three of us."

"Shall we perform the final scene when the merchant's son finds his princess?" asked Armistead.

She nodded, then was sorry she had, for her head spun more with every passing moment. The scratch of tables and chairs being pushed aside added to the burgeoning pain along her forehead. As the others took their places on the makeshift stage, she closed her eyes and tried to dredge up energy to speak her lines. She heard another guest being greeted and guessed this was the person Armistead had been awaiting to arrive.

Brienne had no chance to think more about the late-comer, because Louisa announced the beginning of the play. As Armistead sought about the room to the laughter of his friends, Brienne waited for him to find the princess and her eleven attendants. She smiled as he turned to her.

With the king following, he approached and dropped to one knee. "My beloved princess, I have found you before the eight days ordered by your father. Marry me."

"Yes, brave sir." She put her hands on his shoulders to urge him to rise. That was what she had intended, but her fingers touched nothing.

He stood and gazed down at her. When his arm slipped around her waist, he drew her to him. "Be mine, and give me your father's lands that will be yours upon his death."

"It and I am yours, brave sir."

When he bent to kiss her on the cheek, she smiled.

This was the end of the play. Now she could take her leave.

Armistead shouted, "Let the wedding be held, so that all the kingdom can know of my good fortune."

"There is no wedding scene," Brienne protested in a whisper.

He chuckled. "If we have the wedding for the princess and her brave hero, we can celebrate the wedding feast the rest of the evening."

"No, I think I should leave." She swayed. "I feel very light-headed."

"I promised our guests that we would do this for their entertainment," he said, as petulant as Angiola could be.

"As long as you promise that I can leave as soon as it is over."

"I do, Brienne."

She tried to focus on his face, but it became a bright blob in the candlelight. As she was turned to a darker shape which had no human form, she tried to stay on her feet long enough for this silliness. Each time she blinked, she had to fight to reopen her eyes.

The voices came from a distant place, but with Armistead prompting her, she replied. Applause told her the play was complete. She thought she heard him saying something, but she could not understand his words.

She started to reply, but everything became black as the room vanished. She surrendered to the dizziness, satisfied that she had managed to maintain her senses until the play was completed. It was her last thought before oblivion claimed her.

Brienne winced as she rolled over in bed. Light oozed through her slitted eyes, and she moaned. Hiding her head in the pillows, she wondered if she had been struck by a dray. Only such an accident would leave her head pulsating with all this pain.

An ache in her left temple kept her eyes from focusing, so she closed them and sank back into the soft mattress. Drifting in a black river of pain, she waited for the discomfort to ebb. She realized it had eased when she could blink her eyes without groaning.

Although she was not willing to trust her still numb toes, Brienne clawed her way up the pillows until she was propped against the headboard. She looked about and frowned. She was in Armistead Porter's house, for past the open bed curtains, she could see the view out the window. It was Grosvenor Square, but not the view from her room.

Why had she been put into another room? Mayhap she had been so ill that she had been quarantined. She touched her forehead. No hint of fever remained. Had she been ill?

She ran her fingers through her tangled hair, pushing it back from her face. That she had gone to bed without braiding it amazed her. The only other time she had done that was when she had fallen asleep in Evan's arms.

Evan. . . .

Tears bubbled from her eyes. In her weakness, she could not deny that she loved him. His touch and kisses brought her alive as nothing else did. Grand-mère had been right when she said that Brienne had just been drifting through life until Evan came along to offer her an anchor. That the anchor was set in sand instead of rock did not matter, for she loved him.

The door opened. Peering past the partially drawn bed curtains on the other side of the bed, Brienne saw a maid with a tray. The thought of food renewed her nausea. "Please, take it away."

"As you wish, Mrs. Porter. Shall I come back to help madam dress?"

Brienne sat straighter, ignoring the ache in her stomach. "What did you call me?"

"Mrs. Porter? Do you prefer to be called something else? Tell me what you wish, madam, and I shall do so."

"I wish you to call me Miss LeClerc."

The maid bit her bottom lip uneasily. "But, madam, a woman does not continue to use her birth name once she is married."

"Married?" She started to throw the covers aside. The bright glint of a gold band on her left hand halted her. In disbelief, she raised her hand and touched the ring on her fourth finger. It had not been there when. . . . She could not recall going to bed the previous night.

She touched her flimsy white silk nightgown. Lace encircled the low neckline. Seeing a matching wrapper at the foot of her bed, she reached for it. Her fingers pulled back in horror as she saw an undeniably masculine one of navy silk lying next to it.

"What has happened?" she asked as she stood, holding tightly to the bed.

"Mrs. Porter—"

"Stop calling me that! My name is Brienne LeClerc! Not Porter." She grasped the dark blue robe. "Who does this belong to?"

The maid smiled. "Why, Mr. Porter, of course."

"Are you telling me that Armistead slept here last night?"

Lowering her eyes, the maid flushed. "Madam, it is customary for a man to spend his wedding night with his wife."

"His wife . . ." She touched the gold band again. It was real, but how had it come to be on her hand? She had not been a part of a wedding ceremony, except. . . . Her face grew cold. There *had* been a ceremony, performed for Armistead's friends as the climax for *The Golden Lion*. "But that was only a play!"

The door opened again.

Brienne held the wrapper to her chin as she stared at Armistead, who was walking into the room. His chest was bare above his half-buttoned breeches.

He smiled when he saw her by the rumpled bed. As he stretched, muscles rippled across his body. Why was he parading himself before her like a harlot on the Dover docks? She flushed at the thought, but it was an icy flush. She must have shared her bed with him last night.

She could not remember anything beyond the black pain that overmastered her. Desperately, she searched her memory, but found nothing. She could not recall being brought to this room or being in Armistead's embrace.

Deep in her thoughts, Brienne gasped when he cupped her chin and kissed her swiftly.

"Good morning, my wife," he murmured. He released her and picked up the dark dressing robe that had fallen from her fingers. Pulling it on, he went to the table where the breakfast tray waited. He ordered the maid from the room as he buttered a muffin. "Don't you want some breakfast this morning, Brienne?"

"Get out! I do not know what made you think you have the right to—"

Grasping her left hand, he held it up in front of her face. His buttery finger tapped the band. "This! This gives me the right to everything you possess. You are my wife."

"Wife?" She laughed, but the sound was hollow. "I cannot be your wife. We were never married."

"But we were. Don't you remember? You could not have been that intoxicated."

"I was not intoxicated! I know we never married."

"But we did." He took a bite of the muffin. "Last night with a dozen witnesses."

She scowled. "You know last night was just play-acting."

"As I acted when I persuaded you that Somerset had told me about your short career on the stage." He chuckled. "Neither of you noticed me in your audience."

"You saw us with the Teatro Caparelli?"

"Enough to know this was the way to make you my wife."

"But it was only a play!" she cried. "I did not mean—"

"It does not matter what you meant." He lifted the lids of the silver serving dishes. Bending to sample the eggs, he glanced insidiously at her. "We are married. Legally and irrevocably."

"I shall get it annulled! I shall—"

He whirled and caught her by the shoulders. Tugging her against him, he growled, "You shall do no such thing. However, I will do what I must to make sure everyone accepts our marriage." He eyed her up and down. "No matter how distasteful."

"If you do not want to—that is—"

His laugh was cruel. "Do you truly believe that you are so appealing? Just because Somerset seduced you, do not think every other man pines for you. I have more selective tastes than Somerset, who will bed any woman he keeps company with."

Brienne flinched. She did not want to believe that Evan had seduced her simply because she had been convenient during their adventures. No, she must not let the insults keep her from asking the questions she must. "Then, why would you marry me?"

"If you have to ask that, you are a greater fool than I had believed!"

When he went back to the table, she drew on her wrapper, tying it at her waist. She would not listen to any more of this. She would leave. She would—

A single step betrayed her. She crumpled to the floor, her wobbly legs refusing to support her. The bedside table rocked, and the trio of figurines atop it fell on their sides, one rolling to shatter on the floor.

"What did you do to me?" she gasped as she grasped the bed to try to pull herself up from the carpet.

"Why are you blaming me for your drunkenness?"

She looked up and wished she could strip away his superior smile. When he did not offer to help her to her feet, she struggled to stand. She fell again. Her fury at his laughter strengthened her, and she stood. Flashing him a victorious smile, she wished she could walk out. She did not dare to move, not trusting her precarious balance any more than she trusted this man Evan had so foolishly.

"Armistead, you drugged my wine. Did your friends have a grand time laughing at a woman who was tricked into a marriage which cannot be legal?"

"Yes, they did, but I tell you, wife, that the ceremony was legal. A minister officiated."

She pressed her fingers to her lips as horror struck her like a blow. *Mon Dieu*, it might mean she was truly married to Armistead Porter. As his smile broadened, he patted her on the cheek. She tried to pull away, but the motion was too much for her weak knees. With a soft cry, she slipped back to the floor. She snarled a French oath.

When he answered in perfect French, she stared at him. "You need not look so surprised," he said with a laugh. "Some of the *émigrés* have made a better life for themselves than you and your so-called *grand-mère*, Brienne Levesque."

"How do you know that name?" Brienne knew it was useless to pretend that he was using the wrong name. If he had overheard a single one of the conversations between her and Grand-mère, he had heard them discuss her lost family.

"Do not think you can run back to Somerset," he said

instead of answering her question. "The staff believes that I have wed you to protect you from those who would cheat a simpleminded heiress."

"How noble of you!"

"Isn't it?"

"I shall—"

Gripping her face tightly, he snarled, "You shall cooperate, wife. If you do not, I will see you dead as soon as I find your sister."

"Sister? You know about my sister?"

He released her, shoving her away. "I know all about the Levesque family. It is too bad you did not discover the truth before this, Brienne. I understand your mother died fairly recently." He laughed. "I wonder what the *duchesse* would have thought of her daughter who whores for a common art thief."

Brienne stared at him in disbelief. She struggled to her feet again. "Armistead, do you know where my sister is?"

"Yes."

"Where is she?"

"Where she is I shall keep to myself unless you give me reason to find her. 'Tis not a journey I want to make when winter is still gripping the Continent. If you cooperate, I shall have no reason to bring your sister here to mourn at your demise while I woo her into being my wife at the same time she claims her place as the new *duchesse*."

"You would not!"

"Do not cooperate, and I shall show you exactly how serious I am."

Holding tightly to the bed, she did not answer as he walked toward the table. Armistead Porter would do as he threatened. She could not allow her sister to become mixed up in this.

When she did not reply, he smiled. She kept her face

blank. Until she regained her strength from whatever he had mixed in her wine, she must be careful.

He served himself a generous breakfast. "You need not lurk in the shadows like a beaten dog. Come and sit while we discuss what we shall do to ensure that Château Tonnere du Grêlon becomes ours soon. We shall enjoy a luxurious life in the late *duc's* fine home."

"Château Tonnere du Grêlon shall never be yours!"

He laughed. "You are now my wife. Everything you possessed belongs to your husband when you wed. Your title for our son—"

"I shall never sleep with you!" she fired back.

Ignoring her, he continued, "Your château is mine as is your slender body."

She clenched her hands. If the marriage had been performed legally, he was right. Everything belonged to him. She refused to admit that the marriage was real.

"Come and eat." Taking her hand, he jerked her toward him. He smiled and stroked her face. She tried to twist away, but he pushed her into a chair. "If you sicken and die now, I risk losing your father's lovely château. You would not want to do that and disappoint your loving husband, would you?"

"You shall not have Château Tonnere du Grêlon!"

"You are wrong. It finally will belong to me as it should have long ago."

"What?"

He laughed. "I guess that is one story your grandmother failed to tell you. How Château Tonnere du Grêlon was supposed to be given to the LaPortes because my father provided the proof that Marc-Michel Levesque was a traitor to the Revolution."

"LaPorte?" she choked. This man was the one her mother had warned her about, for *la porte* translated as "the door." Maman had not been out of her mind with pain. She had been completely lucid.

"We found that the English welcomed us more when we anglicized our name." He smiled. "And it kept our enemies from finding us."

"I am sure you had many enemies after betraying innocent men to death."

He laughed. "The guillotine took care of most of them. Unfortunately the tide of sentiment turned before my father could secure his claim on Château Tonnere du Grêlon." He lifted his fork. "To Armistead LaPorte and his son, the Duc of Château Tonnere du Grêlon."

When he began to eat, she stared at her empty plate. His silence told her what she did not want to admit to. The rest of her life, she would have to give to this man, her husband, everything she owned, including her pride.

Through the meal, Armistead exulted in his windfall. More than once, he looked at her as if daring her to refute his words. She remained silent, but as her thoughts became clearer, she began to plot how she would escape. If he was her husband, she could never completely be free while he lived, but she did not think of that. She must find Evan. With his help, she would figure out how to save Grand-mère and develop a plan to disappear.

Brienne looked up as the door opened again. Her eyes widened when Louisa swept into the room and put her arms around Armistead, her fingers slipping beneath the open front of his wrapper. His glided up along her pale pink wrapper to stroke her as boldly.

"Good morning, my love," Louisa whispered, firing a sly glance at Brienne. "She looks quite shocked. I thought you were going to wait for me to join you before you revealed the truth to her. Have you told her everything?"

He kissed Louisa deeply, then turned to Brienne. "Almost everything. She knows she is my wife, and the château soon will be mine as well." He laughed as his avaricious gaze swept along her. "However, I thought I would save the best until you got here."

Chapter Twenty

Brienne pushed herself to her feet. "I have heard all I wish to hear." Hoping her legs would not fail her now, she edged toward the door.

"Stop her, Armistead!" Louisa cried. "You promised me that I could watch when you told her about what you have done with her grandmother."

Gripping the back of a chair, Brienne turned to stare, aghast, at them. She had never guessed that evil would be dressed in elegant silk and lace. "You? You are Lagrille?" She swallowed hard. "*La grille*. The gate instead of the door? Have you had fun hiding the truth from us?"

"Yes, to be quite honest." He dabbed his lips with a napkin and stood.

"Where is my grandmother?"

"She is unharmed, and she will stay that way as long as you cooperate." His lips curled. "I would not say the same for your paramour."

"Evan!" Her fingers dug into the upholstery. "If you have hurt him, I shall—"

"You shall do as I tell you, and so will he." He smiled icily. "I had not expected you to fall for his well-known seductive wiles when I sent him to find that thunderstone vase knowing the *duc's* daughter should be where it was. I had guessed you would be too wise for that, but it appears you are as foolish and trusting as your father was."

As Evan has been. She never would have guessed the time might come when she would be amazed that Evan had swallowed a clanker whole. He had not trusted LaPorte, but he had counted him among his "friends."

"I believe you shall find that neither Evan nor I will follow your orders willingly," she replied, her chin high.

"Then, you shall be sorry."

"I doubt if I could be much sorrier than I am now to find myself the wife of such a cur."

When he reached for her, she kept the chair between them. He did not let her elude him. Grasping her arm, he tugged her to him. "Look at me," he ordered.

"Let me go!"

"I said 'look at me!' " He smiled as she moaned with pain when his fingers twisted in her hair and jerked her head back. "That is better, Brienne."

"You are hurting me!"

"Which I will continue to do if you do not obey me."

She gasped as he pulled her head back farther, then clamped her lips closed, determined not to give him any more pleasure at her pain.

Releasing her, he growled a curse. He took Louisa by the hand and tugged her to the door.

"But, Armistead, this is fun," his mistress whined. "Why are you making me leave so soon?"

"Because there are some parts of this that you cannot

be a part of.'' He shoved her out the door and closed it. With a low laugh, he locked it.

Tensing, Brienne could not keep from shrieking when he gripped her shoulders and brought her against him. She winced as his fingers combed through her hair.

''You are quite beautiful,'' he murmured against her ear while he reached for the sash at her waist.

''I thought you said I should not take on airs simply because Evan and I ...'' She shoved his hand away. ''Leave me alone.''

''You are my wife. I have a right to do whatever I wish with you.'' He eased a finger under her sash. ''It shall not be difficult to beget a *duc* with you.''

She backed away and choked on her horror when she bumped into the bed. ''Go to your mistress! Let her give you a child.''

''That matter is already taken care of.'' He gave her a boastful smile. ''Most convenient, for now I can concentrate on you.''

''Release my grandmother first.''

''You are in no position to make demands, Brienne. However, I will let you see her if you give me the thunderstone vase.''

''The vase?'' She stared at him in disbelief. ''What do you need it for? I thought you were using it as a ruse to have Evan find me.''

He laughed. ''You fool! Do you think you will be able to walk into Napoleon's court, and he will give you the title and the château? You need proof that you are Levesque's daughter.''

''The vase is gone, destroyed in the fire.''

''Don't think me as witless as your lover! I know it was not destroyed because you were seen carrying a bag out of the salon and heard to tell your grandmother that it must not be dropped.'' He smiled and rubbed his hands together in anticipation. "No more talk, wife. I want to see you naked. Undress!"

"No!"

His eyes sparkled with malicious expectation as he drew off his robe and threw it over a chair. "Obey me, or I shall make this very unpleasant for you."

He reached for her. She screamed and turned to run. Her weak legs betrayed her. As she collapsed, he scooped her up and tossed her onto the bed. She slapped him, but he shoved her viciously into the mattress. Her breath was ragged in her ears as she struggled to escape.

"Good," he murmured, pinning her legs beneath his. "Fight me, Brienne."

"Stop! Stop this. Please! I will give you the château. It is yours."

"It can be mine only with you as my wife." He gripped the front of her wrapper and tugged until it came open. With a smile, he reached for the hooks along the back of her nightdress. The threads holding them snapped. When she opened her mouth to cry for help, he covered it with his own and reached for the hem of her gown.

Twisting away to avoid his mouth, Brienne realized he was not going to waste time in undressing her. He would rape her immediately, then return to do the same for the rest of the day ... for the rest of her life. Tears rolled along her cheeks as she sought anything to halt him.

Her fingers struck the side of the table next to the bed. As he pulled the neckline of her nightdress lower, she gripped another of the figurines clustered there. She raised it and smashed it over his head.

He dropped heavily onto her. Shoving him aside, she wiggled out from beneath him. She fell onto the floor with a thump.

Rising, she rushed to the dressing room door that was ajar. She smiled when she saw her clothes tossed on the floor within. Quickly she dressed, then went to the hall door and slid aside the lock.

Brienne opened the door and peered both ways along the hall. She smiled. Armistead's determination to keep anyone from hearing him rape her must have banished the servants from this part of the house. Louisa would be pouting in her room, so Brienne need not worry about her. If Brienne could reach the ground floor, she could slip out without anyone being the wiser. She needed only to look as if nothing were amiss, and no one would take note of her until it was too late. That was something she had learned from Evan.

She faltered as she walked toward the servants' stairs. LaPorte knew where her grandmother was. If she left now. . . . She quivered with horror at what would happen if she remained. She must find allies who would help her help Grand-mère.

As she began to pick her way down the shadowed stairs, she knew the price of failure. She would be returned to LaPorte as his wife. Her father's legacy would be handed over to his enemy's son. Worst of all, she feared for Evan's life and her grandmother's. LaPorte would not allow Evan and Grand-mère to be witnesses against him when he went to claim Château Tonnere du Grêlon.

Brienne could not fail in this and let him capture her again.

She could not.

Evan stood with his hands folded behind his back. When he realized he had stood just like this so many times in this room, he let his arms drop to his sides. He had to be careful what he said. The wrong word would be disastrous now.

"Do you have something to say, or did you only wish to see if I would receive you?" Lord Sommerton scowled from where he sat in the leather chair in his favorite room, looking out through the branches of the trees in the middle of Berkeley Square. A fire played on the hearth, but was dimmed by the sunshine coming through the window that swept from floor to ceiling. Dozens of pieces of artwork were displayed on the mantel. That love of art was something he had bequeathed to his son, whether he was glad of that or not.

A cup of steaming chocolate waited on a table near his father's hand, and the day's newspaper was folded neatly beside it. In the decade since Evan had left Sommerton Hall, his father had not altered his habits, it appeared.

"I find it advisable to choose my words carefully," Evan replied.

"A change."

He smiled coolly as he shook his head. "Quite to the contrary. My words to you, sir, have always been well thought out."

"If you called only to tell me that you have not changed, I see no reason to continue this conversation."

Evan started to reply, but the door opened, striking him in the center of the back and pushing him forward into a chair. Before he could even curse at the pain scoring his shin, someone ran past him.

"I tried to persuade her to wait," he heard the butler say.

His head snapped up when another voice, the very voice that filled his sweetest fantasies, said, "My lord, forgive the intrusion, but I have nowhere else to go. Nowhere else to turn. I need your help."

In disbelief, Evan stared at Brienne, who was kneeling by his father's chair, grasping his father's sleeve. She was here? How had she gotten here? He had been very careful not to let her know that his parents kept a townhouse on Berkeley Square, because he wanted to protect her from the sharp edge of his father's tongue. If she had inquired about the location of this house among the *ton* or the lower classes, he would certainly have heard of it. He scowled, knowing what must have sent her fleeing here.

He put his hands on her arms and drew her to her feet. When she cried out his name and flung her arms around him, he pressed her cheek to his chest. Her trembling told him that the tale he had not wanted to believe must be true. Curse Devereux for failing to find him until not more than an hour ago!

"Miss LeClerc," said his father, coming to his feet, "please sit down while I ring for another cup of hot chocolate."

If his father thought he could ease her despair like this, he was a fool. His father locked gazes with him, and Evan knew his father was not a beef-head. The earl wanted to give Brienne a chance to compose herself before asking her how she had gotten here and why. That was something Evan wanted to know, too. The information Devereux had given him was the very reason that Evan had come here.

"I am so glad you have decided to return my call," Lord Sommerton continued.

Evan's frown deepened. *Return his call?* Brienne had not mentioned that his father had given her a look-in at Grosvenor Square. He shook his irritation from his head. The past no longer mattered. He had admitted to that when he arrived here just before Brienne.

Softly he said, "I am glad Father visited you, honey, if that is how you knew where to come for help."

"What are you doing here, Evan?" she asked.

"The same as you." He gave her a weak grin. "Looking for any help I can get to find your grandmother."

"LaPorte has her!"

His frown returned. "LaPorte? Who is that?"

"Armistead Porter. His real name is LaPorte. He is

French." She choked, "And he hired you under the name of Lagrille to find me."

"Lagrille. LaPorte. Porter. All so close to the same word in English." He swore. "How have I been so blind?"

Lord Sommerton said quietly, "It is said that love is blind. Mayhap it is blinding as well."

As Evan stepped aside to let the maid put another set of cups on the tray where the chocolate pot waited, he did not answer. His father might be more correct than Evan wished to admit. Lost in his delight with Brienne, he had failed to see the facts in front of him.

His father began, "Miss LeClerc—"

"Miss Levesque," Evan said quietly.

" 'Tis LaPorte now." Her hands shook as she sat where his father had indicated. "Madame LaPorte."

Lord Sommerton cursed, then said, "Forgive me, Miss—Mrs. LaPorte."

"Brienne would be easier, if you do not mind the informality." Brienne was glad when Evan sat beside her. She did not care what the earl thought when she wove her fingers through Evan's. That Evan had not reacted to her comments warned her that he already knew of the marriage. Nothing remained unknown among the *ton* for long. "Evan, we have to get Grand-mère away from that horrible man."

"He said he had her?" Evan's face was drawn, and she guessed he had not slept since leaving the house.

"Yes."

"Did he give you any hint where?" asked the earl.

She took the cup he handed her, but did not raise it to her lips. "I suspect she is still within the house. That would explain why no one on the square saw anything unusual."

"And the servants could be easily controlled so they would be where Porter—LaPorte wanted them to be."

Evan stood and paced from the settee to the hearth and back. "That means we must go back there and find her."

Brienne nodded, although her stomach roiled with fear. "Yes. I thought that would be our only choice. It has to be quickly, or he might hurt my grandmother." She caught Evan's hand as he passed by her. When he looked down at her, she whispered, "He wants the vase."

"To prove you are the *duc's* daughter?"

"Yes," she said again, not surprised that Evan understood immediately. "Do you have it?"

"In a very safe place." He smiled tightly. "Don't ask, honey. That is information I would like to keep to myself for the moment." Sitting beside her again, he added, "*This* is the reason I called on you, Father. I know you have nearly as many connections in the government as I do at the docks."

The earl sighed. "None of which will be of any use in this matter. With the blockade around England and fear of an invasion, no one is going to risk anything that might focus Napoleon's government's wrath on us. This LaPorte must have allies in that government if he is so bold."

"Then, we shall have to handle it ourselves."

"Son, I believe it would make the most sense if you and I were to pay a call on your erstwhile host."

"No!" Brienne cried. "I shall not be left behind again. After what happened this time, I cannot risk that."

Father and son exchanged a look she could not decipher. Then, Evan asked, "How did you slip out of the house, honey?"

"Through the laundry and out the back gate. Just the opposite of how we slipped in."

"Past the cellar door?"

"You think he has imprisoned Grand-mère in the cellar? That place has a malodorous reek coming from it."

She fisted her hands in her lap. "That bastard is no better than his father."

Evan's brow threaded. "His father is part of this, too?"

"Not now. His father is dead, but before he died, he arranged for my father's death in hopes of claiming my family's estate." She shivered. "Like father, like son."

When the earl laughed, Brienne regarded him with amazement. She was not sure what she had said that was humorous.

Lord Sommerton came to his feet. "I would like to disagree with that, but it appears that you may be right. Certainly my son is as stubborn as I am. Evan, I believe you and Miss—Brienne have matters to discuss. Be assured that I am willing to help in any way I may to rescue her grandmother from this ignoble Frenchman's schemes which have the stench of froggish greed." He gulped. "Excuse me, Brienne. I did not mean to disparage all French people with my comment."

"No need to apologize, my lord. I quite agree with you." She was amazed she could smile. "Although I may have been born along the Loire, I am, as my mother lamented so often, very much an Englishwoman."

The earl walked to the door, then turned back to them. "Son, I never thought I would say this, but I am proud of you."

"You are?" Evan asked.

Brienne elbowed him. "Where are your manners, Evan? Say thank you."

"Allow the lad a chance to be surprised." Lord Sommerton's smile vanished as he added, "I was wrong to act as I did at Lady Jacington's assembly. Even though you apparently have not changed since you left Sommerton Hall, I, too, know how to make queries about Town, and I have learned that you have gained respect as a man who values his word and his friendships. I suppose I should ask no more of my son than that."

"Thank you, sir."

"Let me know when you are ready to make that call on LaPorte." He rubbed his hands together. "This should be most amusing."

Evan was silent until the door closed behind his father, then he chuckled. "That is what I like best about him. His hypocrisy!"

"What a thing to say!"

" 'Tis the truth, and he would be the first to admit to it. He will never forgive me for leaving Sommerton Hall because he and my mother tried to mold me into the perfect heir, never saying or doing something that was not proper." He arched a brow. "You can guess how impossible that was for me."

"Completely." She leaned her head against his shoulder, longing for the rapture that would make her forget even this horror.

"Now listen to him. He is ready to gird his loins and do battle with LaPorte."

"A most chivalrous thing to do."

He laughed again. "Mayhap you are right. Mayhap he has changed as little as I have. Brienne?"

"Yes?"

When he took her by the shoulders and drew her back so he could see her face, he started to speak more than once. He cleared his throat, but said hoarsely, "Brienne, I have to ask you. You need not answer, but I must know."

"No, he did not consummate our marriage." She put her hands up to his cheeks. "I was senseless until this morning, and then, when he tried, I left *him* senseless. I broke one of his precious figurines over his head." She laughed, halting herself when she heard its hysterical tinge. "What am I going to do?"

"Do not fret about your marriage now. Now we must

get your grandmother away from him. Then we will deal with other issues.''

Although she wanted to counter that her marriage was not just an "issue," she nodded. Grand-mère's well-being was more important than anything else. "So what do you have planned?"

"Right now? Kissing you."

He enfolded her in his arms as his mouth slanted across hers. The craving that only grew stronger each time he touched her detonated within her, shattering her worries as she savored his tongue sliding along hers. It took all her willpower to pull back when she wanted to remain in his arms. She must think of Grand-mère.

"Evan, be serious!"

"I was." He brushed her lips with his. "It seems as if it has been a century since I last was able to do this."

"I know," she whispered. She drew back again and squared her shoulders. "Evan, what do you have planned?"

He stroked her back as he murmured, "Honey, we both know that LaPorte will not let you or your grandmother go while he believes he can use you to claim Château Tonnere du Grêlon."

"I know."

"So we shall have to persuade him otherwise."

"How?"

"With the help of my father and a friend or two."

"Evan!"

He chuckled at her frustration with his elusive answers. "You are going to have to trust me on this, honey. I know how difficult that is for you."

"No, it is not so difficult." She stroked his cheek. "I find that easy to do now."

"As I find it easier to say this." He balanced her chin on his crooked finger. "I love you, Brienne. I want you to know that I would marry you today if I could."

Her eyes widened. "Marry me? I thought you had no use for a family."

"I did say something to that effect, didn't I? You are going to make me admit that you are right, and I was mistaken."

"Yes, but I do not understand why you have changed your mind."

"A man changes when he is shown how empty his life is without the woman he loves." He combed his fingers through her hair. "My love, my Brienne, will you marry me as soon as you can?"

"Yes."

As he kissed her and pulled her into his arms, she answered his eager passion with her own. She did not want to think that this one perfect moment might be the last one they would know.

Chapter Twenty-one

Brienne stood on the corner of a street that led to Grosvenor Square. If she had looked past the building beside her, she would be able to see the square and LaPorte's townhouse. On the street in front of her, a dark carriage with bright red trim was stopped. Evan was giving last minute instructions to his father. So much depended on Lord Sommerton persuading LaPorte that he was calling on a matter that had nothing to do with his son or Brienne and her grandmother.

Evan stepped up onto the walkway as the coachman slapped the reins to send the carriage around the corner. He adjusted his simple coat that would be suitable for a delivery lad or a lower servant. "This will work, honey."

"I hope so."

"My father can talk longer about nothing than anyone I know. He will fill LaPorte's head with so many governmental figures that you will find yourself feeling sorry for LaPorte."

"That is unlikely."

He ran his finger along her lips. "Smile, honey. Just to keep yourself in practice for when we find your grandmother."

"I wish I had your confidence."

"Something I learned to have years ago. If I refuse to admit that I might fail, it is amazing how many times I don't." He hesitated, glancing around the corner, then said, "If you want to switch tasks, I will be glad to."

Brienne shook her head. "Even though it smells, I would rather go down into the cellars than up to the attics. There is less chance I will encounter someone."

"Watch for my signal."

"I will."

He drew her into his arms and kissed her deeply. Brushing her hair back toward her cap that would make her look like one of the household maids, he whispered, "Just stay away from LaPorte."

"I will," she repeated with a shiver. "You, too."

"That is a promise." Reaching under his coat, he pulled out a knife in a sheath. "Just in case, honey."

Although she did not want to take it, she did and hid it beneath her apron. A threat with this might give her grandmother time to escape. "Thank you."

"Thank me when you and your grandmother are safe. I can think of some special ways I would enjoy letting you thank me, Brienne." He tapped her on the nose, then loped along the street.

Brienne waited and counted slowly to fifty. That would give both Evan and his father a head start. This plan seemed too simple to succeed. If LaPorte refused to receive the earl. . . . If she or Evan chanced to run into someone who recognized them. . . . If Grand-mère was not in the house. . . .

No, she would not think of failure. She must be as brazen as Evan and assume that everything would work out just as they had hoped.

Walking another street beyond the square, she turned to come along the walkway behind LaPorte's townhouse. She edged toward the back gate. When she had fled from here this morning, she had not guessed she would be returning so soon.

Brienne smiled when she saw the sheets were still hanging on the lines strung across the laundry yard. Picking up a wicker basket, she walked among the lines. She bent to touch a sheet as if to test if it was dry when another maid walked past on the other side of a line.

Her breath burned in her chest, but she did not dare release it as she entered the laundry room. More laundry hung from lines. Keeping her basket in front of her, she peered into one of the vats of hot water if someone came too close. Steam hung in the air. It would help conceal her face.

Edging along the wall, she reached the cellar door. Her nose wrinkled as she smelled the damp that seeped around it. She hoped she would find Grand-mère down there, but just thinking of LaPorte imprisoning her grandmother in such a horrible place added to her rage. She forced it away. She must not let her anger blind her to danger.

No one turned as she opened the door and slipped through. She drew it shut behind her, glad there was not a bolt on the outside. Waiting on the top stair, she gave her eyes a moment to adjust to the darkness. There was a hint of light, and she suspected there must be a small window that opened to the gardens. The windows that looked out on the square would open into rooms that were not connected with this section of the cellars, Evan had told her. She wondered if he had explored those rooms or if he was just guessing.

Brienne edged down the stairs. The room was empty, save for puddles between the stones on the floor. A darker abyss gaped to her right. Stretching out her toe, she discovered a deep hole that might be some sort of well. The stench that came from it made her retch.

Turning, she looked at the opposite wall. She slid her feet along the floor, wanting to make sure she did not step into another hole. She glanced under the stairs, but saw nothing. That was no comfort because the shadows concealed most of the area.

Brienne smiled when she saw a door with a bolt on it. This must be it! Who else would LaPorte be hiding? She pushed it open. Light came from a narrow window high up in the wall to show that the room was empty. A narrow cot and a pail warned that the chamber was meant as a prison.

If Grand-mère was not here, where was she?

She cringed as she heard shouts from overhead, then a gun firing. They had been found out. She must leave. No, she could not go without her grandmother.

Trying to pull open another door, she realized it was jammed. She withdrew the knife Evan had given her. She stuck it between the door and the frame and tugged. The door sprung open. She looked in and gasped, "Grand-mère!"

Her grandmother raised her head from where she was hunched on a cot identical to the one in the other room. "Brienne, child, you must go! Porter is—"

"I know." She hurried in and assisted her grandmother to her feet. "We have to go. Something has gone wrong."

Grand-mère lurched against her as Brienne steered her out of the small room. Nodding when Grand-mère warned her to avoid the hole beyond the stairs, she assisted her grandmother up to the door into the laundry room. She inched the door open and recoiled again when she heard another gun fire.

"*Mon Dieu*," groaned Madame LeClerc. "Are they mad?"

Brienne did not reply as she looked both ways. The

laundry room appeared deserted. She heard screams from the kitchens and hoped they came from the laundry maids who were fleeing. "This way," she whispered.

Even though she swayed on every step, Grand-mère went with Brienne to the back door. Brienne opened it, then froze as she heard the unmistakable click of a pistol's hammer. Her grandmother moaned, and Brienne looked back to see LaPorte on the other side of a clothesline.

She did not close the door as he walked toward them. Stepping between him and her grandmother, she knew he would not kill her. He had to keep her alive until he could be certain he could find and marry her sister.

"You are as stupid as Somerset," LaPorte growled.

"You were the one who got some sense knocked into his head," she returned as she saw the drying blood in his hair from where the ceramic had cut him.

"I should have guessed this was all a ploy for you to get that old woman." He sneered at Grand-mère. "Why do you want her so badly?"

"She is my grandmother!"

"Does she have the vase?"

"No, she does not have the vase." She laughed. "But she did. If you had not been in such a hurry to sneak her out of here so you could get rid of Evan and drug me, you might have found it."

"You should consider yourself fortunate that I was willing to wed you despite the fact that you are no longer a virgin."

"Willing to marry her?" Grand-mère laughed bitterly. "You have been salivating to get your greedy hands on her and her title. You would have wed her if she had been as old as I am."

"You are right." He kept his thumb on the gun's hammer and stepped toward them, still on the other side of the clothesline. "Where is Somerset?"

Brienne gave a careless shrug to hide her shock. If he

had not been firing at Evan, then whom? She shivered as she feared for the earl. "How should I know? Weren't you the one who told me that you would have him dealt with? You should know where he is."

"Brienne!" gasped her grandmother as LaPorte raised the gun toward Brienne. "Take care."

"Yes, Brienne. Listen to your grandmother." His voice dripped with sarcasm as he shifted the pistol so it pointed at Grand-mère. "She would tell you to come with me before I put a ball in the center of her chest."

Brienne once again stepped between her grandmother and the gun. "If you kill me, you lose your best chance to get my father's estate."

His thumb stroked the hammer. "But it might be worth it to see you die."

"Save your posturing for someone else." She slipped her hand under her apron and curled her fingers around the haft of the knife. In one motion, she swung the wet clothes at LaPorte. They hit him in the face, knocking him backward. "Run, Grand-mère!"

A shot struck the door as Grand-mère rushed out at the best speed she could manage. Splinters cut into Brienne's arm. Seeing LaPorte reach to reload, she whirled to follow her grandmother. He reached over the line and seized her arm, shoving her back against a vat. She shrieked as she burned her hand on the cast iron. Fury strengthened her as she drove the knife into his arm.

He fell to one knee between her and the back door. He cursed her and tried to reload his gun.

She ran up the stairs. She might be able to go along this upper floor and flee out the front door. Hearing LaPorte behind her, she ducked into the nearest room, slipping behind the open door.

She held her breath as he peered into the chamber and then rushed along the hallway, shouting to Hitchcock.

Easing back out into the hall, she rushed back down the stairs. Would he guess she had gone this way?

A hand reached out and grasped her arm. She opened her mouth to scream, but choked on it when she stared at Evan's colorless face. Blood coursed along his right arm.

Before she could ask, he said, " 'Tis nothing but a scratch. I will be fine, and Father is out of harm's way."

"So is Grand-mère."

"Then, let's get ourselves out of here, too." He paused with a curse as shouts came from outside in the garden.

When Brienne turned toward the front of the house, the clatter of footfalls echoed along the hallway beyond the laundry room door.

"That is LaPorte!" she whispered.

"I know. There is no place to run." He threw open the cellar door and led her down the steps. "Did you see a place where we can hide?"

As they reached the bottom, she pointed to the area under the stairs. "There. Be careful. There is a deep hole on the other side of the stairs."

"A deep hole? What sort of hole?"

"Evan, we have to hide!" Giving his usual curiosity free rein could betray them. "Now!"

He bent and looked beneath the risers. " 'Tis not much, but 'tis better than standing here and waiting for him to find us."

When he stumbled against her on the first step, she put her arm around him and guided him into the shadows. Evan must be hurt more than he was telling her, but she would ignore it as he was. What had happened to either of them was less critical than what was about to happen.

She helped him sit against the damp wall. Kneeling beside him, she flinched when something struck her leg. He pressed a pistol into her hand.

"I cannot fire it, honey," he said in a voice laced with

agony. "LaPorte got my right arm. You can fire it. After all, you did well against Marksen's men."

"But—"

"You can if you must."

Nodding, she hoped he was right. She held his hand as she listened to the footfalls banging down the stairs. Not just LaPorte, but several other men who held lanterns. Her breath caught painfully in her chest when she saw the men stride across the cellar toward where she had left the doors to the prison cells ajar. They peered into the corners that were laced with spider webs. When one bent to look under the stairs, she closed her eyes, wishing she and Evan could suddenly become invisible.

Evan squeezed her hand, and she opened her eyes to see the man had turned away. LaPorte's man had not noticed them in the deepest shadows.

"Mr. Porter, there is no one down here," called one of the men. "Where else should we look?"

"Everywhere!" LaPorte growled. "Damn that woman!"

Brienne was sure her heartbeat would betray them as the men hurried back up the stairs. It pounded in her ears like thunder.

"Go!" LaPorte shouted. "They will be trying to sneak out of the house. Stop them!"

"What of Madame LeClerc?"

"Do not worry about that old bat! It is Brienne I want."

"And Somerset?"

"Kill him, and bring my wife back to me unharmed!"

As Evan's fingers stroked hers, Brienne wished for his arms around her. The steady beat of his heart would have calmed the terror within her. Breathing shallowly, she strained to hear the door closing at the top of the stairs. It did, and silence filled the cellar.

Slowly, so slowly she could sense every tight muscle moving, she looked at Evan. He nodded. She eased out of the space and reached back to help him. There was no time to spare. They must hurry if they were to—

She screamed as her arm was clasped. She was twisted away from Evan to stare into her husband's face. As LaPorte opened a dark lantern to splash light across the cellar, she saw blood dripped along his arm, too. He hammered her wrist sharply. She cried out as Evan's gun skittered away into the shadows. Shoving her away with a vicious curse, he smiled victoriously.

"It is time to finish this, Somerset," he chortled with malicious glee.

A gun fired. Brienne screamed, then realized the sound had come from the floor above. Had the earl returned with help?

LaPorte flinched, and his gun wavered. Brienne leaped to grab it. As if she were a fly, he swept her aside. She fell to the hard floor, her breath erupting in a painful rush. Clinging to the wet stones, she fought to remain conscious. She could not let her husband kill Evan.

Desperately she struggled to sit. LaPorte's tone warned he was taunting Evan, but his words were distorted as if they came through thick mesh. She moaned when she saw LaPorte had two handfuls of Evan's shirt. Forgetting her aching head, she jumped to her feet again. She pummeled him, but he knocked her aside.

Evan swung his left fist at LaPorte, but it missed widely. She moaned as LaPorte struck him. When he wobbled, LaPorte's fist hit him again. Evan folded up and dropped to the floor.

"No!" she screamed.

LaPorte faced her, setting the lantern on the floor. "He is taken care of for the moment, dear wife. Now for you." As he stepped toward her, she backed away. "I had planned to take you upstairs in my bed, but the floor here shall do just as well."

Spinning, she fled toward the stairs. He caught her arm,

dragging her to him. He pressed his lips over hers, grinding his mouth down into hers.

She twisted her face away. "I shall not be yours," she stated through gritted teeth.

"You have no choice." He chuckled as he thrust her toward the room where Grand-mère had been imprisoned. "You are mine, Brienne. You and everything you possess. First I shall kill your lover, then I shall have you."

As he reached for the gun he had stuck in his belt, she shoved against his chest with all her strength.

"You fool!" he shrieked as he reached for her. "You are mine. I—"

A shadow moved behind him. Something on Brienne's face must have betrayed what she had seen, because LaPorte whirled to face Evan, then cursed as Brienne tore the gun from his hand. Before she could aim it, again he knocked it out of her grip. She kicked it aside before he could retrieve it. He raised his fist.

Evan grasped LaPorte's coat and tugged him away from Brienne. "Don't touch her."

"She is my wife. I can do whatever I want to her."

"She is not your wife."

LaPorte struck him in the stomach, sending Evan to his knees again. When Brienne moaned and tried to get to Evan, he shoved her toward the stairs. More shots were fired upstairs.

With a curse, LaPorte said, "I don't have time to waste on this. She is my wife. Married in front of a minister."

"In front of my friend Devereux, who was keeping an eye on her."

"You are lying!" LaPorte screeched.

Coming to his feet, Evan smiled. "Do you think I would have let her come back here to rescue her grandmother if I thought you could capture her and steal her father's legacy to her?"

Brienne stared in astonishment. Why hadn't Evan said

something about this before? Mayhap he was just trying to betwattle LaPorte. She edged toward where LaPorte had kicked the gun. LaPorte whirled and shoved her to the floor.

His blow staggered Evan. "Too bad you cannot stay and watch me consummate my marriage to Brienne."

"You bastard!" Evan's fist hit LaPorte's chin, sending him reeling backward.

Brienne cried out as LaPorte teetered, then vanished. She heard a crash as he struck the bottom of the hole by the stairs.

Evan shouted, "LaPorte! Are you hurt?"

She watched as he lifted the lantern and then held it down into the hole. When she stepped forward, he halted her.

"You do not want to see what is down there," he said in a taut voice.

"LaPorte?"

"Dead. A broken neck, I would guess, by the way he's lying on the other corpses."

"Others?" she choked as he set the lantern on the floor and stood.

"I suspect they are your sailor friends who failed him by being so foolish as to risk killing you by setting the salon on fire."

With a sob, she threw her arms around him. He groaned, but embraced her with his uninjured arm.

A sound intruded, and she gasped, "Evan!"

"I heard it. The door." He backed toward the space under the stairs.

Before she could slip beneath them, someone ran down the stairs. She heard Evan laugh with relief. Turning, Brienne saw Lord Sommerton and Evan's friend Devereux standing on the steps.

"It is safe to get Miss LeClerc out of here." Devereux

frowned as he looked around the cellar. "Where is LaPorte?"

Evan hooked a thumb toward the hole, then grimaced. "I think I should get this arm tended to." He fell to his knees. "Right away," he murmured before collapsing to sprawl on the floor.

Epilogue

"Good morning!" sang Brienne as she pulled back the curtains on the bed.

Evan glared, and she laughed. He did not like staying at his father's house and being dependent on anyone for his care. When he started to sit, she shook her head.

"The doctor said you should stay quiet. That bump you have on the back of your head from where you hit the floor is not a minor injury."

He took her hand and drew her to sit on the bed. With a roguish grin, he brought her back to lie on the pillows beside him. "I rest best when you are with me. Are you going to succumb to proprieties and stop sharing my bed until we are married?"

"No talk of that until you are better." She laughed as she pointed to his arm in a splint. "I do not want to bump that and hurt it worse."

"Your touch might help it heal faster."

Leaning on one elbow, she looked down into his face which remained gray. "I have made a decision."

"Have you?"

"Yes."

"Are you going to tell me?"

She twisted a lock of his hair around her finger and smiled. "Your father has offered to advance me the funds I need to rebuild L'Enfant de la Patrie."

"If you want my opinion—"

"I told him yes."

He chuckled. "Did you think I would step between you and your dream? I have seen how despairing you looked each time you spoke of how impossible it was to rebuild the salon." He ran his finger along her cheek. "How did you persuade Father to part with even a farthing?"

"He said if it fails, it will be your inheritance that suffers." She laughed as she nestled beside him again. "But it will not fail. Grand-mère cannot wait to get back to cooking."

"Neither can you."

"And what of you, Evan? If you do not wish to be tied down to the salon and a wife and—"

He captured her lips before whispering, "You have changed me, Brienne. I want to spend every possible minute with you. It does not matter if it is in your salon or where."

"If the war continues, it may be years before we can return to Château Tonnere du Grêlon."

"I am not LaPorte, honey. I do not want you for your father's legacy, just for the sweet kisses you can share with me." He smiled sadly. "And mayhap, by the time we can get to France, we will have found your sister."

"And my brother."

"Your grandmother said she believed he was dead."

"Mayhap, mayhap not. I do not deem anything impossible since you persuaded me to fall in love with you."

She kissed him lightly, then whispered, "Shall we get married in the new L'Enfant de la Patrie?"

"I do not want to wait that long." He reached across the bed and picked up a slip of paper from the bedside table. "This special license was delivered a few minutes ago. We can get married this afternoon, if you are willing."

"By your friend Devereux?" She laughed along with him. If she had not been so drugged, she would have recognized Evan's friend who had been sent to guard her while Evan searched for Grand-mère. Evan's explanation had helped her understand why he had not been surprised by the announcement of the so-called marriage. He had not told her that the marriage was false, because he had not wanted to chance LaPorte forcing that information from her and making the marriage real.

"I thought you might want to ask Père Jean-Baptiste to come here and marry us." He chuckled. "Open the drawer of the bedtable."

Brienne did so gingerly, not trusting the glint of amusement in his eyes. When she drew out the thunderstone vase, she lay back in the pillows and cradled it. "Where did you hide it?"

"In the room where we spoke with my father. I just slipped it amid all the other pieces on the mantel. The best place to hide something is in plain sight, and I figured you would be able to find it if necessary."

She set the vase on the table and cuddled closer to him. "You are a scoundrel, Evan Somerset."

"I am."

"And I am a respectable *duchesse*." She laughed. "Or mayhap not."

His mouth descended on hers as his arm slipped beneath her shoulders. The hunger that had grown more whetted while they were apart seared her as he kissed her face.

"Don't become too respectable," he whispered against

her hair, his breath caressing her ear. "I have loved you as an actress and as a runaway wife. You lost your heart to a smuggler and thief. If we become too respectable, we might lose what we have."

She drew back in dismay. "Do you believe that?"

"Of course not." He laughed. "I just do not want you to think you have changed me completely. I have to tell you a few tales to keep you on your toes, honey."

She drew his face toward hers. "On my toes is not where I wish to be with you. I would rather be in your arms."

As their lips touched, the vow was branded into their hearts. At last, she had learned what destiny the thunderstone vase had brought her.

A love for all time.

Author's Note

I hope you enjoyed reading the first book in the Shadows of the Bastille trilogy, *A Daughter's Destiny*. When these characters first came to me, it was as part of a writing exercise. I set them aside, because, after all, I thought, it was just a writing exercise. Needless to say, they refused to be forgotten. As their adventures unfolded, I found I wanted to explore the secrets in Brienne's past and learn more about her family that had been scattered by the French Revolution. My next Regency is *A Christmas Bride,* available in November 2000. Who would have guessed that a simple lie about an imaginary betrothal could get so complicated?

I like hearing from my readers. You can contact me by email at: jaferg@erols.com or by mail at: Jo Ann Ferguson, P. O. Box 843, Attleboro, MA 02703

Happy reading!

BOOK YOUR PLACE ON OUR WEBSITE AND MAKE THE READING CONNECTION!

We've created a customized website just for our very special readers, where you can get the inside scoop on everything that's going on with Zebra, Pinnacle and Kensington books.

When you come online, you'll have the exciting opportunity to:

- View covers of upcoming books
- Read sample chapters
- Learn about our future publishing schedule (listed by publication month *and author*)
- Find out when your favorite authors will be visiting a city near you
- Search for and order backlist books from our online catalog
- Check out author bios and background information
- Send e-mail to your favorite authors
- Meet the Kensington staff online
- Join us in weekly chats with authors, readers and other guests
- Get writing guidelines
- AND MUCH MORE!

**Visit our website at
http://www.zebrabooks.com**

If you liked *A Daughter's Destiny,* be sure to look for Jo Ann Ferguson's next release in the Shadow of the Bastille series, *A Brother's Honor,* available wherever books are sold in October 2000.

When French privateer Dominic St. Clair seized an American ship attempting to sail through Napoleon's blockade of England, he found more than a valuable cache of guns and ammunition—he found the captain's daughter, Abigail Fitzgerald. Now, as fate sweeps him and Abigail to England's shores, and into the path of danger, Dominic must, at last, face his destiny . . . and fight for the woman who holds his heart in her hands.